ISBN-4: 978-1-7320671-4-1
ISBN-5: 978-1-7320671-5-8

Printed in USA
To purchase wholesale orders email
Shataya.Simms@gmail.com

NYCE

SHATAYA SIMMS

Dedicated to those who gave me a chance as a new author. I hope that this book is just as fulfilling as the last.

<u>ONE</u>
Philadelphia-1990

Suddenly, I wake up. It's freezing in here. I look across the room at my twelve-year-old sister Viola, who is shivering under her covers. Pulling the covers off my bed, I walk over to her and climb in.

"Thanks Jimmy," she says through the chattering of her teeth. I watch the cold air form clouds that sneaks out of her mouth as she bundles up next to me. Her stomach growls which is a reminder that I am starving too.

"Hungry?" I ask her.

"Just a little," she lies. I guess she feels bad because I snuck and gave her my dinner last night when I knew she wasn't full.

"I'll be right back," I tell her. I walk into the kitchen and open the fridge. Nothing as usual. I open the cabinet and find a box of Cheerios.

"Thank God," I say as I excitedly open the box. To my disappointment, there's only a handful of Cheerios left. I walk back into my room and hand Vi the box.

"Thanks Jimmy," she squeals and digs her hand in. "You want some?" She asks.

"No. I already ate a little bit. You eat it." I watch her eat the dry cereal as my stomach growls at every crunch I hear her make.

"Get ready for school. I'll be right back," I tell her. Walking out the room I go down the hall to my parent's bedroom and knock on the door.

"Come in," my mom's voice softly responds from the other side. I walk in and find her wrapped in the covers holding my six-year-old sister Morgan, who is also tightly bundled up in the blankets. My mother smiles at me.

"Good morning baby. I'm sorry it's cold. I called the Super about the heater twice. Hopefully he fixes it today," she says sweetly.

"It's okay mama. I'm not that cold," I lie.

"Are you hungry? Did you eat?"

"Yes. Vi and I just finished the box of Cheerios," I lie again. "There is still a pack of oatmeal left for Morgan to eat."

"Okay baby," she smiles.

"Do you have school today?" I ask her.

"Yes and your father is still working doubles so I need you to take care of your sisters please." My mom works at the local daycare while attending night school where she is working towards becoming a teacher. My father just got hired at SEPTA Transportation and has been busting his ass off since. I haven't really seen him in almost two weeks.

"Okay mom. I promise to take care of my sisters." She smiles at me.

"You really are my little man. Come crawl in the bed with me."

"Ewe mama no. I'm 14 now. I can't be laying in the bed with my mom," I laugh. She cocks her head to the side and stares at me.

"No stealing today James," she scolds.

"But mom, there's no food and it's cold in here."

"God will provide. No stealing. Promise me."

I climb into bed with her and take Morgan out of her arms. I know she's awake because she starts to giggle.

"YIMMY," she yells trying to scare me. I playfully jump and pretend that her scare tactic worked.

"Organ, you scared me," I tell her as she laughs. Morgan has been calling me Yimmy since she could talk. In return, I call her Organ to play off of her little speech impediment of not being able to pronounce her J's.

"I have a basketball game today. You coming?" I ask my mom.

"I have to work baby, I'm sorry. Look in my purse. I think I have a few dollars in there," she says. I walk over to her purse and open her wallet. There is only a $5.00 bill in it.

"Do I have any money in there?" She asks.

"Yeah. You have $15.00. I took $10.00 for me and Vi to get some food and left you $5.00 so you can eat," I lie to her and rush out the door.

"James, we're going to be late for school. Hurry up," Vi utters passing me in the hallway.

"I'm coming. Wait for me." I dash into the bathroom, brush my teeth with baking soda, use soap chips to wash my face, and hurry to my room to throw on the clothes I wore on Monday. It's Friday so hopefully no one will notice. Grabbing my coat, book bag, and basketball, I rush out the room and meet Vi at the front door.

"Your coat is too small. Did you tell mom you need a new one?" Vi asks me as we're walking out of our housing project.

"No. Not yet. I'm fine."

"They're gonna tease you James and if you fight and get kicked out of school again, daddy is gonna kill you," she warns as we enter the school yard.

"I'll be fine Vi. I'll drop off some lunch or some money to your class soon." My little sister looks at me.

"Don't worry James. Daddy is gonna figure it out. He always does," she says walking inside the building.

Being poor fuckin' sucks. I'm tired of starving, recycling clothes, and crazy gluing my shoes back together. I look across the street and watch the corner boys hustling. They never seem to be hard up for cash.

"Yo Nyce, let me see the rock," Tone yells at me referring to the basketball I'm holding. Tone gave me the nickname Nyce after I had to school him and his boys in a game of basketball last summer. My mom and dad always tell me that I am not allowed to hang out with Tone and his crew because they are trouble; *they are what's wrong with the black community* but they show me nothing but love. They give me money when I'm broke and my mom has no idea that the money she randomly finds lying around the apartment is Tone's drug money - and not money that she accidentally thought she misplaced.

"What up man?" I greet Tone and hand him the ball.

"You're looking skinny my dude. You eating? You can't be the next Jordan on the court if you're famished on the court. You got a game today, right?" He asks.

"Yeah,"

"Here," he says handing me a hundred dollar bill. "Take care of yourself and remember, you always have a spot on my team," he winks.

"Five-O, Five-O, Five-O," the lookout yells as the men disperse.

"Be cool Nyce. I'll catch you later," Tone says climbing inside his hooptie. I'll never understand why he drives that piece of shit when I know for a fact he owns both a Benz and a BMW.

I walk to the corner store.

"Not today," Mr. Paul says to me as I enter.

"Come on Mr. Paul. Every time I've stolen from you, I've paid you back. I have money today anyway," I tell him holding up the hundred dollar bill. He looks at me with sympathy in his eyes.

"You want me to make you a sandwich?" He asks.

"Yes please." I cruise up and down the aisles buying groceries, soap, and toothpaste.

"You're going to school today, right?" Mr. Paul asks when I approach the counter.

"Yeah. I have a game today," I respond as he rings up my stuff.

"I'll be there to support you kid and I'll bring up some sandwiches or pizza for you guys." That's Mr. Paul. He gets mad when we steal from his store but he always looks out for us kids by making sure we eat even though he complains about it. I guess he does it as a way to give back and help out. It seems to work because his store is the only store that never gets robbed in the hood. Yeah we steal random stuff from him but Mr. Paul has never been robbed for his cash. That's the thing about the hood; we never forget whose there for us when times are hard.

I walk back to our housing unit, enter the building and step onto the elevator. As the doors are closing, a kid that I've never seen before jumps in. He doesn't push any buttons. The only lit button is to my floor. I know everybody in the projects but this kid I don't know so my red flag is up. He is bigger and stockier than me. He has to be at least sixteen.

The elevator finally stops on floor 7. The kid steps off first as I stay on. I let the elevator doors close and push floor 9. On floor 9, I wait for about 10 minutes before pushing the button to return back to my floor. I step off the elevator, walk to my apartment and open the door. I kick the door back to shut it but I don't hear it slam. Alarmed, I turn around and the kid is standing in my doorway.

"I don't want to kill you so give me your groceries," he says with a gun pointing at me. I drop my groceries on the floor.

"I'm not giving you my fuckin' groceries dawg," I tell him staring into his eyes. Yeah I'm scared shitless but I can't let him see that. I'll be damned if I let him have my shit so my family can go hungry for another week.

"I will shoot you niggah I swear," he threatens.

"Then you better kill me because I am not willingly giving you my shit." The kid steps in and shuts the door. I look up at the clock. It's after nine so my mom is safe at work.

"You really want me to kill you?" He asks.

"Shoot," I challenge. He walks all the way up to me and points the gun at my head.

"You sure?" He questions towering over me.

"Do what you gotta do." The kid takes a step back and I make my move. I punch him in the nose as blood squirts out and quickly snatch the gun out of his hands.

"You dumb ass. You tried to rob me wit' a toy gun?" I yell at him.

"Man, I'm sorry. I'm hungry," he says holding his nose. Shaking my head, I walk into the kitchen, grab the dish towel, and walk back over to him.

"Thanks," he says taking the towel out of my hands. I hear his stomach growl; a feeling that I know all too well.

"Look, I'll make you something to eat but then you gotta roll." I pick up the groceries and walk back into the kitchen to fix him a sandwich.

"Thanks," he says when I hand it to him. He greedily bites into it.

"What's your name?" I ask curiously.

"Marquise," he says in between mouthfuls. "You think I can have some water or something?" He asks as he continues to devour his sandwich. I walk over to the cabinets and remove a glass. When I turn around, he is standing behind me.

"Sorry," he apologizes.

"It's coo…"

When I come to, I am lying in the middle of my kitchen floor.

"MOTHAFUCKA," I shout, picking myself up off the floor. My jaw is swollen.

"THIS NIGGAH TOOK ALL MY SHIT," I yell angrily at my missing groceries. I grab my coat, hat and book bag and run back to Mr. Paul's store.

"Mr. Paul, I got robbed. I'm sorry but can you make a sandwich for Viola and I'll pay you when I can?"

"What's wrong with you kids? You don't rob and steal from each other," he says annoyed as he hands me four premade sandwiches.

"You come back here tomorrow and sweep out front and help me clean up this store," he says. "And put some ice on your face. He got you good," he chuckles.

"Thanks," I tell him stuffing the sandwiches in my book bag and running out the store. Finally making it back to the school, I run inside and head straight to Vi's class.

"Ms. Andrews, can I see my sister for a second please?" I ask Vi's teacher while standing in the doorway. I step out into the hall and hold up a sandwich. Ms. Andrews looks at me, rolls her eyes, and nods at Vi.

"Bitch," I say under my breath.

"What happened to your face?" Vi asks me once in the hall.

"I'm fine Vi. Here," I tell her handing over two sandwiches.

"I told you the kids were gonna tease you. Did you get in trouble James? Daddy is gonna beat you," she says. Ignoring her, I kiss her cheek and run to the other side of the building to my class.

"Nice of you to join us Mr. Hennessey. Do you have a note?" My teacher Mr. William asks.

"No. Sorry. I was robbed on my way to school." I take off my hat so he can see my face. He shakes his head at me and tells me to have a seat.

The school day breezes by and I am now in the gym getting my teammates amped up for the game.

"WHOSE HOUSE?" I yell to my team in our huddle before the game.

"OUR HOUSE," they shout.

"WHOSE HOUSE?"

"OURS."

"LET'S GET 'EM," I say hitting the court. I am the captain of the team. I love being in charge and being in control. The court is where I feel like myself. There are no worries or the stresses of everyday life on the court. Your only concern is stopping a niggah from making a shot.

I am the next Jordan and I will get my family out of this fucked up life. I can't be stopped. I won't be stopped.

"Dang. In yo' face," I taunt number 34 as my shot goes in. I hear Tone yell my name.

"THAT'S MY NIGGAH NYCE," he yells. I give Tone a head nod and come alive.

"Uh...again. You can't stop me," I mock. Number 34 is getting annoyed and frustrated as I throw him off his game. Playing mad is never good. That's how you make stupid mistakes.

I strip the ball out of 34's hands and run it up the court. I can't dunk yet but I'm getting there. I go for a lay-up.

"You gotta be faster than that," I taunt him as he watches the ball go in. "Tell your coach I'm too much for you," I laugh and jog back down the court.

"You gettin' on my fuckin' nerves," he grits through his teeth.

"BALL," I yell at my team mate to pass me the ball.

"I'm gonna send you home cryin' to yo' mama," I laugh. As I start to step around him, he pushes the shit out of me. Purposely and dramatically I fall to the floor.

"FOUL," my coach yells as the whistle blows. I step up to the free throw line and wait. The crowd knows what I want to hear.

"NYCE, NYCE, NYCE," they chant. It's like music to my ears.

I shoot my first free throw - nothing but net. I own the court and I never let my opponent forget it - just like MJ.

We straight blow the other team out. My team mates and I celebrate our victory with our audience. I notice Tone and run up to him and his crew.

"CHAMP. I KNEW YOU COULD DO IT. I HAD MONEY ON THIS," he excitedly says while handing me $200.00. "Here's your cut."

"Thanks man." I eagerly grab the money.

"What the fuck happened to your face?" He asks examining my swollen jaw.

"We live in the hood, man. What can I say?"

"You don't have to live like this youngin'. When you ready, come see me."

"OVER MY FUCKING DEAD BODY. I TOLD YOU TO LEAVE MY SON ALONE. DIDN'T I, PUNK?" My dad shouts out of nowhere. He charges at Tone, grips him up and grabs him by his neck.

"DAD CHILL...CHILL," I yell as me and Tone's boys try to stop him from choking the life out of Tone.

"DAD, YOU'RE GONNA KILL HIM," I scream when it becomes evident that my dad has no intention of letting go.

"Remember mom, me, Viola, Morgan. How are we going to survive if you are in jail?" I ask calmly trying to get my dad to come to his senses. He finally let's go of Tone. It all happened so fast I don't even know what to do at this point. Tone straightens his clothes and laughs.

"It's cool Mr. Leonard. You got that one. Don't let it happen again though," Tone warns my dad as he tells his crew to back off.

"Nyce, I'll see you later," he says winking at me before exiting the gym.

"You stay away from him James. I told you to stay away from him."

"Dad he's cool. All he does is try to help me."

"HE'S TRYING TO RECRUIT YOU," my dad snaps and grips me up by my jersey.

"Daddy, don't kill James," Viola cries. I didn't even notice her this whole time. My dad lets me go and looks at me sorrowfully.

"Let's go," he says softly as he heads towards the exit. Vi and I look at each other and then walk quietly out of the gym. The walk home is awkward. My dad hasn't said anything since we left the school. He looks stressed and bothered like he's carrying the weight of the world on his shoulders.

"The lights are out," is the first thing my mom says as soon as we enter the apartment. She hands me a candle.

"How much is the bill Annette?" My dad asks as he takes the flashlight out of her hands.

"One-fifty-seven. When's your first check?"

"Next Wednesday."

"I can ask Rachel if we can run an extension cord from her place," she suggests. My dad looks at me, then Viola, and then back at my mom.

"Do what you feel is necessary. I'm going to go see if I can find some quick money at the loading docks or something. I'll see you later."

"Leonard, you haven't slept in almost two weeks. You need to rest."

Morgan yells my mom's name from the bedroom.

"I'll be back. Lock the door," he says kissing my mom. "Great game tonight son. I'm proud of you my little Hoya."

"Thanks dad." My dad looks worn out, tired, and old as I hold the candle up to his face.

"You're the man of the house so take care of our women while I'm gone," he says.

"Always," I tell him as he walks out the door. My mom rushes into her bedroom and slams the door behind her.

"James, I'm hungry," Vi whines.

"I'll be right back," I tell her walking out the door. I walk up the block to the Chinese store and order some food. As I am walking back to the apartment, somebody calls my name.

"NYCE. COME HERE," I hear him say. It's Boom, one of Tone's boys.

"What up Boom?"

"Nothing. Good game kid."

"Thanks."

"Tone will be here in a second. Chill for a minute."

"I can't. I have to go feed my family."

"Chill. You have time," Boom says with a look of seriousness on his face. A moment later, Tone's hooptie pulls up to the curb.

"Hop in," Tone commands. I climb inside the car.

"Tone man, I'm sorry about my dad."

"It's cool youngin' but now you owe me."

"Owe you how? I'm not slinging dope for you, Tone."

"You love your dad?" Tone asks me as he starts to drive towards the projects.

"Yes."

"Then you owe me," he says pulling up to my unit.

Son of a bitch. Can today possibly get any worse?

"Tone man, I promised my mom that I would never sling."

"Little Nyce, now you don't have a choice. If your parents give you shit, tell your dad you're doing this to keep him alive. Now get out. I'll be in touch."

I hop out the car.

"Oh and Nyce, snitching niggahs end up in ditches, niggah. I always have somebody watching," Tone warns before driving off.

I enter the apartment and walk into the kitchen. Morgan, Viola, and my mom are sitting at the table bundled up in blankets. There are candles lit everywhere and the oven door is wide open giving off some warmth.

"I got food," I say to them.

"Yes. Finally," Vi squeals.

"Where did you get money from Jimmy?" my mom asks.

"I had a game today mom and I betted on myself," I shrug.

"What did I tell you about gambling?"

"I won mom. That's all that matters. Now eat."

"You first," she says. I bite into a chicken wing and spoon some rice into my mouth.

"I have to go to the bathroom. Please eat mom. There is plenty," I tell her before excusing myself from the table. I walk down the hall and into my parent's room. I dig inside my mom's bill box, fish out the electric bill and stuff it into my pocket before joining them back at the table.

"I thought you had class tonight," I say to my mom.

"Yeah. I didn't go. Maybe I should take a semester off so I can help your dad out more."

"Dad won't let you even if you tried. He just got the job at SEPTA. His first check is coming. Things will get better. I promise," I assure her. She looks at me.

"Your heart is special James. Don't let this cold world change you. This isn't the life I dreamed of," she says quietly as a tear rolls down her face. She quickly wipes it off before we could take notice but it's too late. I already saw.

"Mom, it will be okay," I tell her. Cocking her head to the side, she smiles.

"I know baby. One more year of this shit. Just one more year. Lord, God, give us the strength," she says as she smashes a roach that creeps across the table with a napkin.

"In one more year I'll be done school, I'll get a decent paying job and we are getting out of here. I promise."

"Good 'cause I hate it here," Vi blurts. I turn and give her a stern look. She shrinks in her chair and mouths sorry.

"I hate it here too baby girl", my mom sighs agreeing with Vi. "What's the plan you two?"

"Graduate from high school, graduate from college, establish a career, and then love will find me," Vi and I say together. It's something that my mom annoyingly makes us repeat at least twice a month.

"That's right. Falling in love will throw you off your path. Never get off your path."

"Do you regret falling in love, getting married and having kids young?" I ask her.

"No baby. I love your father and I love you kids. This is just a temporary situation," she assures us. "But to avoid situations like this, I urge you guys to get your education first. That is how you get ahead in life."

"Don't worry mom. I am the next Michael Jeffery Jordan. I'm gonna get drafted right out of high school," I beam with pride.

"James," my mother scolds, looking at me sternly. I let out a heavy sigh.

"I'm a Georgetown Hoya, mom. I'm gonna go to college and get my degree."

"And what other colleges will you be applying to? You can't just apply to one. You have to have options."

"Duke, Notre Dame, Kansas City, OKC, Michigan and of course, UNC."

"You only want to go to UNC because MJ went there," Vi blurts.

"So." If it's good enough for my idol then it's good enough for me.

"All Division One colleges, huh? You just remember why you are there - to get an education. Life is more than basketball James."

"I know mom, but you already know that I am a Georgetown Hoya," I smile, flexing my muscles. My mom laughs.

"And what about you little lady?" She asks Vi.

"I'm gonna marry a rich man just like they do on TV," Vi beams.

"I hope you do baby," my mom chuckles as I kick Vi under the table.

After dinner, we sit at the table doing homework. I wish my mom could be my teacher for real. She has a way of breaking stuff down that helps me understand better. I know she is going to be a great teacher someday.

"No baths tonight. It's too cold. Go gather the blankets," my mom instructs us once we are finished our homework. Vi and I grab all the blankets and sleeping bags and bring them to the kitchen. My mom already moved the table out the way so Vi and I can make our spots on the floor to sleep.

"No. This isn't going to work," mom says thoughtfully.

"What's wrong?" I ask her. I look at the floor covered in blankets. It doesn't look any different than the other times we went without heat so I don't understand what she is saying.

"Help me pull the mattresses off our beds and drag them in here. We can't pay the bill until next Wednesday so we might as well be comfortable," she says.

We drag our mattresses into the kitchen and make one giant bed. Mom reads Viola and Morgan a story as I lie listening to her soothing voice. I love to hear my mom's voice. She sings her words when she talks. *Mom I promise, we're not going to live like this forever,* are my final thoughts before I drift off to sleep.

The next morning I wake up early to run to the store before my mom and sisters wake up.

"Good Morning Miss Wendy," I greet Mr. Paul's wife.

"Good Morning Jimmy. How's your mom?"

"She's fine," I tell her. I cruise up the aisles and grab grits, eggs, and some bacon.

"I owe you guys some money from yesterday. Mr. Paul gave me four sandwiches for me and Viola," I tell Miss Wendy at the counter.

"Don't worry about it baby. Tell your mom I said hi for me, okay?" She says as I pay for my groceries.

"Okay. Thanks."

I sneak back into the apartment, sit the food on the table and grab the electric bill before making my way back out the door. I hop on the trolley and ride down Center City to pay the electric bill. Afterwards, I check my pockets to see how much money I have left. Shit. I am right back where I started yesterday morning…broke, cold, and hungry.

As I'm walking into the building, I see the Super.

"Hey. You're supposed to be fixing our heat," I tell him.

"What for? You don't even have any electricity. I saw the cords running this morning. I'm going to call the city on you," he says to me.

"I need to call the city on you. You have a woman and her kids up there in the freezing cold," I bark back.

"You people are all the same. Blame society for your problems as if you don't create your own problems. Tell your mother to shut her legs and she wouldn't be in this predicament."

"I'm gonna let you have that because my mom and sisters are cold but mark my words, one day, you will be begging me to keep your life and if you talk bad about my mom again, that one day, will turn into today," I tell him calmly even though inside I am ready for war. This mothafucka. I swear I can't stand his ass.

"Our electricity is back on. I expect to see you upstairs soon and if not, I'll be back for you," I state sternly so he can comprehend how serious I am.

"You and what army?" He challenges.

"I am my own army," I tell him jumping on the elevator. I walk to my apartment and see the front door wide open with extension cords running from Miss Rachel's apartment across the hall into ours.

"Mama, turn on the lights. They just cut our electricity back on." I yank the cords out of the wall and shut the door.

"How? Who paid?" She asks me, turning on the lights to see if I'm right.

"No one. I saw the electric dude downstairs and asked him what unit was he here for. He told me that the electric company has been making mistakes with people's bills this month and they are out here fixing the accounts that were overcharged. We were on that list so now we have a zero balance."

My mom cocks her head to the side and looks at me thoughtfully.

"I knew they were overcharging us. Your dad didn't want to believe me," she beams happily. "And thank you for the groceries baby," she says giving me a kiss. "Now come and eat some food."

It's one in the afternoon, my belly is finally full, there is heat circulating in our apartment, and Viola is outside not getting on my nerves. Things are good. I'm sitting on the couch playing with Morgan.

"Say Nyce," I tell her.

"No way," she says and sneezes in my face. A snot bubble shoots out of her nose.

"Yuck Organ." I think about the night before and how we didn't have any heat. She must have caught a cold.

"Don't worry baby girl. One day your brother is gonna be the man and you won't have to worry or want for anything. I got us," I tell her while wiping her nose.

"Jimmy, can you go get your sister and tell her to come inside please?" Mom asks me.

"Well, the peace and quiet was good while it lasted, right?" I jokingly say to Morgan.

"Yup," she responds giggling.

I get up and grab my coat.

"Can I come too, please Yimmy?" She whines.

"No. I need you to babysit mom. Can you do that for me?" I wink at her before heading out the door.

I find Vi up the street roller skating and playing with a girl that I've never seen before. I know all of Vi's friends because I want to make sure her friends are good influences for her.

"James, this is Keisha. She is here visiting her dad. Keisha, this is my brother James."

"Hi," the girl says to me smiling brightly.

"Hey," I respond to her. "Mom wants you, Vi."

"Okay. Bye Keisha."

"Bye Viola. Bye Nyce."

"How do you know my name?" I ask her.

"Because everybody knows your name," she smiles and skates away. I like her but I don't *like* her. She has a sneaky vibe - but I like her.

"You're staring creep," Vi says.

"No I wasn't," I smile to myself.

I am in a deep sleep when mom bursts through my bedroom door.

"Vi. Jimmy. Wake up. Get ready for church," she says waking us up.

"James, can you play the piano today while I direct the choir? Your dad isn't going to make service today."

"Sure mom." I hate going to church. Don't get me wrong; me and G are good, I just hate being there all damn day. My mom acts like she don't know how to leave once we are there. Not only is she the choir director, she is also the church treasurer, the Sunday school teacher, and leads the women's Bible study group on Wednesday nights. What can I say? Mama loves church.

I'm sitting at the piano playing *Lord I Lift Your Name on High* while the choir sings along. I glance at the clock. It's only 11:30 am. The Eagles are playing today at 1:00 which means Pastor Michaels sermon should be short. He thinks he's slick but I know, and the members of the congregation know that when the Eagles are playing, Pastor Michaels will be dismissing the church at exactly one o'clock. Hopefully, my mom doesn't linger around and talk to all the other women who seem to enjoy church just as much as she does.

I glance over the audience and spot Marquise; the boy who stole my groceries. It's taking everything in me to continue playing this damn piano and not haul off and fuck dude up in the middle of church. What the hell is he doing here anyway? I've never seen him in the hood before, and now it seems like I am seeing this dude everywhere. I keep my eyes on him as Pastor Michaels starts preaching a few words about taking care of your fellow man as the collection plates begin to circulate around the church. When it gets to Marquise, he swiftly grabs the cash out of the plate and tosses a handful of money back into the plate. *What the hell?* I think, wondering why the hell would somebody steal money out of the plate just to put money back in? He finally looks up and sees me. I give him the look of death as he cracks a smile. I hate this kid. Church can't end fast enough because I swear after service I'm going to hunt him down and beat his ass.

After offering, mama dismisses the choir and I take my seat in the front pew next to Morgan who crawls into my lap. I hate that my mom makes us sit here. Especially now because I can't keep my eyes on Marquise if he is sitting behind me.

After the boring sermon, Pastor Michaels dismisses the church on time just as I predicted. I jump out of the pew with only one goal in mind- get my revenge. Marquise sees me and quickly starts moving towards the door. I follow him outside and he bolts. I hurry and run behind him.

"YIMMY…YIMMY. WHERE YOU GOING?" I hear Morgan yelling trying to run behind me. What the hell? Having little sisters is annoying as fuck. I stop chasing after Marquise's dumb-ass to tend to my little sister.

"THAT'S IT? THAT'S ALL YOU GOT?" He taunts, laughing and runs around the corner.

"Damn it, Morgan. Why are you following me?" I snap. "And where's your coat?"

"I'm sorry Yimmy," she cries. I take my coat off, wrap it around her, and carry her back to church to wait for mama.

By two o'clock, we are still at church waiting for mom to hurry up and count the money that the church has collected. The treasurer's door finally swings open as Morgan, Vi and I stand, relieved to be leaving. Just as I thought we were finally escaping, Mrs. Michaels calls my mom over to her and begins talking. Damn it. I'm missing the game.

"James, can I go to the store to get some chips?" Vi asks me. I dig in my pocket and hand her my last two dollars.

"Get me a hug and some hot cheese popcorn. What you want Organ?"

"I want some Now & Laters," she says.

"No candy," I tell her.

"Fine," she puffs. "Can I have some chips please?"

"Sure. And hurry back Vi. I better not have to come out looking for you," I tell her.

I'm off to the side holding Morgan's hand while mama is still running her mouth. Why can't she be like everybody else who comes to church? Come, hear the word and be anxious to go home and return to their sins. Finally, she stops talking and walks over to us.

"Can you believe that one of the collection plates had a bunch of fake ones in it? Who would do such a thing?" Mama says to me. Clever. Marquise done robbed the damn church right in our faces.

"Jimmy, where's your sister?" She asks.

"She ran to the store."

"Well can you go get her please? I am just about ready to leave." *Yeah right*, I think as I grab Morgan's hand and walk out the church in a quest to find Vi.

I spot her standing on the corner talking to Keisha. Keisha looks good. I don't know what it is about her that I like. Maybe it's her lips or the mystery behind her dark eyes.

"Mom's ready to leave, and what I tell you about standing on corners," I scold Vi.

"I know, I know. Geez. Don't have a cow, Nyce," she says.

"Oh, since when have you started calling me Nyce?" I question.

"Since Keisha told me to," she smiles brightly.

"Hi Nyce," Keisha finally speaks. I watch her lips part into a smile.

"What's up?" I say to her trying to sound cool.

"I want to call you Nyce too Yimmy," Morgan whines.

"You should. It makes him seem cooler," Keisha chimes in.

"You wanna go to the movies or something?" I ask her. Oh shit. Look at that. I just asked a girl out. I've never done that before.

"I don't think so," she says bluntly. What? Damn. She just rejected me.

"Why not?" I ask her.

"Uh...because I don't want to," she says walking away. Vi burst out laughing.

"Oh she dissed you," she laughs.

"Shut up Vi."

"Serves you right for trying to mack my friend."

"Nyce has a girlfriend," Morgan teases.

"Nyce just got dissed," Viola mocks.

"Yeah, alright. She'll be mine one day. You'll see," I say accepting the challenge.

For the past two weeks, I've been cutting through the alley ways trying to avoid running into Tone. I know he's going to catch up to me eventually but I'm trying my best to stay clear. Vi and I just picked Morgan up from afterschool care and are now walking back home.

"Why do we have to go this way Nyce? We've been going the long way all week," Vi whines.

"Because I am trying to avoid Tone."

"Why? I thought you guys were friends."

"Nah. He just wants me to work for him."

"You should. He makes money. Way more than mommy or daddy," she says.

"You don't know what you're talkin' about Vi," I tell her.

"All I'm saying is that he dresses nice, has a nice car, and doesn't seem to ever be hungry."

"Yeah but everything has a price tag. When's the last time you spoke to Keisha?" I ask her changing the subject.

"She doesn't like you Nyce," she teases.

"Whatever. What's her story anyway?"

"Well, her parents are going through a divorce. Her dad now lives with her aunt and she is forced to visit him every other weekend."

"So she'll be here this weekend then?" I ask her. Viola smiles.

"Yup and we are going to hang out."

"You remember where you come from. Don't let that girl be a bad influence on you."

"Says the boy who is trying to get wit' her."

We're sitting at the table doing homework when there is a knock at the door.

"Shhhh…be quiet," I tell my sisters. Our parents aren't home and these are the projects. I grab my baseball bat and approach the door.

"WHO IS IT?" I yell through the door trying to put as much base in my voice as possible.

"Terry," the voice yells back. Terry is one of Tone's flunkies.

"Fuck," I say under my breath. I open the door.

"What's up little niggah? You're wanted," he says to me.

"I can't. I have my sisters," I tell him.

"Not my problem," he replies walking away. I grab my coat.

"You can't leave us alone," Vi whines.

"I'm not Vi. I'll be right back." I walk across the hall to Miss Rachel's apartment.

"Hey man," she greets me.

"Hi Miss Rachel. Can you watch my sisters while I run to the store please?"

"Sure but only if you can pick me up some soda, chips, and a pack of cigarettes please."

"Sure," I tell her. She hands me $2.00 and some food stamp coupons. Mama said that we don't need food stamps. She said people on them get content and forget what they have to do to survive life. I want to tell her that the people on them look fed and not hungry but I would never disrespect my mom like that.

I walk outside and climb inside the backseat of Tone's car. He's sitting in the driver's seat, another man in the passenger seat, while Terry sits next to me.

"You've been avoiding me little niggah?" He questions.

"Yeah I have but you know where I live so you wasn't looking for me too hard," I tell him. He chuckles.

"That's why I like you. You got heart and show no fear. You know I will kill your little ass and throw you in the fuckin' river and yet you talk to me like I'm some chump," he laughs as he lights a blunt.

"Y'all niggahs find something to do," he orders as the men obediently file out of the car. I grab the door handle to leave too.

"Not you Nyce. Hop in the front seat. Let's take a ride."

"Fuck," I accidently say as I climb in the front seat.

"You owe me," he says.

"I don't owe you shit so go ahead and dump my body. You'll be doing me a favor," I tell him. He shakes his head at me.

"Why you not scared to die Nyce?"

"I am scared but you're gonna do what you wanna do anyway. Ain't no point for me to cry about it."

"I'm not going to kill you Nyce. I will kill your dad though."

"Go ahead. That niggah gets on my nerves anyway," I challenge. Of course I don't want him to kill my dad. I'm just trying to call his bluff.

"Hmmm…so you don't care about your dad? Shit. I don't care about mine either but I be seeing your mom and your little sisters around a lot and…"

"Say no more," I buckle as my adrenaline begins to flow with rage. "What do you want from me Tone?" I snap.

"Nothing yet but starting tomorrow, consider yourself in training."

"Training for?"

"That's it. Get out," he says unlocking the doors. I hop out the car.

"Oh and Nyce," he says.

"Yeah."

"You got one more time to say some slick shit to me. Kids ain't exempt from gettin' knocked the fuck out," he warns pulling off.

Vi and I take our normal route to school the following day. Tone and his corner boys are in their usual spot.

"Nyce. Get over here," Tone commands.

"Shit. Go inside Vi," I tell her.

"Okay. Hi Tony," she greets him.

"What's up Princess?" Tone responds. Vi smiles brightly and walks across the street and into the school yard. I make a mental note to beat her ass later for speaking to a grown man.

"What's up?" I ask Tone when I approach.

"You gotta game today?" He asks me.

"No. Just practice," I tell him.

"After practice, meet me here."

"And don't be late little niggah," Terry chimes in. I never did like his bitch ass.

"Niggah, I don't work for you," I tell him.

"What you say?" He steps to me.

"I said I don't..." my words are cut short by Terry punching me in my mouth.

"You hit like a bitch," I spit and swiftly grab an empty 40 bottle that is conveniently lying on the sidewalk and smash it upside Terry's head.

"Whoa...whoa...whoa. Y'all niggahs chill," Tone says laughing while standing between me and Terry who now has blood leaking down his face. "You gonna need stiches Ock," he says examining Terry's head.

"I'm gonna fuck you up you little bastard," Terry threatens trying to break free from Tone.

"Nah. Nyce is off limits. He's mine. Y'all challenging him is like y'all challenging me. Understand?" Tone says looking at each man.

"Go to school Nyce. I'll meet you here later," he dismisses me.

The school day goes by faster than I wanted it to. Normally, I would be glad but today I am dreading meeting Tone and becoming one of his bitches.

"HENNESSEY. WHAT'S THE PROBLEM SON? YOU'RE PLAYING WORSE THAN MY DAUGHTER," the coach yells at me during basketball practice.

"Sorry Coach. Distracted," I tell him.

"You can't get into Georgetown playing like this," he says shaking his head at me.

"You just better be ready for Wednesday. Practice dismissed," he says blowing his whistle. I throw on my clothes and head for the door. I think about running home but what good would that do? The niggah knows where I live. I walk outside and look on the corner. Empty. Maybe he finally got arrested. Just as I am coming out of the schoolyard, Tone's black Mercedes Benz pulls up.

"You wasn't thinking about running from me were you?" He asks.

"Thought about it," I tell him as I hop in the backseat. There is a big, burly niggah sitting in the front.

"This is my partna, Bo. Bo, this is the little dude I was tellin' you about."

"What's up kid?" Bo greets in a deep voice.

"Hi," I nervously reply because I don't know who this big ass niggah is or what their intentions are.

"So, you was gonna run? You know, niggahs beg me to be part of my team. Why you so different?" Tone questions as he pulls off. I roll down my window.

"You see there?" I ask pointing at Mr. Tommy.

"Who? That crack-head over there?" Bo asks.

"Yeah. His name is Mr. Tommy and he used to be a school bus driver. He would buy me and Vi water ice in the summer but now he's a full fledge junkie. And there goes Stacy," I say pointing. "She was pretty once. Smart too from what I remember. She got her kids taken away from her last year. I watched her give Terry head for a rock. And there goes Peanut. He's only 15. I don't even know what happened to him," I say as I name some of the many crack-heads walking around. "You feel nothing for the lives you're fuckin' up?" I ask Tone.

"Man, listen. Them mothafuckas would still get high with or without my help. It's a choice youngin," Tone nonchalantly explains.

"Whatever. It's wrong," I tell him.

"You wasn't saying that shit when you accepted all my damn money that I gave you over the years. You can't hate what the Devil does and still eat off his table."

"You right. I won't take another dime from you," I assure him. Tone is silent for the remainder of the drive. I have no idea where these niggahs are taking me. Maybe Tone decided to kill me after all.

He pulls up to some castle looking house. I look up at the house as him and Bo hop out of the car. Tone gives Bo a giant duffle bag before jumping back into the car.

"Get in the front," he orders.

"Where are we going?" I ask hopping in the front seat. Tone doesn't answer as we leave the city and head towards the suburbs.

"I bet you never left the hood before, huh?" He assumes. Wrong. Grandma Norah lives in Wynnewood but there is no way I'm telling him that.

"I'm taking you home with me," he finally says.

"Man Tone, I ain't into that shit. I will kill you first before I allow you to touch me," I snap with my pocket knife already in my hand.

"What niggah?" He barks and abruptly pulls the car over. "Get out," he demands, swinging his car door open. He comes around the passenger side door, yanks it open and grabs me out the front seat, throwing me to the ground.

"Say that shit again," he yells, kicking me in my stomach. "Little Nyce gonna learn to fuckin' respect me," he snaps, punching me in the eye. I can feel my eye immediately swell.

"Now get your ass in the damn car," he commands lifting me to my feet but I buckle back to the ground. "You got five seconds to recoup niggah," he threatens pulling out his gun. I gather my strength and climb back inside the car. We ride in silence for a moment.

"You good?" He asks, breaking the silence.

"Fuck you. I ain't gonna be little forever," I tell him. He laughs.

"Little Nyce. You gonna learn. I'll make a deal with you. You can talk to me grimey all you want but not in front of the homies. I can't have mothafucka's thinking I'm soft BUT if you accuse me of some pedophile bullshit again, that's your ass. Cool?"

"Why me Tone?" I ask.

"Let's just say I see something in you. A real boss; a true leader. I like that. You're not a knucklehead like these other dicks are. We're here," he announces pulling in a driveway.

"Where are we?" I ask looking at the nice two-story suburban home.

"Villanova," he answers. I follow him inside.

"DADDY," a cute little girl squeals leaping into his arms.

"Hey baby girl," he smiles scooping her up.

"Hey baby," says the finest woman I've ever seen. She walks into the room and gives Tone a kiss. I check her out. *Damn.* Fat ass and big titties. *Shit.* I'd come home to that every night too.

"Stop staring at my girl niggah," Tone says popping me upside my head.

"I'm sorry Miss but damn, you bad," I boldly tell her. I couldn't resist. She giggles before turning to look at me.

"Oh my God, what happened to your face sweetie?" She asks, cupping my face in her hands. Damn. She even smells good.

"A misunderstanding," Tone replies. "Can you get him some ice, babe?"

"You need to pick on somebody your own size Tony," she playfully scolds winking at me. Tone slaps her on her ass before she bounces off and disappears.

"First lesson," Tone says turning to face me. "Always keep a bad bitch by your side. She's gonna be the one that silences your demons and sees you for who you really are. If she loves you, she'll try to make you leave the game but you got to live by the code: Money over Bitches. You can fuck wit' other bitches too, but never give them your all. You give them bits and pieces. Just enough to keep them coming back beggin' for more.

"The gold-digger; the skank bitch, she'll fuck you good and help you move the weight. She'll always be in your pocket wanting something though. *Always* use protection youngin'. These bitches will see you and try to trap you," Tone says as his bad bitch comes back with a bag of ice.

"Here you go suga," she smiles, handing me the ice.

"Thank you Miss."

"Nina," she corrects me with a smile as she picks up the little girl and walks out the room.

"I didn't know you were a father, Tone."

"There are a lot of things you don't know about me," he says lighting a blunt. He passes it to me.

"Nah. I'm good," I tell him. He laughs.

"Second lesson. Only smoke or drink when you think you are safe enough to let your guard down. Never get intoxicated with people you don't trust. And third lesson, only people you trust should know where you live. Never stash your shit in your house. Not drugs…not money…always keep your house clean. Have a stash house. A place that only you know about. Keep your money there. Never keep your money and your drugs together," Tone babbles as he exhales the smoke. I look over at the clock.

"Tone, it's 7:30. I gotta go before my mom calls the cops thinking I'm shot up somewhere," I tell him.

"A'ight…a'ight," he says putting out his blunt. We walk outside. Tone has three luxury cars sitting in his driveway but we climb inside his hooptie.

"Tone, why do you drive this piece of shit when you have way better cars?" I ask.

"Lesson number….shit…what number are we on?" He chuckles. I laugh and shrug my shoulders.

"Anyway, never move weight or product in a fancy car. Cops already target us niggahs so never give them a reason to pull you over. Buy a car that says I am a blue collar working man. Keep that shit clean. No tints, no loud music. Never bring attention to yaself.

"You need to build a team. People you trust. You always need a right hand man; a brother that is going to have your back no matter what. Always keep an alias name. Stop giving people your government. You stay hidden. Mysterious. Even the bitches you're screwing don't need to know your name. Bitches will sell you out just as fast as your homies will," he says pulling up to my unit. I sit in the car and wait.

"What you waitin' for? Get out." He commands.

"I thought you were gonna give me something to sell."

"Nah. You ain't ready. Like I said, you're in training. You just worry about school; Georgetown right? Start payin' attention in class and getting ready for your game Wednesday. That is your only job for right now." Confused, I hop out of the car and head inside.

I hang out with Tone almost every day after practice depending on my mom's schedule. He takes me to his house, makes me do my homework, and even checks it. His girl Nina and their daughter Toni become my second family. Nina cooks almost every night like it's the Last Supper. At first, I would steal some of their food to take home. After Tone caught me and fucked me up for stealing from him, he started giving me $100.00 a week.

I convince my mom that I have a part-time job bagging groceries on the weekends. I pay Miss Rachel to watch my sisters on the nights that I'm at Tone's house and give my sisters $5.00 each to keep their mouths shut.

41

So far, so good. Tone still hasn't made me do anything for him. All he does is talk to me about life; about the game. What to look out for and who to trust. I develop a love/hate relationship with him. He's like the older brother that I always wanted and yet I have to be mindful of the role he is training me to play.

<u>TWO</u>

It's Friday and practice has been cancelled. I walk around the school yard looking for Vi so we can walk home together. Instead of running into Vi, I run right into Marquise. Without hesitation, not even thinking, I ball up my fists and swing first. I crack him right in his jaw. He's way bigger than me so I keep swinging; trying not to give him a chance to regain his composure.

"YOU OWE ME FUCKING MONEY FOR STEALING MY GROCERIES," I yell punching him in the face. My punches seem to not have any effect on him. Yeah he's bleeding but he doesn't back off as we exchange blows. A crowd forms and I hear people instigating and being hype.

"FUCK YOU NIGGAH. I'D DO IT AGAIN TOO," he yells before punching me in my mouth. Fuck, that hurt. He hits harder than Terry's bitch ass as I try to regain my composure and catch my footing. *This niggah hits hard as shit* I'm thinking as I try my best to duck out of his way to keep his punches from landing. I know it's only gonna take that one good hit from him before I'm stretched out on the pavement and as soon as I think it - it happens.

"Nyce. Nyce. Get up," Vi yells slapping my face.

"FUCK. Did I win?" I ask her.

"No stupid. I wouldn't be trying to lift you off the ground if you won," she scolds helping me up. "Your face is swollen," she tells me.

"Thanks for enlightening me" I sarcastically respond. She acts like I don't feel the shit.

"Why you always fightin' somebody bigger than you anyway?" She asks as everybody else is asking me if I'm alright?

"Every man bleeds," I tell her as I take my shirt to wipe the blood off my face.

"Well, the only blood I see is yours." I ignore Vi as I walk home in silence trying not to be embarrassed by the L I just took. Everybody is used to me fighting but I am not use to me losing. We walk inside our building and catch the elevator up to our apartment.

"DADDY," Viola screams.

"Hey sweetie," he says scooping her up. He looks at me.

"What happened this time son?"

"A misunderstanding, Pop," I tell him. He puts Vi down and sits at the kitchen table.

"Go to your room Vi. I want to talk to James."

"What's up?" I ask.

"What is this?" He asks, tossing money at me. He found my stash.

"It's money dad."

"Where did you get it from?"

"I earned it. I work at the supermarket on Broad Street bagging groceries on the weekend."

"Uh-huh," he utters as he stands up towering over me. My dad is built like an ox; 6'5-solid muscle. *Damn!*

I think as I watch him take off his belt. I just got my ass beat in the school yard and now I'm about to get my ass beat at home too.

"I'm gonna ask you again. Where did you get this?"

"It's not what you think," I tell him swallowing the lump in my throat. With no hesitation, he cuts the belt through the air. I try to dodge it but it lands on my back.

"AHHH DAD. IT'S NOT WHAT YOU THINK," I yell trying to dodge his blows. This doesn't help. He grips me up and starts really beating my ass.

"DADDY…DADDY…STOP," Vi pleads grabbing my dad's massive arm.

"YOU WILL NOT SELL DRUGS IN THIS HOUSE," he rages.

"I'M NOT," I shout. I hear the front door swing open and slam shut.

"LEONARD! STOP IT," my mom yells running into the kitchen.

"DADDY," Morgan cries and throws herself in front of me taking the last blow. She lets out a harrowing scream as the whole kitchen falls silent. I scoop Morgan up.

"I'm sorry Organ," I repeatedly say to her as she cries hysterically in my arms.

"Pumpkin. I'm sorry. Daddy didn't mean it," he says taking Morgan out of my arms.

"Jimmy go to your room," my mom commands. I walk down the hall and into my room. My body is on fire. Between the ass kicking I took earlier from

Marquise and the ass whooping my dad just delivered, I feel like I just got hit by a fuckin' truck.

"Nyce. You okay?" Vi asks handing me a bag of frozen peas.

"Yeah," I tell her putting the peas on my face. "Is Morgan okay?" I ask.

"Yeah. She's fine," she responds plopping down next to me on my bed. I take off my shirt.

"Oh my God," she gasps. I can feel the welts on my back with every move I make. Vi jumps off the bed and runs out the room. She comes back with peroxide and cotton balls. As she's catering to my wounds, my mom walks in with Morgan.

"Jimmy, come into the kitchen so we can talk. You girls stay here." I follow my mom into the kitchen and take a seat across my dad.

"I'm not raising you to be a liar son," he starts. "So I am going to ask you one last time. Are you selling drugs?"

"No sir. I'm not," I tell him truthfully.

"Jimmy, where are you getting the money from?" My mom asks.

"I already told you. I bag groceries," I lie.

"I love you son but you will not live under my roof or be welcomed into my house if you are selling dope."

"Dad, I promise. I'm not doing anything wrong."

"Then I'm sorry for spanking you," he says handing me back my money.

"You keep it," I tell him.

"No son. You earned it. It's yours." This makes me feel like shit as I take the money out of his hands.

Yeah, I'm not lying to him about selling drugs but I *technically* didn't earn the money either.

"I'll start dinner," my mom says getting up from the table.

"So how was school Hoya?"

"It was fine dad. Basketball got cancelled though."

"You can still practice shooting and running drills."

"I'll probably hit the courts sometime tomorrow."

"Maybe we can make a Hoya game this year," he suggests.

"It's cool, Pop," I tell him not wanting him to waste his money. Before Morgan was born, before my dad got laid off at the factory, he used to take me to the Georgetown Hoya games all the time. I use to love our road trips; just me and my dad chillin' for the day as he talked about his Alma Mater...well, his almost Alma Mater. He had to drop out his junior year when my mom got pregnant with me. I know that attending and graduating from Georgetown will make my parents proud; my father in particular. He's been brainwashing me and calling me Hoya since I can remember.

I spend the rest of my night with my family and enjoying my dad's company. I miss him being home and wish that every night could be like this; minus the ass whipping. A home filled with love and for those brief moments, we forget our everyday struggle of being poor and living in the projects.

I wake up the next morning and look over at Vi and Morgan who are still sound asleep. Tiptoeing out the room I go into the kitchen to get some cereal. I make a bowl of Fruity Pebbles and start devouring it while watching Saturday morning cartoons. Morgan comes waltzing in holding her doll and sits down right next to me invading my space.

"Can I have some?" She asks. Man. Having little sisters is a pain in the ass. I get up and walk into the kitchen to make her a bowl using the rest of the milk.

"Here Organ," I call her into the kitchen as I sit the bowl on the table. "I'm gonna run to the store to pick up some stuff to cook mom and dad breakfast."

"And me too?" She asks.

"You're eating cereal," I tell her.

"Yeah but I like when you cook. Especially when you make panycakes," she says. I laugh.

"Pancakes," I correct her.

"That's what I said. Panycakes." I bend over and kiss her forehead.

"Love you Organ."

"Me too Yimmy," she says putting a spoonful of cereal into her mouth. I get dressed and head out.

"Hi Miss Wendy," I greet her when I walk into the store.

"Hey sweetie," she replies as I grab a basket and cruise the aisles. I'm filling up my basket with food when I run into Keisha.

"Hey you."

"Hey. What happened to your face?" She asks.

"I got into a fight," I smirk trying to impress her.

"Did you win?"

"Of course."

"It sure doesn't look like it," she giggles.

"Is that going to stop you from going to the movies with me?"

"Boy, no. I don't want to go to the movies with you."

"Why you tryin' to play me? You always speak to me and smile."

"I speak and smile at everybody."

"Well stop. I only want you to speak and smile at me." She giggles.

"See. I can make you laugh" I tease.

"Bye Nyce," she says walking out the store. Watching her leave, I purchase my items and walk back home.

"Dad. How can I get a girl to like me?" I ask at the table as we eat breakfast. I cooked them pancakes, eggs, and sausage. Mom made sure I knew how to cook by the time I turned eight.

"What girl is this?"

"Just asking," I tell him.

"He has a crush on my friend Keisha," Vi teases.

"Shut up, Vi," I sneer, kicking her under the table. Looking at my mom, she cocks her head to the side and smiles at me.

"Why didn't you ask me?" She questions.

"Because you are not a man," I answer.

"Yeah, but I am a woman so I do have the inside scoop."

"Okay mom. What should I do?"

"Treat her nice. Compliment her. Buy her flowers and be persistent," she says, gracefully standing up from the table. "Girls, help me clean the dishes and thank your brother for making this meal."

"Thank you," they both respond as they stand up and start to clear the table.

"Hoya," my dad whispers. "You get a woman's attention by ignoring her," he tells me with a wink.

"And how does that work?" I ask confused.

"Trust me. Start ignoring her. It'll work. Women hate being ignored. It drives them crazy," he affirms. Huh? Now I am left even more confused because I don't know what the hell he is talking about. How does ignoring somebody make them want you?

That afternoon as I am watching TV, someone starts knocking on our door.

"I'll get it," I yell. When I open the door, Keisha is standing there looking beautiful as usual.

"Miss me?" I ask with a smile.

"Please. I am here to see Vi," she says sucking her teeth as I block her entrance inside. "Are you going to let me in?" Keisha asks.

"Are you going to give me a hug to be let in?" I reply.

"Ewe...no," she says rolling her eyes.

"Ewe?" I question.

"Yeah...ewe," she says with an attitude.

"Nyce, move," Vi says pushing me to the side. Damn! Keisha is crushing my ego.

"You look beautiful anyway even though you're mean to me," I tell her still trying. She ignores my compliment and walks past me.

I grab my basketball and coat and walk to the park. It's cold as shit outside but people are still in the park scattered around. Kids playing, crackheads being crackheads, and the corner boys occupying the benches. I spot Tone, Terry, and Boom amongst them.

"Nyce, let me see the rock," Boom yells at me. I toss him the ball. He tries to make a 3-pointer but it was nothing but air. I start laughing at him.

"You know what? You're a cocky mothafucka for you to only be fourteen," he laughs. "You ain't even that good," he says playfully.

"Wanna put some money on it?" I challenge.

"I got this," Terry says. "How much you got on it?" He asks.

"I got about $200.00," I tell him.

"Put your money where your mouth is," he challenges taking a cheap shot. I watch the ball go into the net as Terry gives me a cocky look. Obviously, Tone and Boom never warned Terry about me. Looking over at the bench, I watch Boom and Tone placing bets. Terry and I play a little one-on-one. I purposely let him think that he is better than what he is so that I can hustle him out of his money.

"Game point," he announces and cuts around me, dunking the ball into the basket.

"Good game," I tell him while handing over the $200.00.

"I knew you wasn't shit," he mocks as he collects his money. I laugh to myself. Just like I thought, he takes the bait.

"I guess not. You the man," I say shrugging my shoulders. "Must be off my game today. This fourteen-year-old boy almost had you," I taunt.

"Niggah, please. You ain't have shit," Terry snaps back.

"Then let me win some of my money back?"

"What for? You lost. You broke now anyway."

"Nope. I got another $100.00 to put up."

"Just $100.00 huh? When you get $500.00 then come holla at me."

"I got that," Tone says handing me $500.00. "What's up? $1000.00 to the winner," Tone schemes as Boom starts collecting money for round two.

"Bet. Winners court," Terry exclaims snatching the ball out of my hands. Twenty minutes later, I'm walking out the park with $500.00 in my pocket after paying Tone back. I stop by Mr. Paul's store and purchase some candy and a little teddy bear. Walking back to my apartment, I'm hoping that Keisha is still there.

"I got you something," I announce to her when I walk in interrupting her and Vi playing jacks. I hand her the bear.

"Uh…thanks," she says standing up off the floor. "Vi, I'm going home."

"Don't let my dumb brother chase you off," Vi interjects.

"Nah. I can handle him. I just have to check in with my dad. I might come back and if not, I'll call you," Keisha says putting on her coat and leaving without taking the bear. Vi shakes her head at me.

"Just stop trying boy. She don't want you," she laughs.

"Yes she does. She just doesn't know it yet," I tell her. I look down at the bear. I'm pissed that I just spent my money on it and she didn't even fuckin' take it.

For the remainder of the month, every time I saw Keisha, I would tell her how pretty she is. However, that does nothing. I bought her flowers, she said she was allergic. I bought her chocolates, she said she wasn't allowed to have them. I even bought her a bracelet out the bubble gum machine and she told me that she doesn't wear cheap jewelry. I am at a loss. I keep striking out with this girl.

At the end of the school day, I pack up my bags and start to cut through the school yard to go to the gym for practice. I spot Marquise across the street talking to some guys. I put my bags down and casually walk over to them.

"Hey," I say tapping him on the shoulder before swinging with all my might. I hit him square in the jaw and watch him drop to the ground. His boys grip me up.

"Nah. Let 'em go," Marquise says standing up and spitting blood out of his mouth. "You wanna knuckle up little niggah?" He asks throwing his hands up. I brace myself. Now, this niggah done knocked me out twice already so I gotta think fast, move my feet and...

"FUCK," I say hitting the ground.

"Young bol, you got heart," Marquise says standing over top of me before everything went black.

Later that evening, Tone picks me up from basketball practice. We are riding in his car as I am applying ice to my busted lip that I had received from Marquise earlier.

"So, you wanna talk about it?" Tone asks laughing.

"Not really," I mumble.

"You know, I got something for that," Boom says pulling out his gun.

"Nah man, I'm straight," I tell him.

"What? You scared to pop a cap in somebody's ass?" Terry asks.

"No, but the niggah don't have to die for busting my ass." Tone laughs.

"See…leadership. That's what I keep tryin' to tell y'all knuckleheads," he says shaking his head. "I can't believe a fourteen-year-old gets it and y'all grown ass men; scared to take an ass whoopin'. Good job Nyce. You only shoot a niggah when you have to," Tone says. I see Terry cut his eyes at me.

We drop Terry and Boom off and head to Tone's place. When we walk inside, Tone's daughter comes running up to me.

"Uncle Nyce," Toni greets and jumps into my arms.

"What's up Peanut?"

"Wanna play dolls with me?" She innocently asks.

"Sure," I tell her not meaning it. Between her and Morgan, it's a wonder how my ass ain't gay.

"Hey suga," Nina greets, coming out of the kitchen and kissing my cheek. I blush as I feel a hard on coming on. I watch her ass sway back and forth before running into the bathroom to beat off. When I come out, Tone is standing in the hallway waiting for me.

"I'm gonna let you slide wit' beating your shit off to my girl in my own house."

"I wasn't," I lie embarrassed.

"Uh-huh," he laughs, throwing a dirty magazine at me and walking away. I put the magazine in my book bag before walking into Toni's room to play dolls. Twenty minutes later, Nina calls us down for dinner. Thank God.

"So babe, I think little Nyce here has a thing for you," Tone teases while we are sitting at the table. I almost choke on my juice.

"Don't embarrass him Tony. Come see me in ten years kid," Nina says smiling and then winks her eye at me. When we're all done eating, Nina stands and starts clearing the table.

"Ten years; twenty years, I don't care if I'm fuckin' dead, I will kill you if you ever try to take what's mine," Tone says whispering in my ear laughing but I know he's serious.

THREE

I'm chilling on the block when I see bitch ass Marquise swiftly run past me almost knocking me over. He is being chased by a clerk from Rite Aid.

"THIEF. SOMEBODY STOP HIM," the clerk yells. I think about chasing his bitch ass down. Not because he stole from Rite Aid; we in the hood; don't nobody care about that- but to get my revenge. I know, I know. He beat my ass 3 times already but I am determined to win at least once. I watch Marquise cut through the schoolyard and decide to go after him. The Rite Aid clerk gives up his pursuit so it's just me following Marquise on the sly. I watch him cut down an alleyway, and climb through a hole in the gate. Tracing his steps, I follow closely behind him without him noticing. He cuts through someone's backyard and enters a rundown house. Marquise leaves his front door wide open as he rushes inside. Following behind him, I tip-toe up the stairs.

"MOM, NO," I hear him crying. "I GOT THE MEDS MOM. NO. PLEASE WAKE UP," he yells. I stand in the doorway in shock watching Marquise hold a lifeless body on a dirty mattress while trying to insert a needle in his mother's leg.

"MOM…WAKE UP," he hollers at her. I'm stuck. I can't move.

"MOMMY," he yells again. His cries are agonizing. Painful. I stand stuck in place watching Marquise sit on the floor holding his mother's body with tears streaming down his face. I walk slowly towards him.

"Should I call somebody?" I ask softly. Alarmed, he turns to looks at me.

"Just go away," he mumbles. I try to leave but something is stopping me. Call it sorrow, or sympathy but I can't leave him like this.

"Mama, please wake up," he whispers tearfully. I walk closer to him.

"NIGGAH, WHAT ARE YOU STILL DOING HERE?" He snaps.

"I just want to help. We'll let bygones be bygones. Let me help you."

"GET OUT," he barks.

"You know where I live," I tell him before turning to leave. Marquise and his dead mom's body play heavily on my mind that night. The next day, I wrap up a breakfast sandwich, cut school, and go back to his house. I knock on the door this time but no one answers so I let myself in. I find Marquise still sitting next to his mother's body. He looks at me with tears running down his face.

"I don't know what to do," he cries.

"You have to call somebody. You can't just leave her here," I tell him.

"There is no one to call. If I call the ambulance, they will ask questions which leads to the cops coming and me getting taken out of here and placed in a group home."

"You don't have any family?" I ask.

"No. Not really."

"If I leave, will you stay here until I get back?" He nods his head up and down and starts crying again. I walk back home to get mama.

"Mama. Can you come with me please?" I ask her when I enter the apartment.

"James, why aren't you in school?" She scolds. I don't know why but tears start to fall from my eyes.

"Baby. What's wrong?" She asks alarmed pulling me into her arms.

"Can you please come with me?" I whisper. She grabs her coat and silently follows me to Marquise's house.

"We have to go upstairs," I tell her as she looks around the rundown, empty house. She follows me upstairs into the room. Marquise is still sitting, holding his mom. My mom quietly walks over to him and wraps an arm around him. Marquise grabs on to my mom, holds her tight and starts to cry. I mean, really cry. My mom lets him have his moment as she rocks him in her arms.

"James. Go call the paramedics," she says quietly.

"NO," Marquise says breaking out of my mother's embrace. "No. I'm not going back into a group home," he exclaims. My mom cocks her head to the side and sits quietly for a moment.

"I have to call somebody to come and get her. If I don't, she will rot. I need you to say goodbye and walk with James back to our home. Can you do that?" She calmly asks him. Marquise nods his head. He kisses his mom a final goodbye and walks out the room.

"Jimmy, go with him," my mom orders shooing me away.

"Are you going to be okay?" I ask not wanting to leave her by herself.

"Yes. I am going to use the phone to call the paramedics. I will call your father and Aunt Ruthie too. I'll be fine."

I walk down the stairs and out onto the porch. Marquise is sitting on the steps looking pitiful.

"You ready?" I ask him. He looks up at me with an empty expression.

"Why?" Is all he says. Understanding his question, I reply;

"I have a mom too." He nods his head in understanding and stands up. We walk back to my apartment in silence.

"Do you want something to eat?" I ask once inside.

"No," he mumbles as he sits down on my couch.

"Do you want to call somebody?"

"Like I said, there is no one to call. All of my so called family lives in Cleveland."

"Is that where you're from?"

"Yeah," he says. He closes his eyes and quickly falls asleep. About an hour later, I hear the front door open and close.

"Is everything okay?" I ask my parents while they're walking in. Behind them, my mom's sister, Ruthie and Grandma Norah are here too. I greet them both with a hug.

"Yes. The paramedics came and removed the body," my mom says. "Where is his family?"

"He said that he is from Cleveland and he doesn't have any family."

"Well he needs to get in contact with somebody for funeral arrangements," Aunt Ruthie says. "What's his name? Maybe I can look them up."

"His name is Marquise."

"Marquise what?" Aunt Ruthie asks. I shrug my shoulders.

"I don't know. I just know him by Marquise."

"Well, where is he?" Grandma Norah asks.

"Sleeping on the couch." Grandma Norah walks into the living room and stares down at a sleeping Marquise.

"Poor baby," she shakes her head in sympathy.

"Annette, what are you going to do with him?" Grandma asks.

"When he wakes up, I guess we will track his family down in Cleveland. He can stay here for now. He must be exhausted," my mother replies.

"There isn't any room here," my Grandma says turning up her nose and looking around. "I don't know why you won't come and stay with me for a while. There is plenty of room at my house."

My dad looks visibly annoyed and walks out the room.

"We're fine mama," my mother responds. "Jimmy, I am going to work. Please pick up Morgan from after school care. I'll be home on time tonight to cook dinner. Let your father rest if you can. I love you." My mom comes over to me and wraps her arms around me.

"See you sweet pea," Aunt Ruthie says.

"Jimmy, come give your Grandma a hug before I go." I get up and hug my Grandma. "You know you're my favorite right? Don't tell the others," she whispers in my ear while sliding some money in my pocket.

"I love you Grandma," I smile.

"I love you too."

I sit in the living room watching TV for most of the day. Marquise still hasn't budged from his spot. Around two in the afternoon, he finally wakes up.

"Shit. What time is it?" He asks, yawning.

"Don't curse in my parent's house and it's two." He gives me a funny look.

"I guess I'll be going then," he announces.

"Where you going? My mom said that you can stay until she contacts your people."

"I already told you; it's just me."

"Your dad?"

"A pimp in Memphis somewhere."

"Aunts? Uncles? Cousins?"

"Listen man. This ain't nothing new. I've been in and out of group homes for the majority of my life. Them niggahs didn't care then. I doubt they would care now."

"Why were you in the homes?" I question.

"Because," he says. I leave it alone. Obviously there is a backstory there.

"Are you hungry?" I ask.

"Nah. I'm good. Do you think I can take a shower?"

"Are you going to steal from us?" I ask not fully trusting him in my home. He laughs.

"Nah. I ain't gonna steal from you."

"You better not because then I would have to fuck you up for real," I tell him getting up off the couch.

"You can try to knuckle up with me but we both know how that's going to end. You already hit the pavement three times now." He laughs.

"Fuck you. You're bigger than me."

"Whatever man. Can I use your shower or not?" I walk him down the hall to the bathroom.

"I'll be right here," I tell him.

"Niggah, is you gay?"

"No but you're a thief in my home and I don't trust you." He looks around.

"Don't worry little Nyce. Y'all ain't got shit worth stealing anyway," he says slamming the bathroom door in my face. This shit ain't gonna work. I feel bad for him but I still don't trust him. He can't stay here if I don't trust him. Hell, I don't even like his bitch ass. I wait for him by the door for about 20 minutes before he swings the bathroom door open.

"Damn. You really don't trust me," he says walking past me and back into the living room.

"Where you going?" I ask avoiding his question and following behind him.

"I'm going to mind my business and don't try to stop me," he says putting on his shoes.

"I don't give a shit what you do."

"Funny how I can't curse in yo' mama's house but you don't show her the same respect," he accuses putting on his coat.

"I live here. You don't."

"Whatever," he says walking out the door.

Mama comes home around 6 o'clock. My dad, Morgan, Vi, and I are in the living room watching TV.

"Hey baby," my dad gets up to greet her.

"Hey honey," she says as they engage in a kiss.

"Where's the little boy?" She asks my dad. "James, where is your friend?"

"He's not my friend mom. He's just somebody I know."

"Well you displayed concern for him so I thought you guys were friends."

"Nope. That's the guy that keeps beating him up." Vi laughs.

"Hoya, you had the kid that keeps kicking your butt up and down the streets in my house? What's wrong with you son?" my dad asks confused.

"Leonard, leave him alone. He has a heart of gold. What you did today for him was an act of human kindness. You did nothing wrong," my mom assures me sounding like an after school special. "Do you know where he went? He can't roam these streets alone. He is still just a child."

"I don't know mom. I didn't ask him." My mom cocks her head to the side and looks at me thoughtfully. Without saying another word, she disappears into the kitchen.

By the next day, everything is back to normal. I walk Vi to her class and then cut around the building to go to my class. School is school. I can't wait until I'm done with this shit. I only go so I can play basketball, and I make good grades because that is the stipulation my mom lives by. Bad grades equal no basketball.

I dominate the court as usual with Tone and his boys cheering me on. Mr. Paul brings pizza for everyone and I spend time with my team celebrating our victory. Afterwards, I sit with Tone in his car as he preaches.

"So have you thought about a stash house?" He asks me.

"Yeah."

"Where?"

"I'm not supposed to tell you."

"It's me."

"I don't trust you." He smiles.

"I'm glad that you listen to me but that hurt little niggah," he chuckles. "But that's right. Your stash house will only be for you and your top lieutenants to run product out of. Always watch your back. Never drive your own car. Circle the block a few times and always check your mirrors. Niggahs will try to rob you once they know who you are," he repeats sounding like a broken record.

"Nobody is going to know who I am. Rule number one...don't get caught. I plan on never getting caught. I'm going to remain inconspicuous. Never bring unwanted attention to myself. Remain incognito. I will be a shadow. Few people that I trust will know but majority will not."

"Good...good," he says beaming.

"So if these are your rules, why don't you live by them?" I ask.

"What do you mean?"

"I mean, well, the hood knows you're a drug dealer."

"Do they? Have you ever seen me sell drugs?"

"No," I answer truthfully.

"Have you ever seen a feign come up to me?"

"No."

"That's right. It's all speculation. You *assume* I sell drugs. All you know about me is that I like to hang out with my friends on the corner and talk."

"Yeah but…"

"But nothing. I'm from this neighborhood so I come back frequently to talk to the people I grew up with. I am a business man. I own a detail shop, some real estate, and I pay my taxes. I'm married to a law student, we have a daughter, and I live in the suburbs. I go to PTA meetings; every parent/teacher conference; every field trip. My daughter's friends play in my pool in the summertime and their parents, who are doctors, lawyers, and judges come to my house for my end of the summer Barbecue's. I am a law abiding citizen and a likeable dude. I'm non-threatening to the white man. I'm just a simple business man trying to raise a family."

"Tone? You're married?" I ask surprised. He smirks.

"Like I said, there is a lot that you don't know about me. The world operates like a chess board Nyce. You have you. You are the king. You are your empire. You have your queen. For some that may be their lady. For others, that is your right hand man. In my case, Bo is my right hand. Very few people know that because nobody needs to know. The less people know, the more mystery and protection you build.

"Anyway, the King & Queen; the President & Vice President. You have your other key players that you trust that are going to protect you at all times. Those are the pieces you move on your board to make big moves; to make big deals. To move weight. To sell to your top notch clientele. They are the CEO's, COO's, the directors and shit like that. Then you have your pawns. Your pawns are disposable. Those are the ones you keep on the streets to push nickels and dimes. They are the ones who get locked up and take the rap for you. You grease their palms a bit. Make them feel like they are a part of something. Feed their books while they're locked up and take care of their families. The pawns, you treat like the annoying kids of the bitch you're trying to fuck. You're only nice to them because you have to be," he says to me.

"Huh?" I ask confused trying to keep up.

"Just remember what I'm sayin'. You don't understand now because you are still young and green but you'll get it one day. Your pawns are your laborers; your workers. They are on the forefront like in all corporations. They are under paid, over worked, and take the biggest risks. Treat them with respect. They're disposable but they are valuable.

"So am I a pawn?" I ask curiously.

"You haven't listened to a word I've been saying," he says annoyed. "Get out," he tells me.

"Just help me understand," I say to him.

"We wouldn't be having this conversation if I thought you were just a pawn. Like I said, I'm grooming you."

"Grooming me for what?"

"OUT," he barks at me and tosses me three one hundred dollar bills. I climb out the car confused but I'm always confused when it comes to Tone.

NYCE

Friday is finally here and this is the weekend Keisha comes to spend time with her Dad. After school, I purchase her a gold necklace with a butterfly pendant. After putting some money in my parent's bank account (they still have no idea that I feed their accounts so we can stay afloat), I treat myself to a haircut, some jeans, and a new button up shirt. I wish I had the money for some fresh kicks too but I have to treat my sisters to a little something.

I walk up the block hoping to run into her. I find her and Vi in the park sitting on a bench.

"What y'all doin'?" I ask joining them.

"Minding our business, now go away Nyce," Vi blurts.

"Shut up Vi. Hi Keisha," I say turning my attention to her.

"Hello."

"Can I talk to you for a moment?"

"I'm listening."

"In private please."

"I'll be right back girl," she says to Vi. Vi rolls her eyes at me. We walk a little bit away from Vi.

"I got you something," I tell her smiling and pulling out the necklace.

"It's nice," she says nonchalantly.

"You don't like it?" I ask.

"No. I wish you would stop and leave me alone," she says harshly as she begins to walk back to Vi. Bitch. She just crushed my soul.

"Hey," I say catching up to her.

"Nyce, leave her alone," Vi huffs.

"I just have somethin' to tell you," I say to Keisha grabbing her arm. She quickly snatches her arm away from me like I have cooties.

"What is it?" She hisses.

"One day, you are going to want me so bad that it's gonna make you sick. You'll be begging me to be with you," I promise her and begin to walk out the park. As I'm turning the corner I run into Marquise.

"Yo punk," he insults.

"We can square up right here," I say to him with my guard up.

"Man, sit down somewhere. Ain't nobody trying to knuckle up wit' you."

"What you doin' around here then?" I ask.

"I just left from your place. I took your mom some flowers as a thank you."

"Don't be going to my house when I'm not home niggah," I say getting angry.

"Relax. I like your mom. I wouldn't do anything to her and I won't allow anybody to fuck wit' her either."

"I protect my mom. She don't need you."

"Like I said, relax man. We're good and now I owe you one for helpin' me."

"You don't owe me shit"

"Nyce, let's let bygones be bygones," he says extending his hand.

"Fuck outta here," I snap stepping around him.

"Thanks anyway. It's not often that people have shown me they care. My mom was all I had."

"You're welcome," I say with a twinge of guilt for acting like an ass.

FOUR

Summer is finally here and the school year has ended. You would think I would be excited about being on summer vacation, right? *Wrong*. My mom makes me, Vi, and Morgan do book reports, math and reading assignments *every day*. It's cool though. Once we do an hour of each, she lets us enjoy our freedom.

Summertime in the hood is the truth. The loud systems blasting out of people's cars, the girls in their short shorts; busting open fire hydrants to cool off; playing tag and hide and go get it when the street lights come on; the endless summer league games and Mr. Paul giving us free ice cream and popsicles during heat waves. I love summers in the hood.

I spot Keisha walking with one of my classmates Ashley. Taking a chapter out of my father's book, I walk towards them.

"Hey Nyce," Ashley speaks. Let's see how Keisha likes being ignored.

"What's up Ashley?" I greet her giving her a hug.

"Nothing. You tell me what's up," she says.

"Be careful what you ask for," I flirt, smiling at her while caressing her cheek.

"So is Ashley all you see?" Keisha interrupts.

"You tryin' to go to the movies later Ashley?" I ask, ignoring Keisha.

"Yes," she answers eagerly. "But I have to ask my mom first."

"Cool. Just give me a call," I tell her and hand her my number before walking away.

"Hey Ashley," I yell out her name. She slowly turns around.

"Yes," she answers.

"If your mom says yes, wear that yellow sundress you got. You look really pretty in it," I tell her before walking down the street. I turn my head slightly to where the girls are standing and see Keisha out the corner of my eye staring me down and looking like someone just slapped her across the face. *Good,* I laugh. I go home to chill and watch some TV. I'm in the middle of watching *Thunder Cats* when the phone begins to ring.

"I'll get it," I yell to my mom. "Hello."

"Is Vi there?" Keisha asks on the other end.

"Nope," I tell her hanging up. The phone rings again.

"Hello," I answer.

"You ain't have to hang up on me," Keisha says with an attitude.

"You didn't call for me so why the hell would I stay on the phone?"

"What if I wanted to leave a message?"

"Would you like to leave a message, Keisha?" I sarcastically ask.

"Yes. Please tell her that I called."

"Isn't that obvious?"

"What?"

"Nothin'. Bye," I tell her hanging up.

Later on that night I meet up with Ashley. I take her out to see *Home Alone* and for some pizza after.

"Did you like the movie?" I ask her as I am walking her home.

"Yes. I thought it was soooo funny," she giggles. "I'm a little surprised that you asked me out though."

"Why?"

"Because I thought you had a thing for Keisha."

"If I had a thing for Keisha, I wouldn't have bought you this," I tell her handing her the butterfly necklace that I had originally bought for Keisha.

"Do you like it?" I ask.

"Yes. Thank you," she beams and gives me a kiss on the cheek. I walk her to her door.

"I'll call you later, okay?"

"Okay," she says smiling before walking inside her house. I walk back to my crib and as soon as I step foot inside the door, the phone starts ringing.

"Jimmy, the phone's for you," my mother shouts. I walk into the kitchen and take the phone out of her hands.

"Hello."

"How in the hell you just gonna give Ashley the necklace you bought for me?" Keisha yells.

"You said you ain't want it," I laugh.

"That's foul Nyce."

"Whateva. What do you want Keisha?" I ask trying to sound annoyed while holding in my laughter.

"Nothing. I just think that you are rude and an arrogant jerk."

"What else do you think about me?"

"Nothin'. You're so whack."

"Have you heard from DT today?" I ask her.

"Who?"

"Dial Tone," I say before slamming the phone down in her ear.

I continue to ignore and be rude to Keisha throughout the summer. As my dad predicted, it seemed that the more I acted like a dickhead towards her, the more she paid attention to me. So I ignore her most of the time. Not because I don't want her but because I have to teach her a lesson; never play ya boy.

Later that night, I meet up with Tone and we are riding through the city cruising the streets. He finally parks his car on the hill at Fairmont Park; what we call the Plat for short. It's where niggahs hang out to smoke, shoot dice, and to show off their bikes, cars and dogs.

"Reach in the glove box and hand me that bag of weed," Tone says to me. "Can you roll?" He asks.

"No. I don't smoke."

"You've watched me enough times to know. Roll," he demands. I do as he says as best as I can making a mess.

"Damn Nyce. What the hell is this shit?" He asks when I try to give him the rolled blunt.

"I told you I didn't know how," I laugh.

"Smoke with me Nyce."

"Nah. I promised my mom."

"You gonna do everything that your mama says? I bet she told you to wait until you're married to have sex too, huh?" He teases.

"So," I reply.

"Nyce. You a virgin?"

"Yeah. You make it sound like a bad thing."

"You're almost fifteen so yeah, it is. I lost mine at thirteen to my babysitter."

"You didn't lose your virginity. Niggah, you got molested," I laugh.

"Niggah watch yo' mouth."

"I'm saying. How old was she?"

"Nineteen I think."

"And you don't see an issue?" Tone thinks about it for a moment.

"Shut up, Nyce. I hate talkin' to you sometimes," he says hitting the blunt. "You just haven't made the change yet."

"What change?"

"The change where all you want is pussy and money. That change. I'll give you until next summer, maybe sooner. You still have a lot of kid in you despite your maturity level. What's up with you and that little light-skinned girl that be hanging around you and your sister? I see how she looks at you."

"Keisha? Nothing's up. I'm letting her digest the fact that she didn't want me when I was chasing her so I fell back. She got to chase me now if she wants me."

"SEE. NOW THAT RIGHT THERE IS WHY YOU MY LITTLE NIGGAH," Tone shouts cracking up. "That's some shit I would do."

We go back to Tone's house and I change into my swim trunks. I walk out to the backyard and Toni tries to tackle me.

"Uncle Nyce, come play in the pool with me," she says chasing me.

"Alright Peanut but only if you can catch me," I tell her as her little legs start running a little harder. I glance up and see Nina come out wearing an orange bikini. I'm staring so hard at her that I trip over the garden hose and skin my knee.

"Uncle Nyce are you alright?" Toni asks. "You're bleeding," she says. I don't give a damn about the blood leaking down my leg. All I can do is stare at Nina who is now running towards us with her titties bouncing up and down.

"Oh my gosh baby, are you alright?" She asks me. I just sit on the ground not saying a word trying to hide my boner.

"He a'ight Nina," Tone laughs handing her the peroxide and cotton balls. Nina cleans my knee up as Tone is making faces and teasing me for my woody behind her back.

"Daddy. What are you doing?" Toni asks.

"Nothing baby girl. Teasing your Uncle Nyce there," Tone replies, cracking up.

"All cleaned up," Nina says placing a Band Aid on my knee. She stands up and turns to walk back into the house. As she walks away I watch her ass bounce with every step. *Damn.*

"Snap the fuck out of it," Tone laughs popping me in the back of my head.

"Shut up man. I need a minute," I tell him trying to get my wood down.

"Jump in the pool dummy. Your shit should shrivel right up," he suggests picking up Toni and walking in the house. I stand up and hop in the pool.

"All better?" Tone asks me when I sit down at the patio table.

"Shut up Tone," I respond while spreading mustard on my hot dog.

"Here chump." Tone throws a box of condoms at me. "Never leave home without 'em."

"I don't need these," I tell him.

"Just in case," he says.

"Daddy, what are these?" Toni asks.

"Parachutes darling," he answers winking his eye at me. I laugh.

"Tony, don't corrupt that boy," Nina says sitting pasta salad down on the table.

"I ain't doing nothing that he ain't gonna do naturally on his own," he says.

For the remainder of the night, I chill at Tone's house and play with Toni. When Bo and his girl Rasheeda comes, I watch and learn how to play Spades and Dominos in between Toni bossing me around.

The following day, I wake up early, get dressed and hop a bus to Grandmom Norah's house in Wynnewood. At least twice a week during the summer I try to visit her. I love Grandma Norah; she's mad cool but more importantly, she treats me like a kid. At home, I feel like I have to be and think like an adult. Here it's different. Grandma Norah's house is my escape to just be a kid. I like sitting on her porch, eating cookies, drinking lemonade and listening to her chatter about the good old days and when Pop-Pop was alive. It's a nice change of pace for me without the worry of bills getting paid and putting food on the table. Sometimes I miss just being a kid.

FIVE
1992

September 1992 and ya boy is about to turn sixteen already-standing at 6'3 and 170 pounds of muscle. I've been lifting weights in the gym and it got my body lookin' right, I mean, hella right. I can't keep the females off me but I ain't trying to either. Between having small town celebrity status with my basketball skills and having a "bad boy" image from hanging out with Tone's crew, chicks always come flocking when they see me. Keisha hates it. We break up to make up. Yeah, it's official. Keish is my girl and I love her but it's like once I got a taste, now I have an insatiable appetite. My dick seems to have a mind of his own but I'm always careful. I only go raw wit' my chick who ain't talking to me at the moment. See, women don't understand. Men can fuck other women and still be in love wit' one. Keisha ain't going nowhere anyway. As long as I keep her flyy, give her money when she asks, and continue to dick her down good, the little fights and arguments we have are minimal.

Tone and I still hang tight and I still have not touched any drug product. I continue to shadow him as he talks his jibberish. It's all good though. He pays me almost $1000 a month to do nothing but listen to him talk so I can't complain and I like the fear that niggahs get when I'm around due to my association with Tone and his crew. I can hold my own though. I still be knocking niggahs out when need be. Had to knock one out the other night for stepping to my fourteen year-old sister and I ain't having it - even though she's a hot ass. Not sure if she's fuckin' yet but I wouldn't be surprised. I try to keep her out of trouble too but she acts like an ungrateful spoiled little brat. She's another female that is always in my pocket wanting something but I love her so of course I take care of her.

My moms finally graduated and is working as a middle school teacher out in Overbrook. She seems happy with her job and I am happy for her. My dad is still busting his ass for SEPTA but at least they gave him a nice raise. Now that my parents finally got their shit together, I no longer have to pay the bills in the house. Life is good.

I'm on a high walking home from school after a winning game when all of sudden Tone's car screeches to a halt.

"Get in," he demands.

"What's up? I didn't see you at my football game," I tell him hopping in the backseat of his car. Bo is sitting in the front.

"My bad," Tone says.

"We need you to get your ass on a plane and fly to Oklahoma City and make this drop," Bo advises.

"WHAT?"

"Listen. You remember everything I taught you, right? I'm gonna give you $25,000 in cash to fly to OKC, buy product and drive it back. I don't mean to put you on the spot but you're the only one I trust with that kind of money," Tone explains.

"Man...Tone," is all I manage to utter. I don't even know what to say other than the fact that I don't want to do this shit.

"Remember that favor you owe Tone for keeping your dad alive little niggah? Well today is the day you pay up," Bo barks.

"Bo, chill. I'll handle this," Tone intervenes.

"Nyce, I do need you now and you owe me this," Tone says seriously.

"I'm scared to fly," I confess hoping that somehow I can get out of this.

"Niggah, you better get yo' ass on that damn plane," Bo snaps. Tone slaps his arm before pulling the car over and turning his body around to face me. He looks me dead in my eyes.

"This is pay-up time. Don't make me do something that we both are going to regret."

"When do you need me to do this?" I ask. My head is spinning on how I am going to get out of this without anybody getting hurt.

"By the end of the month. I'm working on plans with my cousin now who is hooking me up with the connect. This is your first test, Nyce. Don't disappoint me," Tone says.

"You're using me as a pawn. You said that I wasn't a pawn," I challenge Tone. He says nothing in response as he sits quietly staring at me.

"Just do what the fuck you're told and shut the fuck up," Bo snaps. I look at Tone who is still saying nothing.

"I'll work out the details. You just find someone who is going to help you drive back. Now get out," Tone barks maliciously.

What the fuck am I going to do? I knew this day was going to come but I didn't think he would make me do some shit like this. I thought I would be doing little shit; like picking up and dropping off locally. On the walk home I have all types of thoughts running through my mind.

"JAMES," Morgan greets me at the door as I pick her up.

"What's up, Organ?"

"I'm eight now and I don't say your name wrong anymore so stop teasing mine," she says.

"You don't want to be my little Organ anymore?" I ask her.

"I will always be your Organ but can you please call me Morgan now?"

"As long as you continue to get good grades and make me proud, I promise to call you Morgan."

"Good," she exclaims kissing my cheek and jumping out of my arms.

"What up, Pop?" I greet my dad as I enter the kitchen.

"Good. You're finally home," my mom says entering. "I want to talk to you guys. VI…MORGAN…get in here. Your father and I have some great news."

"Yes," Morgan and Vi answer, taking a seat at the kitchen table.

"WE'RE MOVING," my mom excitedly blurts out.

"Yay. Where to?" Morgan squeals bouncing in her seat.

"To Overbrook Park. It's like a small suburb in the city. 5 bedrooms, 2.5 bathrooms, basement. Oh my goodness I am just so happy," my mom beams full of excitement and passes Polaroid pictures around the table. This might be the answer to my prayers. I just have to make sure that my sisters don't tell anybody so Tone and Bo won't catch wind.

"YAY. Closer to Keisha," Vi points out bouncing in her chair.

"Yes. You will more than likely be going to the same school," my mom confirms.

"When are we moving?" I ask anxiously. I want to put as much distance between me and Tone as possible.

"Next weekend so start packing," my dad answers.

By the end of September, we officially move out of the projects and into our new place. My parents allow me to have the entire third floor and bathroom to myself. Finally, no little sisters to bug and nag the fuck out of me. The first night we're there, I walk around the neighborhood casing out the area, making my way down to Overbrook High School; the school that Vi and I will be attending. It takes me 4,526 steps to walk from my house to the school; approximately 30 minutes in time.

As I walk, I take mental notes of the area. Whose backyard can I cut through? What houses have dogs? What hiding places I can fit my body in? The neighborhood is so quiet; too quiet. I'm not use to that. Being in the suburbs, I no longer have the protection of city noises to mask my heavy footsteps or breathing if I need to run and hide.

I wake up early the next day to get ready for my first day of school.

"Come on Nyce," Vi says eagerly as she busts into my bedroom. I hate the fact that we are two years apart but only one grade behind each other because Vi's smart ass skipped the second grade.

"You need to learn how to knock," I tell her as I'm getting dressed.

"Well hurry up. I don't want to be late for our first day," she whines. Vi is hype to be attending a new school but I am terrified. That just means more fights that I will get into because of her. When I'm done getting dressed, I meet her outside on the porch as Keisha is walking up the steps.

"Hey baby," she smiles brightly, greeting me with a kiss. She looks really pretty wearing a red dress with white Reeboks.

"Hey. You look pretty," I tell her grabbing her ass.

"I'm tryin' to look good for my man. You being in my school now is scary. I'm gonna be fighting bitches off you. Just remember where and who you belong to," she warns. As if Tone wasn't enough to worry about, I now have to worry about Keisha's ass blocking me from getting some new ass.

"There's nothing to worry about babe. I'm all yours," I assure her.

"Uh-huh. Hey girl," she says greeting Vi as she steps out of the house and onto the porch.

"Hey girl."

"You nervous," Keisha asks Vi.

"A little. I wish we were in the same grade so I at least know somebody."

"Don't worry about that. I got you. You will be hanging out with me and my girls in the caf. So when people see you hanging out with a bunch of 10th graders it will enhance your popularity. Trust me," Keisha assures her.

"I'll meet up with y'all," I tell them.

"You're not going to walk with us?" Vi asks

"Nah. Y'all good. Here," I say to her giving her $20.00 for lunch.

"And what about me?" Keisha asks with her hand sticking out.

"Here." I hand her a $10 bill.

"Why are you holding out on me Nyce?" She whines with her lips poked out.

"Because you're holding out on me," I point out before walking down the stairs. Keisha has put me on "punishment" by not giving me any sex because she caught me cheating, again.

"I'll just see you in school, Nyce," she mutters rolling her eyes.

Damn. Overbrook High School got some nice looking women and they're so helpful in helping the new student. I've collected five numbers already and it's not even ten o'clock. I got a white girl named Wendy's number. I haven't smashed a white girl yet but it is definitely on my to-do list.

The student body is very diverse; something to get used to. I'm in my Social Studies class half listening to the lecture when I decide that I need a break and ask to use the bathroom. As I'm roaming the halls trying to find more victims, I mean, women to add to my collection, I spot some big dude breaking into lockers. *What the hell is this niggah doin'?* I think to myself as I watch him steal somebody's Walkman, Gameboy and lunch. I casually walk by him but then the guy stops me.

"Well, if it isn't little Nyce. What you doin' in these parts?" Marquise asks me.

"Niggah, ain't you too old to be stealing people's lunches?" I laugh.

"You know how it is. You want some?" He asks opening up a fruit roll up.

"Nah. I'm good. You go to school here?"

"Yeah. Something like that," he snickers while breaking into another locker.

"So, we friends now or what? I kind of run this school," he says stealing someone's jacket.

"Don't count on it," I tell him walking away. This niggah's crazy.

The first two months of school is pretty dope. Not the classes but the socializing part. On top of that, Wendy has been extremely helpful in keeping me from missing my girlfriend from back home. She understands that we have to keep our relationship on the low for now because my girlfriend's cousin Keisha goes here. I tell all the girls I'm fucking the same lie but Wendy, I kind of like. She's pretty cool for a Snow Bunny. Plus, she knows how to cater to a niggah. She brings me lunch and does my homework but most importantly, she doesn't get on my fuckin' nerves with pressuring me to leave my girl and trying to force me to commit to her.

Marquise was right. He does have the school on lock. Everyone fears him. He doesn't bother me at all but I still keep my distance. I always watch his small entourage cater to his every whim out of fear.

I make some new friends too; some real friends. I've never had that before because I learned early on to not trust niggahs in the hood. Maurice is a cool dude. He's on the football team with me, and we pick up females together at away games. For him to be pitch black, he has a way with the females. Because this niggah is pitch black, I started calling him Black. Once I did, the name just stuck. I also befriend Calvin but everyone calls him Mookie. Not sure why he has that stupid ass nickname but I'm not about to ask him either. Mookie has a couple of screws loose in his head; like anything will set him off but he's a cool dude and one of my new friends.

I'm walking home from football practice when a car screeches to a halt.

"GET THE FUCK IN," Tone yells out the window. *FUCK!* I drop my shit and take off running as two of Tone's goons chase me. I dodge in between cars and cut through someone's backyard going towards the alleyway to get to my hiding spot. I glance behind me and the men are still chasing me. I finally make it to the alleyway but my plan to shake them off isn't working.

What the fuck did Tone do? Hire Emmit Smith's nephews to chase me 'cuz these niggahs are on my heels.

I cut down the alley as the men turn the corner. No time to hide so I just keep running. I am almost through when I see three men at the opposite end waiting. I slow down to turn back but the other two men are approaching me fast. *FUCK. THINK FAST.*

I try to hurry and hop the fence into someone's backyard but I am quickly snatched off the gate.

"FUCK," I yell as my body hits the pavement. The men swarm around me and start kicking me. I do a swift Bruce Lee move and roll out the way, quickly bouncing to my feet. I start swinging for my life as I randomly hit these niggahs and they start hitting on me— one against five. Yeah I'm getting a little fucked up but I'm taking these niggahs down too as I watch one hit the ground.

"YO," I hear a familiar voice yell. I don't know who it is because I am too busy concentrating not getting my ass beat. As I am swinging, knocking these niggahs back, they start hitting the pavement like flies; getting knocked the fuck out. When two of them are stone cold on the ground, I am finally able to look and see who the hell is knocking these niggahs out with me.

"MARQUISE?" I shout surprised to see him out of all people. We are now two against two.

"Yo," he casually answers. Marquise swings at the guy he is squaring up with, throwing his mighty fist and in one blow to the jaw; I watch the other guy's teeth come out of his mouth as he hits the pavement face first. *This niggah hits hard as hell.* I move out of Marquise's way so he can take care of the last guy, in which he does with little to no effort.

"Uh...thanks," I tell him.

"You good?" He asks me.

"Yeah. You?"

"I'm good. So what was that about?"

"Stupid, long story," I reply as I hear someone clapping in the background. I don't have to turn around to know who it is.

"Little Nyce," Tone says still clapping while a lollipop hangs out of his mouth. Bo and Terry are with him. "You did all of this?" He asks looking at his fallen soldiers.

"I had help," I tell him truthfully noting that both Bo and Terry are wearing brass knuckles.

"Uh-huh. Niggah you owe me. I thought we was better than that."

"Look man. I don't want to hustle for you."

"You don't have a choice."

"We all have choices," Marquise interjects ready for action. "He said he don't want to be bothered with you so leave him alone." Bo steps up but Tone gently holds him back. Tone turns to Marquise.

"I heard about your little bitch ass. They told me that your hands are deadly."

"Then you know when I say to leave him alone, I mean it."

"Niggah, if you don't cut that shit out. You're from the streets. You know how this works. Now I'm about to make both of y'all put in that work."

"I ain't doing shit," Marquise snaps stepping to Tone. In one swift move, Bo pulls out his gun.

"And what's that supposed to do? Shoot niggah," Marquise challenges not backing down. Bo points the gun at me. BANG...BANG...BANG. I damn near jump out of my skin as I Moonwalk across the pavement while Bo continues to shoot at my feet. Terry laughs.

"ALRIGHT, THAT'S ENOUGH BO. STOP," Tone yells at him.

"STOP," Marquise shouts and then stands in front of Bo without hesitation.

"This is between me and Nyce so I suggest you back the fuck up," Bo spits.

"I am my brother's keeper so now it's between me, you, and him" Marquise challenges, still not backing down. Bo and Terry start cracking up as Tone's goons start to come to.

"Nyce, I ain't playin'. I may not know where you live now but I do know where your peoples work," Bo says.

"You made your point Bo," Tone tells him.

"I'll see you tomorrow when you get out of school. I'll be waiting in front of the steps. If you run from me again, I swear on my life I will put a bullet in your back," Tone says tucking Bo's gun away.

"Get the fuck up," Tone yells kicking the other men who are still lying on the ground. "Y'all niggahs better find your own way home; gettin' knocked out by children and shit. Disgrace," he spits annoyed as him, Terry, and Bo walk up the alley.

"Thanks man," I say to Marquise as we begin to walk.

"What you gonna do?" He asks me.

"What can I do? Why did you help me?"

"Because you needed help," he replies with a shrug of his shoulders. We walk in silence for a moment.

"Where are you staying?" I ask.

"Here and there."

"Do you need a place to stay, Marquise?"

"Nah, I'm good. I have until 11 o'clock to make it to the shelter."

"You can come to my house. At least come and get something to eat."

"So, we friends now?" He asks with a smile on his face.

"Something like that," I tell him. This niggah just somewhat saved my ass so I guess I can let bygones be bygones...for now.

"Do you want to take a shower or something?" I ask him once we're inside my room.

"Yeah," he mumbles, greedily slurping up the spaghetti I made the other night.

"Towels and washcloths are in the bathroom closet and here." I hand Marquise a t-shirt and some sweatpants to throw on.

"Thanks man," he says grabbing the items. I go downstairs and chill in the living room for about 45 minutes before Marquise makes his way down the stairs.

"Where your parents at?" He asks.

"My mom will be here soon. She's probably tutoring somebody and my dad more than likely is still at work. He won't get home until later this evening."

"Hey Jimmy. Who's this?" Morgan asks entering the living room.

"Damn. She got big," Marquise says.

"Nyce, Keisha has been lookin' for you," Vi says coming into the living room.

"Hi," Marquise greets, acknowledging Vi.

"She's fourteen and I will kill you," I warn.

"Damn, Nyce. All he did was say hi," Vi says walking out with an attitude.

"You straight homie. I would never violate like that," he says.

"Just remember what I said."

"It's all good. So, what's the deal wit' them niggahs in the alleyway?" He asks.

"Morgan, go read a book or something," I tell her. She huffs but does what she's told.

"Man. I got caught up in some dumb shit. He wanted me to fly to Oklahoma and drive back with kilos of drugs. That was over two months ago. I have no idea what he wants me to do now."

"Don't worry. Take the meeting and see what the fuck he wants. We'll take it from there," Marquise proposes making himself comfortable on my couch.

When I walk out the doors of Overbrook High School the next day, I see Tone sitting in his hooptie parked across the street, as promised. I walk down the stairs to an awaiting Marquise eating a bag of chips.

"You good?" He asks me.

"As good as I'm gonna get. Wait here," I tell him as I reluctantly proceed to walk across the street.

"Little Nyce," Terry sarcastically acknowledges me when I hop in the car. I suck in my breath.

"What up, Tone?" I say ignoring Terry and a pissed off looking Bo.

"Here," Bo says handing me bundles of white packages. "The packages are labeled. H for heroin and C for coke or crack. You remember how to cook it, right? I know Tone has showed you more than a thousand times."

"I thought you said that you would never make me a corner boy; a pawn," I say to Tone as I hold the bundles in my hands.

"That was before you moved without telling me. We no longer have that relationship. That's about $1500 worth of shit-$5 per bag. I will meet you here next Friday to collect. Don't be late and more importantly don't be short," Tone says curtly.

"And what if I can't sell it all?"

"You better…and Nyce?" Bo hisses.

"What?"

"I'm sorry about Keisha," he laughs.

"What?" I ask confused.

"I was gonna go after your mom but Tone stopped me on some pussy shit. Go check on your girl, and get the fuck outta this car," Bo barks with his gun already pointing at me. I jump out his car slamming the door hard. I hear the window shatter but I don't look back as I start running home. I hear Marquise's heavy footsteps running behind me.

"What the fuck we runnin' for?" He asks when we make it to my front porch. I open the door and walk into the kitchen. Morgan is sitting in my mother's lap crying.

"What happened?" I ask taking Morgan out of my mother's arms and trying to console her.

"Keisha is in the hospital. Some guys robbed her and beat her up pretty good. Your father and Vi just left to go see her. Morgan is shaken up a bit. Had I known that we would still be facing this type of bullshit, I would have never moved here," my mom utters. I put Morgan down and go upstairs to think. Thirty minutes later, there is a knock on my door. Without waiting for an answer, Marquise barges in.

"WHAT?" I snap.

"Man, chill. I called you a cab. They're waiting outside for us," he says.

At the hospital, I stop by the gift shop and buy Keisha a bear and some roses. Marquise and I find her room and knock before stepping in.

"Hey baby," she greets me with a smile. She has a bandage on the side of her face, scratches on her neck, and her hand is wrapped up in an ace bandage.

"What happened?" I ask as I take a seat on the foot of the bed.

"Marquise? What are you doing here?" She asks confused.

"Hey Keisha," he greets.

"Keish, what happened?" I ask again.

"I don't know. I was walking home from school and three guys robbed me. They took my book bag, my purse, and the necklace you gave me. I fought back and that's when one of the guys punched me in the face; splitting my skin. I sprained my hand...my face," she explains in between sobs.

"I'm sorry, baby," I try to console her giving her a kiss and a hug. My dad and Vi enter the room.

"About time you showed up, Nyce," Vi snaps.

"Shut up, Vi."

"Where were you? Why didn't you protect her," Vi screams at me with tears in her eyes.

"That's enough, Viola," my dad says.

"No. He walks around here like King Tut and..."

"I said that's enough Vi," my dad demands with a stern look on his face.

"Are they keeping you overnight?" I ask Keisha.

"No. I'm just waiting for my mom to get here."

I feel like shit. I mean pure shit. Keisha took a beating for me. I'm fuckin' pissed. Tone and his goons crossed the fuckin' line. He has to go.

I lie awake all night thinking of a way to get rid of him and Bo's ass without the worry of his goons coming to hunt me and my family down.

I look on the floor at a sleeping Marquise snoring loudly. I'm not sure how I got stuck with this niggah. I'm not even sure if I fully trust him yet.

The next day at football practice, we are running suicide drills when I spot Marquise waiting for me on the bleachers. When the coach finally blows his whistle to dismiss us, I start walking over to him.

"Where you going?" Black asks me.

"I have something to handle," I tell him and Mookie.

"With Marquise? That niggah is bad news."

"Nah. He's straight."

"You need me to handle him?" Mookie asks.

"And what you gonna do, Mook?"

"I'm gonna handle some business, niggah," he replies.

"Nah. I'm cool," I tell him finally reaching the bleachers.

"Nasty Nyce," Marquise says giving me dap. "What y'all niggahs want?" He asks Mookie and Black.

"Nyce, all you gotta do is say the word," Mookie states staring at Marquise.

"What niggah? You tryin' ta knuckle up wit' me?" Marquise barks taking his stance. I step in between the two of them.

"Chill. Nobody is doin' nothin'. Black, Mook, I'll catch y'all later," I tell them as Marquise and I start walking out the yard.

"What's in the book bag, homie?" I ask.

"Your drugs, niggah. We're going to some chick's house I know. She's gonna cook it up and increase the supply; try to put some cash in our pockets."

"Marquise, what about customers? Who the fuck am I going to sell this shit to?"

"You think these white kids up in here don't get down? You're trippin'. Word of mouth spreads fast. Start here, build a team, and start spreading out to the 'burbs," he says sounding like Tone.

We finally reach our destination as I follow Marquise around back and into the garage. The garage is fully decked out with a kitchen, living area, bathroom, and one bedroom. There are travel posters and brochures hanging on the walls and on the tables. Three white girls from school are sitting on the couch, watching TV and passing a blunt around.

"Hey you," Becky greets Marquise with a kiss on the cheek.

"You sure you know what you're doin', Beck?" Marquise asks her handing her the bag.

"Yeah. I got this BUT it's gonna cost you," she says.

"What?" I ask.

"Some product of course. You can make the money back if you stop by Friday night. I know a few people who wouldn't mind having a local around instead of us driving all the way down into the city to cop shit."

"Cool," I tell her while silently praying in my head for her not to fuck this up. I watch her divide the bag in half.

"Keep this to sell coke," she says handing the soft powder back to me. I start to seal the bag back but was quickly interrupted

"Uh-uh. You have to pay your dues before sealing that bag. Tobi, see what we're workin' wit'," Becky says motioning for the other girl to come and test the product. I hand Tobi the bag, watch her scoop a small portion out and make a line on the table. She digs in her purse, takes out a cut straw and inhales the powder, clearing the line.

"Shit," she says holding her nose with her purple fingernails. "That shit's good," she says mopping the table with her finger and putting the remainder of the residue in her mouth. "Like, good-good...pure," she continues.

"Let me get on this," the girl from my math class says. I think her name is Lisa or Lucy. Something with an L.

"Go for it Lucy. You won't be disappointed," Tobi says handing her a straw. I watch Lucy repeat the same exact steps as Tobi.

"Yeah. This is the shit right here," she says holding her nose with her blue fingernails.

"Well fellas. It looks like you have your first two customers," Becky says as she walks over to the stove with the other half of the product. I watch her cook it up and whip it with a bent hanger. Tone's method is a bit different.

"You just have to cut it up now," she says handing me a giant rock with crystals sparkling out of it.

"What the fuck did you do to it?" I ask her. It looks nothing like Tone's product.

"I improved it. Trust me," she says.

"Nyce, hand it here. I'll cut it up and have one of them smoke it to test it out," Marquise says. I watch Marquise cut up the giant rock using a razor blade. When he's finished, he hands a rock to Lucy. I watch her retreat to the couch and test the product.

"This is the shiiiittt," she says before passing out.

"Oh my God, is she dead?" I ask running over to her.

"No silly. She's just high," Becky laughs.

"Beck, let me talk to Nyce in private for a moment," Marquise says to her.

"Okay but can you break me off before you leave?" She asks seductively while placing her hand on his dick. He whispers in her ear. She laughs and motions for Tobi to follow her. Lucy is still in her drug induced coma.

"What's up?" I ask Marquise while walking over to the table.

"You said that Tone only gave you $1500 worth of product right?"

"Yeah. That's what he said."

"Well whatever Becky just did with the crack, we're already looking at $800. You know what this means?"

"Yeah. Money in our pocket," I tell him slapping him five.

We leave Becky's garage and walk back to my house. I hide my book bag full of drugs under my bed and anticipate what's going to happen on Friday. Hopefully, Becky has enough friends that are willing to buy the product.

I spend the rest of my week catering to Keisha and making sure she's good. I'm in her bed holding her in my arms when she looks up at me and says:

"Nyce, can you please stop cheating on me? I know you're fucking some of the girls from school. You told them that I was your girlfriend's cousin? Wow. That's hurtful," she sobs with tears coming down her pretty face. I look at her, kiss her nose and wipe her tears.

"They're lying. Why would I jeopardize what we have?"

"Do you love me?"

"You know I love you."

"Then stop. Why am I not enough for you?" She asks as she begins to cry.

"Babe, stop. Stop," I tell her climbing on top of her. I hate seeing her cry.

"I love you," I whisper in her ear as I slide myself inside of her. I make love to my girl in hopes to ease her mind.

"What are you thinking about?" She asks me after our little session.

"I got into some shit Keish." I confess to Keisha about Tone and how I am now one of his bitches. I leave out some of the details so she wouldn't put two and two together about what really happened to her and why she got robbed, but I tell her enough for her to know that I am a fucking drug dealer and somehow I managed to bring Marquise along with me.

"It might not be so bad babe. You can stack enough money to get us out of here," she beams.

"You don't get it. What if I get caught? I can't go to Georgetown wit' a record. I can't get into any colleges wit' a record. Why would I want to chance that?"

"Well, you can look at it this way. Who is going to pay for us to go to college? Yeah you'll get a scholarship but what about your necessities? Food, spending money, clothes. Just be careful. Make moves and stack your money and when that day in August comes when we finally leave, you retire as a dealer and become a fulltime college student who's gonna get drafted into the NBA," she smiles.

"You really don't think that what I am doing is wrong?"

"To an extent but the money and opportunity is here so why not take it? It beats being broke. A temporary solution to your temporary problem. We only have two more years left of this bullshit and then we're out."

"And if I get caught?"

"I'll hold you down and wait for you. Promise," she says sticking out her pinky finger. I laugh and wrap my finger around hers.

<u>SIX</u>

"You ready?" Marquise asks barging into my room as I am packing up the drugs to hit Becky's party. I think Marquise lives here now. My mom gave him his own room, he's never late for curfew, and he even helps Morgan with her homework.

"Yeah, I'm ready."

When we finally make it to Becky's house, we walk inside the garage and I am surprised to see that half of the school is there along with other people I've never met.

"Hey Nyce. This is my cousin Jeff. He goes to Lower Merion." Becky introduces us as soon as I walk in. "Jeff, this is the guy I was telling you about."

"Two-hundred. Heroin," Jeff requests holding up his money. I dig in my bag and give him two-hundred dollars' worth of heroin. "Do you have any pills?" He asks me.

"No. What are you talking about?"

"Percs, xany's, valium, the good shit."

"Nah. I may be able to get some for you though."

"Cool. I need to talk to you before the party is over. Don't forget about me," Jeff says before walking away.

"Yo, I sold all the coke," Marquise says handing me the money and throwing his heavy arm around me.

"How? We only been here for like 10 minutes."

"Man, I told you. White folks know how to party," he laughs.

By the end of the night, Marquise and I get rid of all the product. *Every single thing.* I look at all the high ass people around the room and shake my head. Maybe I've been stereotypical my whole life but I had no idea that white people got down just as hard as black people. I see now that white people just know how to hide it better or it may be just how the media portrays the differences between the races.

"Hey, you ready to talk?" Jeff asks me.

"Sure," I say following him to the couch.

"So, put me on. I can be your man in Lower Merion. I even have somebody for Harriton High," he states referring to the two prestigious high schools on the Main Line.

"Shit. I can help you take over all of the high schools in the area. From Upper Darby all the way up to Norristown," he declares.

"Give me your number. I'll be in touch," I tell him as he scribbles his number on a piece of notebook paper. I see Wendy in the corner talking to Mark, dude from the football team. When she finally looks at me, I motion for her to come.

"I'm not talking to you," she hisses.

"Why. What did I do?" I ask grabbing her hand.

"You lied to me. Keisha is your girlfriend and not your girlfriend's cousin. You made me your fool," she snaps.

"I only lied to you because I really like you and I really like that," I whisper in her ear and grab her pussy.

"I don't care," she says pushing me away. "You're a liar." I grab her, pull her into me and kiss her.

"If I didn't really like you, I wouldn't have kissed you in front of all these people," I whisper in her ear. She takes the bait because the next thing I know I'm fucking her in the bathroom.

"Are you going to leave her for me?" She asks as we are cleaning ourselves up.

"When the time is right," I lie to her. She turns around and I can see the look of disappointment on her face through the mirror. Walking up close behind her, I turn her around and kiss her. Pulling away, I look deep into her eyes and whisper:

"Wendy, I really, really like you. I may have actual feelings for you. Please don't let this me and Keisha thing mess up what we have because I don't know what the future holds," I game her while stroking her cheek. My little lie works because the next thing I know she's jumping up on the counter ready for round two.

"So, how much money did we make?" Marquise asks as I'm counting the money in my room.

"$2305 minus the $1500 we gotta pay Tone," I tell him.

"Cool. You're not supposed to meet Tone until next week, right?"

"Yeah."

"I guess you should ask for more product since we got rid of it so fast."

"I don't know man. This really ain't my thing."

"Understood, but is he going to let you off the hook? I think you're kind of stuck now since he knows that there is money up here to be made."

"I don't know. Maybe I can buy my freedom or some shit," I tell him as I separate Tone's money and split the rest with Marquise.

"Thanks man. The money is good...fast, but I will support you with whatever you decide. I'm goin' to bed," he yawns. Standing and stretching he proceeds to walk to the door.

"Hey, man. What the hell did you say to my parents to allow you to stay here anyway?" Marquise smiles brightly and walks out my room.

"Nyce, Keisha's on the phone," Vi says waking me up out of my sleep. I look over at the clock and it reads 9:30 am. I grab the cordless out of Vi's hands.

"Hey babe," I answer.

"You were kissing Wendy at Becky's party last night? How could you?" Keisha tearfully accuses. *Fuck.*

"What? I did not kiss that girl. Who told you some bullshit like that?"

"Don't play with me, Nyce. I am so sick of going through this bullshit with you."

"I didn't kiss her. We were at a party and the music was blasting so I pulled her to me to whisper in her ear to ask her a question."

"And what was the question, Nyce?"

"It's a surprise...for you...so get dressed. I'll be there around one," I tell her hanging up.

"You are such a filthy liar," Vi snaps. "I know you be fucking half the girls in our school."

"Shut up Vi and since when do you curse and talk to me like this?"

"The moment that you made my best friend your personal whore."

"I get that you are a female and you'll be 15 soon but if you disrespect me again, I will fuck you up."

"Whatever Nyce. I liked you better when we were kids and broke," she yells walking out of my room and slamming the door. I'm not gonna lie, she hurt my feelings with that. Getting out of bed, I walk down the hall and into Marquise's room.

"Aye boi," I say sitting on his bed.

"What up? What fuckin' time is it?" He asks, rubbing his eyes.

"Almost ten. I got to take Keisha out to calm her nerves. She found out that I was up on Wendy last night." Marquise laughs.

"Why not just break up with her and do you?"

"Because I got love for her niggah that's why," I tell him before punching him in his chest and running out the door.

Keisha and I hop on the bus to the mall.

"When are you going to get a car?" She whines as we walk in the cold.

"When you give me the money to buy one."

"Haha, very funny Nyce." We arrive at the mall and I let her rack up on whatever she wants to appease her.

"Baby, I want to get on the Merry-Go-Round," she begs as she pulls me towards the Merry-Go-Round in the middle of the mall.

"Go ahead babe. I'll be right here," I tell her grabbing her bags. She walks over to stand in line. I go to buy a soft pretzel from the stand and watch Keisha jump on one of the unicorns. I'm sitting on the bench eating my pretzel when I hear people arguing on the Merry-Go-Round and a crowd starts to form. I look to see what the hell is going on. As I get near the crowd, I see fists flying and commotion going on amongst a group of women.

"Bitches are crazy," I say to no one in particular. As I'm turning around to get away from the commotion, I see Keisha's hand go up in the air. I know it's her by the gold bracelet she is wearing that I just bought her.

"OH SHIT," I yell as I start pushing people out of my way trying to get to her.

"YOU BITCH. STAY AWAY FROM MY MAN," Ciara yells at Keisha before slamming her fist into her face. Ciara's entourage is holding Keisha so she can't defend herself. When I finally make it to them, I push the shit out of Ciara causing her to stumble back and fall on her ass.

"Let her go. NOW," I shout at the other two females who are holding Keisha.

"That's fucked up Nyce. You're trying to play my girl for this bitch?" Shelby snaps while letting go of Keisha. I look at Keisha's busted eye and grab her.

"It's like that Nyce?" Ciara says to me. "Really? What happened to her just bein' your girlfriend's cousin? You are a fuckin' asshole," she screams at me with teary eyes. Holding Keisha, I push my way through the crowd trying to hurry up before security comes.

"KEISHA, IT'S ALL GOOD. COME HOLLA AT ME. I'LL TEACH YOU HOW YOUR MAN LIKES HIS DICK SUCKED," Ciara yells behind us.

"GET THE FUCK OFF ME!" Keisha yells at me. "I'M DONE. I'VE HAD ENOUGH. IT'S OVER AND I MEAN IT," she barks as tears slide down her face.

"That bitch is lying," I tell her trying to hold her.

"So every bitch who said they slept with you is lying, Nyce? Really? You really think I'm that stupid? You are such a fuckin' asshole," she curses pushing me out of her way and starts power walking towards the bus terminal. I run back to the bench where I was sitting, grab our bags and run to catch up to Keisha. I follow behind her not making a sound, giving her some time to cool off. I stop at one of the food carts, get some ice, and jog to catch up to her, walking next to her in silence.

"Boo, let me put some ice on it," I tell her, breaking the silence.

"Fuck you. I'm fine and we are not together anymore so do not call me boo," Keisha snaps.

"Okay. I won't call you boo but at least let me put some ice on your eye," I say trying to hold in my laughter. She's so damn cute when she's mad.

"I don't need or want nothing from you anymore," she responds with tears running down her face. I say nothing else as we sit silently waiting for the bus.

"Come here. Let me hold you," I whisper in her ear after sitting in silence for almost ten minutes. It's cold as shit outside and I see Keisha shivering.

"Leave me alone, Nyce," she says softly.

"Come here," I tell her pulling her to me. I wrap my arms around her allowing her to use my body for some warmth. I place one of my cold hands on her eye.

"Ouch," she cries out jumping back.

"I'm sorry but you need to apply pressure to it to decrease the swelling. You want some of this ice?" I ask holding up the cup. She digs into her pocketbook and pulls out her mirror.

"God. My face," she utters examining her eye.

"You're still beautiful to me," I assure her.

"Whatever Nyce. I just want to go home."

"But I still have a surprise for you."

"I don't want it."

"Okay," I say. *And 5...4...3...2...1.*

"What's the surprise?" She finally asks. I laugh to myself. Just like clockwork.

"You have to come with me," I tell her. We board the bus down to Center City, Philadelphia. I take Keisha to the art museum, out to dinner, and now we are at the Marriot riding the elevator to our room that Marquise managed to get for me.

Keisha is naked lying in my arms while I'm icing her eye down. I look over at the clock.

"Babe, it's 9:30. We have to get ready to go," I tell her so neither one of us misses curfew.

"One day, I want a house and babies and you by my side forever," she professes.

"I got you, baby."

"Oh yeah?"

"Of course. As soon as we graduate, we will be headed to Georgetown. We'll get an off campus apartment and finish school or I'll get drafted into the NBA and I promise to take care of you."

"Forever? You promise?" She asks sticking her pinky finger out.

"Forever. I promise," I assure her wrapping my finger around hers.

After walking Keisha home, I go to my house. As soon as I walk in the door, my mom calls my name sounding annoyed.

"Yeah mom?" She is sitting at the kitchen table staring at me.

"Boy, sit down," she snaps.

"Man…I didn't do it," I tell her taking a seat.

"You had little girls knocking on my damn door and playing on my phone all damn day, James."

"I'm sorry Ma. What can I say? The ladies love your son," I joke trying to lighten the mood.

"Are you protecting yourself Jimmy?" She asks. I don't know how to respond. I usually talk to my dad about all this stuff. He's the one who feeds my underwear drawer with condoms.

"I know you're not a virgin and no your father didn't tell me."

"Yes mom. I always use protection." My mother cocks her head to the side and looks at me thoughtfully for a moment.

"Remember you have sisters. Would you want your sisters to date someone like you?" She asks. Fuck no is what I want to say.

"Mom, I'm just having fun."

"Yeah but sometimes having fun comes with a price," she warns standing up and walking out the kitchen. I run upstairs and walk into Marquise's room.

"Damn niggah, knock. I could have been beatin' my dick up in here," he says throwing a pair of socks at my head. "I'm about to roll this Dutch," he states pulling a shoe box from under his bed.

"Don't let my peoples smell that shit," I tell him.

"I got it man. They love me like the son they never had. I'm not gonna ruin that," he teases laughing as I give him the finger.

"You want some of this?" He asks, handing me the Dutch.

"Nah. I'm straight. Can't be the next MJ or get into G-Town fuckin' wit' that shit. Shit ain't healthy," I tell him while dribbling an imaginary ball.

"Neither is pussy but you still do it." I laugh.

"Whateva niggah. When I'm a Hoya on my way to the NBA, you gonna wish you had skills like me," I tell him throwing a ball of socks at his head and running out the door.

The school week breezes by with plenty of students coming up to me and Marquise asking if they can cop something. It was like the whole student body caught wind that we are dealing. After practice, I see Tone's car parked across the street. I walk over and hop in.

"Here's your money man," I toss it at him.

"Oh, you can't hand it to me like an adult?" He asks.

"Sorry. I'm just a kid."

"Aw man, you still salty about my boys roughing up your lady?"

"Fuck you Tone."

"Here," he says handing me her necklace. I snatch the necklace out of his hands pissed off that I allow him to dominate my world.

"Don't be salty Nyce. I've done worst; Bo has done worst to niggahs who haven't done half the shit you have done to me." I don't say anything. I just sit in his car mad as hell waiting for him to tell me the next bitch move I have to do for his ass.

"So, I see we can make money out here," he says counting his money. "You're really going to sit here in my car with your chest poked out, niggah?"

"What do you want Tone?" I snap.

"Nothing. Toni wants to see you," he answers while pulling off. As we're driving, I realize he's taking a different way to his house than usual.

"I know where you live regardless," I arrogantly tell him. Since the first time Tone took me to his house over two years ago, I know how to get there with my eyes closed.

"You right. I forgot how smart you are."

"If I'm so smart, why you got me makin' bitch moves?"

"It wasn't my intention. Bo's on some other shit; some greedy shit. He got Terry in the mix and I don't even like that dude," Tone says before stopping himself, realizing that he may have told me too much. We're quiet for the rest of the ride.

"UNCLE NYCE," Toni screams as I enter the house.

"What's up Peanut?" I smile picking her up.

"Nothing. You don't come over here anymore. Who am I going to have tea parties with now?"

"I'm sorry. I'll do better," I tell her putting her down.

"Baby, go on upstairs. Daddy and Uncle Nyce have some things to discuss," Tone says dismissing her.

"Fine," she huffs as she reluctantly climbs the stairs.

"Look man, that shit with your girl was nothing personal," Tone says to me.

"Whatever. You crossed the line."

"Niggah, you crossed the line. We had an arrangement. You lucky I didn't shoot your ass."

"Why didn't you?"

"Because despite it all, I got love for you; my wife and my daughter got love for you."

"I'm like the annoying kid that you have to deal with in order to fuck my mom, right?" I ask mockingly reciting his words. He laughs.

"Oh, you get it now?" He cracks up. "Here," he says handing me money.

"What's this?"

"Your cut," he replies as I count out $500. "And here." He hands me a black book bag. I open the bag to find more drugs.

"You sell pills?" I ask him. He smiles mischievously.

"I do. I'll drop some off to you tomorrow. I don't keep shit in my house. Do you have a team yet?"

"What?"

"A team niggah. What have I been preaching to you all these years? Never get your hands dirty."

"You let me worry about that," I assert.

"Cool. I'm gonna run upstairs to dismiss the babysitter and check on Toni. Meet me in the basement. I'll be back," he says standing up and running up the stairs. I get up off the couch and walk downstairs into the basement. There is a gun sitting on the bar. Without hesitation, I pick the gun up and tuck it in my waist band before taking a seat on the couch. I turn the TV on but I'm zoned out. Thoughts are racing through my head. Heroin, Keisha, coke, dad, pills, Keisha. FUCK. I stand up and start pacing back and forth. Tone comes down the stairs dressed in sweatpants, a t-shirt, and some white Jordan's. *Fuck it.* I pull the gun out and point it at him.

"In my own home, huh?" He asks putting his hands up. My finger is on the trigger but I can't bring myself to do it. Right now, I could end his life and be free of this shit. His goons won't come after me because they have no idea where he lives and Nina is not home so she wouldn't know that I did it. The only person who would know would be Toni. She would know that I shot her dad and left him to die. She would be the one to find her dad dead in a pool of blood. At six years old, it would change her life forever. I lower the gun.

"Goo...," Tone starts to say before I pistol whip him, knocking out a tooth and watching him hit the floor. I stand over top of him with the gun pointed at his head. He doesn't flinch. He's not even scared. He just stares at me with blood seeping out of his mouth.

"We're even," he finally says.

"For?" I ask still holding the gun to his head.

"For Keisha. We're even."

"I want out," I tell him.

"You ever think about your future, Nyce? You'll get a basketball scholarship; that I'm sure of but who's gonna support you while you're there? They won't allow you to work. Books costs money; food; your necessities. Who's gonna pay for those things? Your parents?" He questions, tryin' to bait me in, sounding a lot like Keisha.

"You work for me until that day comes when you are packing up your shit to go off to college. Then you'll be free," he persuades. Gun still pointed at his head, my thoughts are racing. If I continue to hustle for him, I can save some money for me and Keisha without burdening my parents. I just have to do this for two years and then I'm out. Without saying a word, I tuck the gun in my belt, walk over to the couch and turn on ESPN.

"FUCK," Tone grunts getting up off the floor and walking over to the bar. He pours himself a glass of Henny and takes a long gulp.

"Give me my money back niggah. You're paying for my fuckin' tooth," he demands while I watch him make an ice bag for his jaw. He sits down next to me as I dig in my pocket to give him back his money.

"You're really gonna let me live after I hit you?" I ask.

"Yup. We just squashed this shit. There's no bullets in that gun anyway. But had you pulled the trigger, nah, I wouldn't let you live," he avows. "I'm sorry about Keisha. I have no intentions of hurting you or anyone that you love but sometimes you have to make hard decisions. Sometimes it means doing shit that you don't want to do to save face; to send a message that you are a force not to be reckoned with. Never show weakness and never let a niggah slide. As soon as you do, you become human; you become vulnerable and niggahs will remember that you bleed just like everybody else. But yeah, I'm allowing you to live because I see a lot of myself in you. You are a logical thinker; a natural born leader. I like that about you.

"By the way you little shit, I left the gun out on purpose to see what you would do because one day, you may have to pull that trigger. I just want to make sure that you don't pull it on me. So, we even?" He asks with his hand extended. Despite this fucked up situation, I love Tone. He has always been like an annoying ass older brother to me.

"We good, as long as you and your goons don't cross the line again," I tell him shaking his hand.

"Never give me a reason to cross the line, Nyce," he warns squeezing my hand.

"Daddy?" Toni yells down the stairs.

"Yeah sweetheart."

"Is Uncle Nyce still here?" She asks.

"I think my daughter has a thing for you," Tone laughs.

"Yeah, Peanut. I'm still here." I shout back.

"Can I come downstairs now?" She whines.

"We're coming up," Tone says to her as we get up off the couch. We hear Nina come home as we are walking up the stairs.

"Hey baby, how was class?" Tone greets her.

"Baby, what happened to your face?" She asks alarmed rushing to him.

"A misunderstanding," we both blurt out. Nina takes a step back and looks at me.

"You finally teed off on an old man, huh? Serves him right," she jokes giving me a high-five.

"Babe, seriously though?" Tone asks.

"Yup," she laughs picking Toni up and walking out the kitchen.

"I think your wife got a thing for me too," I tease.

"Yeah, a'ight. I will bust a cap in yo' ass right here in my kitchen."

<u>SEVEN</u>

Marquise and I are back at it. Becky cooks up our product increasing the weight, which in return increases our profit. The pills sell just as fast as the other shit so the demand for product becomes high. By the end of the month, Marquise and I made $10,000. The money is fast and easy; too easy. It's making me want more as I start to get a taste of the fast life.

I put Becky's cousin Jeff on. Jeff and his friend Rick work the high schools in the suburbs. Marquise recruited and initiated people from the other surrounding high schools as well. By December, we have eight high schools on lock and twelve pawns working for us including Black and Mookie. Marquise and I no longer make deals ourselves; we simply delegate the work.

I formally introduced Marquise to Tone and Bo so they could familiarize themselves with each other in my absence. Tone seems impressed with the work we put in but Bo, not so much. He be on some hating bullshit for real. Terry's no better with his bitch ass.

Life is good but the more money I make, the more bitches flock and the more bitches flock, the more Keisha fights. This shit is starting to give me a headache because the more Keisha fights, the more we fight. It's like a never ending cycle. I don't know what the hell she wants from me. I do EVERYTHING for her. Anything that she and Vi asks, I do, but it seems to never be enough. I bought myself a Ford Tempo and not only did Keisha bust all my damn windows out, she tried to run me over with the bitch. I had to jump on the hood of somebody else's car to escape her crazy ass.

Okay, so a niggah has a problem with staying faithful. It's not like I do for the other girls what I do for her. I don't spend time with other girls nor do I buy them stuff or hold them after I cum. She just doesn't get it.

By February, Marquise and I saved enough money to purchase a rundown house in North Philly to stash our product. Tone hooked us up with a shady banker who pushed our paperwork through as an inheritance property since I'm a minor and Marquise is barely eighteen. We tell my parents that we both work at the local McDonald's however, we still have to park our cars blocks away from the house so my dad won't get suspicious. Like I said, life is good. Basketball, money, and pussy; it doesn't get any better than that.

"What-up playboy? Great game. Georgetown will be definitely calling you if you keep playing like that," Tone says as I jump in his car.

"Yeah, Uncle Nyce. Great game," Toni beams from the back seat.

"Thanks Peanut." I made the varsity team but I am not the Captain which kind of irritates me but I am the starting Point Guard. Considering that I'm only in the 10th grade, that's not bad at all.

Tone and I make small talk as he drives to his house in Villanova.

I am sitting in the basement watching Tone and Bo count this week's profits.

"It's all there, niggah," I assure Tone laughing.

"I know. I'm still gonna count it. I don't want you to ever get too comfortable where you think you can steal from me."

"Yeah. I wouldn't want to have to kill your stupid ass," Bo threatens. I swear he fuckin' irritates my soul. I'm not even gonna lie. I secretly wish that his ass would die already or at least get caught by the pigs.

What Tone and Bo doesn't know is that with Becky increasing the weight of the product, Marquise and I make damn near an extra $1000. Not sure if that is considered stealing or not since their money is never short.

"You driving yet?" Tone asks me.

"Yeah. My Pop taught me."

"Good. We need you to make a run next weekend."

"What?"

"I need you to drive to Richmond and make a deal," Tone says.

"We're back at this shit again?"

"What niggah? We need you to pick these pills up. You the one who needs them not me. Niggahs in the hood ain't privy to pills yet and I want you to take Terry with you," Bo demands.

"I'll do it but I'm not taking Terry. I have my own team," I tell him.

"You defying me little niggah?" Bo barks standing up from the table. Before I can say anything, Tone intervenes:

"It's cool B. Let him do it."

"Why you keep babying him? Y'all niggahs got something goin' on that I don't know about?" Bo asks looking at us suspiciously as he takes a seat.

"I'm gonna pretend that what you just said never came out of your fuckin' mouth," Tone snaps at Bo. "Nyce, I'll rent you a car and pay for the hotel."

"I need two cars," I tell him.

"Two cars for what?"

"I just need two cars." Tone says no more as he pulls out his stash of weed and starts to roll up while Bo stares at me like he wants to beat my ass.

That night at home, I'm in Marquise's room going over the plan.

"So Becky, Wendy, and Tobi in the one car and we will be in the other," I tell him.

"I get it but why two cars?" Marquise asks.

"Cops won't mess with a group of white girls. We're going to drive down, meet the connect, put the drugs in the girls car and follow them back in another car."

"Cool. I know a guy that will make us fake IDs and shit. We might as well try to party while we are down there."

"That's cool but we have one problem that I haven't worked out yet."

"What's that?"

"What the hell are we going to tell my folks?" I ask hoping Marquise has an answer.

"Basketball tournament. I'll make some fake school papers to make it legit. I'll tell them that I am going with you to keep you out of trouble."

"Whateva niggah but what if my mom calls the school or some shit?"

"Wendy sounds like an adult. I'll put her private line on the forms just in case. You just need to tell her to change her answering machine message."

"Cool."

By the end of the week, Marquise and I have worked up a solid plan. After dicking Wendy down, she agrees to drive back with Becky, Tobi and the drugs. I did have to promise to take her out while we are in Richmond which is fine, as long as it ain't anywhere near home. Marquise comes through with fake IDs for all of us and paperwork from the school for my fake basketball tournament.

We leave early Saturday morning. I load the girls' car up with their bags and Tone's $15,000.00 in cash. I don't tell them that they are riding with the cash. I just sneak it in the trunk with the rest of their stuff.

"Am I riding with you?" Wendy asks me.

"If you want to," I whisper in her ear.

The drive down is pretty smooth and straight forward. We check into our hotel and chill for a moment. Marquise and the girls are passing a blunt around when I sneak off to call Keisha.

"What up baby?" I greet her when she answers the phone.

"Are you with somebody Nyce?"

"Yeah. I told you me and Marquise had business to take care of."

"I mean are you with any females? I find it ironic that Wendy is out of town too."

"Babe, I don't fuck wit' that girl. She's probably at a cheering event or something. You're trippin'."

"Whatever Nyce. Tell me something I want to hear," she says seductively.

"I miss your fat ass especially when you're riding me."

"Tell me something romantic, Nyce," she says annoyed.

"I love you," I whisper into the phone.

"I love you too so hurry back so I can sit my fat ass on you," she says giggling into the phone.

"I will baby. Promise," I tell her hanging up. Marquise comes walking into the room.

"You ready to do this?" He asks. I look over at the clock. It's 2:30pm. We have a meeting with the connect at 3:00.

"Yeah. Are the girls ready?"

"Yeah. I gave them the instructions. They're gonna park around the corner from the drop. We will meet up with them and trade cars and come back to the hotel. They know where the bags will be hidden and they will bring them up. Are you sure you don't want the shit to stay in the car since we are leaving tomorrow anyway?"

"Nah. What if somebody breaks into the car in the middle of the night or some shit?"

"We at a ritzy hotel. Who would break into the car?"

"The valet niggah, I don't know. I'm not chancing it."

We leave the hotel and head towards the connects house. My mind is racing as the plan is on instant replay in my head. The only thing that I am uneasy about is having three white girls sitting in the car by the projects. That shit looks suspicious.

"Change of plans," I tell Marquise as I pull into the Waffle House.

"What's up? Why we stopping here?" Marquise asks.

"I'm going to have the girls stay here until we get back. We're only ten minutes away from where we need to be," I let him know as I watch the girls pull into an empty spot. Marquise and I make eye contact with them as they nod and walk inside the restaurant.

"Ready?" I ask Marquise.

"Ready," he says pulling a gun out.

"What the hell is that for?" I ask.

"I don't know these niggahs. I got you one too just in case," he says pulling out another gun from under the seat.

"Man, you trippin'. Make sure you put these guns in the girls car on the way back."

"How the hell do you think they got down here?" He laughs.

We pull up to the Mosby Court Housing Projects and walk around trying to find the connects housing unit. I notice that we look out of place. Richmond niggahs don't dress like Philly niggahs. I think Marquise catches on to how out of place we look because he is casing his surroundings just like I am.

"We may have to knuckle up with these niggahs," he whispers while adjusting the straps on the duffle bag.

"These niggahs up in here are staring at us looking shifty."

We make it to the unit and knock on the door seven times fast; three times slow; and then two final times as me and Marquise try to hold in our laughter at the coded message.

"Who is it?" Someone barks from behind the door.

"Nyce. Tone's boy," I yell. A big, black, ashy dude steps outside.

"Follow me," he says. We walk around the development, walk down cellar stairs and enter a dark padded room as the door slams shut. I look behind me and realize that there is no handle on the door to let us out. There is just a deadbolt.

"I'm Skeet," the man finally says. "You got my money?"

"You got our product?" I ask. Skeet looks me and Marquise over. I know this niggah ain't thinking about robbing us. I see the door key dangling from the thin chain around his neck.

"So, you're Nyce? Tone told me about you," Skeet says walking over to the washer machine. He pulls out a giant duffle bag, lays it on the table and unzips it.

"Pills, weed, coke, heroin," he says sitting the bundles on the table.

"Nah. We just here for pills," I tell him.

"There must be some confusion because I verified the order myself this morning. He gave you $15,000.00 right?"

"Yeah but…," I start to laugh. "That mothafucka."

"Damn. Tone hit you with the okey-doke," Skeet laughs. I motion to Marquise to hand him the bag of cash. Skeet takes the bag and then pulls out a money counter. I grab the bag off the table.

"If the money is short, you won't make it out the projects," Skeet says.

"If the drugs are short, it's gonna be a Philly vs Virginia showdown," Marquise claps back. Skeet gets up, takes his necklace off and unlocks the door.

"Deuces niggahs," he dismisses us before letting the heavy door slam shut.

"Let's get the fuck outta here," I say to Marquise as we walk back to the car.

We make it back to the girls, switch cars and drive back to the hotel.

"Hey baby. Here's the bags," Wendy says to me handing me the two duffle bags once we are back inside the room.

"Thanks babe," I reply smacking her on her ass and giving her a kiss.

"My cut please," Becky says with her hand sticking out.

"Damn. Can we get settled first?" Marquise asks picking up the bags. "Y'all be gone anyway. Nyce and I got shit to do."

"Here y'all," I say to the girls giving them $100 apiece. "Go to the mall and grab yourselves something so we can go out and celebrate tonight." They eagerly grab the money and head back to their adjoining room.

"Babe?" Wendy turns around before exiting.

"What's up?"

"Do you want me to grab you something too?"

"Nah. Just make sure you look pretty for me tonight," I tell her. She smiles brightly and leaves out the room. Marquise gets up and locks the door. I pull out the bags and start counting the pills.

"Yo, did you bring your scale?" I ask Marquise.

"Yeah niggah I got it."

"Cool," I tell him handing him the bags of coke and heroin.

"Yo, Wendy is damn near in love wit' yo' ass," Marquise says as he's weighing the bags.

"Nah partna, not me. She in love wit' the Mandingo," I laugh pointing at my dick.

"You're a fool, Kunta," he laughs.

"What's the deal wit' you and Becky?" I ask.

"Nothin'. That's my homie."

"Uh-huh."

"Naw it ain't even like that. We met after my mom died. She gave me a place to stay and food to eat. She even bought me clothes and forged papers for me to enroll in school using her address. I never even asked her to do it but she did. She's the most loyal friend I got and I trust her wit' my life."

"Where are her folks anyway?" I have never seen them before and we cook drugs in their garage.

"Pops a deadbeat. Had an affair, got a divorce, and split and her mama gotta fat ass," he laughs. "Her mom lives off the divorce settlement and is too busy tryin' to find husband number two before the money dries up. She's never home and never has time for Becky. What I learned, TV got us niggahs fooled. White people got their issues too."

"That's for damn sure. So how much do you like her?" I ask.

"Like I said, that's my homie."

"So you've never knocked her off?"

"I ain't say all of that," Marquise laughs.

"Soooo, can I test the product?" I ask with a cheesy smile on my face.

"Niggah, I don't care as long as you sharin' Wendy."

"That's on her if she wants to BUT I am tryin' to get this threesome going so if you want to knock her off, it has to be after me."

"Nah niggah. I'm not doing that sloppy seconds bullshit."

"Come on man. This will be my first time in a threesome. Wendy is already down and Becky will be so high tonight she will be down for whateva."

"Only because this is your first time I will allow it. Fuck it. I'll just holla at Tobi or I might meet somebody at the club tonight."

"Bet," I tell him giving him a pound and sealing up the pill bag.

We take the girls out to eat before heading over to the club. These fake IDs Marquise got are fuckin' amazing. We slide inside the club with no problems. I dance a little with Wendy but the shit isn't workin' out; she has no rhythm. Becky however shut down the stereotype that white people can't dance. Her ass tore the club up.

"Here babe," Wendy says handing me a cup.

"What is this?" I ask her.

"Hennessy. Don't you people love Hennessy?"

"You people?" I question her.

"I didn't mean it like that," she says innocently. I take a sip. This shit is nasty. How the hell niggahs drink this shit?

"James Hennessey drinking Hennessy," Wendy giggles.

"Come here. Don't ever say my fuckin' name out loud again. Understand?" I snap at her. I am still a little pissed off by the whole "you people" statement.

"I understand. Excuse me," she says before leaving me to run towards the bathroom. Shit. I just made her cry. Why the hell are females so damn sensitive?

"What you do? Wendy is crying, and Becky and Tobi are in the bathroom with her," Marquise asks.

"Nothing. I'll fix it."

"What you got in this cup?" Marquise grabs the cup out of my hands and downs my drink before I can even respond.

"Sure, you can have it. That shits nasty anyway."

"You gotta build up a tolerance. Is this your first time drinking, niggah?" Marquise laughs.

"Yeah, so. You act like you never met my peoples. I'm surprised my mom didn't make us promise to go to church while we are away."

"Here. Let me break you in. I'll get you a cocktail; a pussy drink," he laughs.

"Fuck you," I laugh.

"You don't want none of this. Who knuckles up better than me?"

"Whateva cocky ass. That's only because you're like a 6'5 giant at 18."

"Nyce," Wendy whispers my name.

"Come here baby," I say grabbing her and tonguing her down.

"Wow. You bitches take all of our men," some light-skin chick says interrupting us.

"Excuse me?" Wendy snaps.

"Bitch you heard me," she repeats with much attitude. Shorty bad as shit too. If I wasn't here with Wendy, I might have graduated into some older pussy.

"How you doin' Miss Lady? Go have a drink on me. It's all good," I tell her handing her a $20.00 bill.

"Our ancestors are rolling around in their graves," the girl says sticking my $20.00 in her bra and starts walking towards the bar with 5 equally bad looking chicks.

"Come on. Let's go," I tell Wendy grabbing her hand. The club is starting to get packed and I'm starting to notice the heated glares that Becky, Tobi, and Wendy are getting. I collect the girls and Marquise so we can head back to the hotel.

"Aye Nyce, pull ova right here," Marquise says from the back seat. I pull into the 24 hour CVS parking lot.

"What you gotta get?" I ask.

"Some condoms and alcohol," he says hopping out the car.

Back at the hotel room, the girls are doing lines, Marquise is smoking a blunt and I am trying to finish my cup of Mad Dog. I start to feel the effects and go sit down in the chair. Marquise is bugging out laughing on the couch as Becky, Tobi, and Wendy are now dancing in their bras and thongs listening to Kris-Kross *Jump* on the radio.

"Ah shit," I say to nobody in particular. I'm drunk as fuck but my dick is hard as shit. I lay my head back and close my eyes trying to regain control. Tone's voice echoes in my head.

"Only drink around niggahs you trust."

I pop my eyes back open. Marquise is on the couch with a drunken and high Tobi sitting on his lap. Becky is at the table doing another line and Wendy is pouring herself another drink. I lay my head back again and I must have dozed off because the next thing I know, I feel my dick slide into someone's mouth. I pop my eyes open and Becky face is in my lap giving me head. I look over at Wendy who now has her bra off and her titties in my face.

"Who does it better Daddy?" She whispers in my ear. Oh shit. It's about to go down.

I wake up the next morning with my head pounding. Wendy and Becky are lying comfortably in my arms. Weirded out, I jump out of bed startling both girls. I promised myself that Keisha would be the only female I would ever hold.

"FUCK. Did we use condoms?" I ask. I remember what happened but I don't remember what happened.

"Relax. Of course we did," Becky says getting out the bed naked. "I'm going to take a shower," she says disappearing into the adjoining room.

"Did you have fun?" Wendy asks all bubbly.

"Of course. Did you?"

"I always have fun when I am with you. Can I get some alone time now though? I miss us," she smiles. I climb back into bed and give Wendy the alone time she asking for.

As I'm packing up my shit, the phone rings.

"Why the fuck you ain't been answering the phone, Nyce?" Keisha yells at me on the other end of the line.

"It's called sleep Keisha."

"Whatever. Who do you think you're talking to? I've known you for almost three years now and I know your ass wasn't sleep at no 10:30 last night."

"I went to the club wit' Marquise."

"Uh-huh. You ain't shit Nyce."

"What the fuck did I do now?" I ask getting annoyed as I jam my clothes in the duffel bag.

"EVERYTHING. I have bitches playin' on my fuckin' phone now."

"That ain't my fault."

"No? If you knew how to keep your fuckin' dick in your pants, they wouldn't be calling."

"My dick is in my pants and if it's not, it's in your pants," I tell her trying to make her laugh.

"I'm not in the mood Nyce."

"Babe, I gotta go."

"No. You better sit on this phone and talk to me."

"Babe, I got to check out the hotel. I'll be home soon."

"Whateva," she says slamming the phone down in my ear.

"Damn that girl is driving me crazy."

"Do you need me to help you release the tension?" Wendy asks dropping to her knees. Of course I don't object.

We check out of the hotel and Marquise and I are now trailing behind the girls on our way home.

"So, how was Tobi?" I ask him laughing.

"She ain't Becky that's for damn sure but she was good."

"Yeah, Becky is a fuckin' freak."

"Yo, the sistahs was mad at us last night," Marquise chuckles.

"Why you think I said that it was time to go? Sistahs be dramatic. I still have a few on my roster but they always pressuring me about Keisha like damn. I'm not leaving my girl for you."

"You had Ciara and Shelby trippin' off your ass. I can't believe that they fought each other over you and they were friends," Marquise laughs.

"I know right," I chuckle.

"You grimy niggah."

"Dawg, it was not like that. I was fuckin' Ciara and Shelby came at me one day in her volleyball shorts. What was I supposed to do?"

"Yeah a'ight. Hope yo' ass don't get caught up."

"Who you tellin'? Ciara be trippin'. Her and Keisha be fighting all the time and now I think she's playing on her phone."

"You better get your lies straight playa."

"You act like you're innocent. You be fuckin' mad bitches too."

"Yeah but I'm not in a committed relationship."

"Keisha ain't goin' nowhere."

"Uh-huh," Marquise says giving me the side eye.

"Don't you even try it. I will drop you where you stand," I tell him half joking and half serious.

"Please. Keisha ain't my type; too needy. You always talkin' about droppin' somebody. We can knuckle up anytime you want. You can pull the car ova right now."

"Knuckle up. That's all the fuck you say. I'm about to start calling your ass Knuckle since you be running wit' it," I laugh. Marquise sits quietly for a moment.

"What?" I ask him when his face gets serious.

"Not Knuckle but Knuck. I like the sound of that because I do be knockin' niggahs the fuck out," he says looking at his large hands.

"Seriously? That's what you want to be called?" I ask him.

"Yeah. You always preaching that I need a street name and to stop givin' people my government so yeah…Knuck…I like it."

"A'ight, Knuck. You want some business cards to go wit' your new name too, niggah?" I tease cracking up.

"Nah, you asshole," he says laughing.

We drop Wendy off first and now I'm sitting in Becky's garage waiting for Knuck to come back from dropping off Tobi.

"Well that was fun. We need to get away more often though. Like Brazil or something," Becky suggests.

"You always talkin' about traveling somewhere," I laugh. She snorts up a line of heroin and then sits next to me on the couch.

"It's a big world Nyce. Don't you want to see it?" She asks excited, laying her head in my lap.

"Is that why you have all these travel posters and brochures?"

"Yup," she says with her eyes closed. "I want to see the world. What about you?"

"As long as I can get there by bus, car, or train," I tell her.

"So there is something you are afraid of," she says popping her eyes open. I laugh.

"I guess you can say that."

"Well, we can at least drive down to the shore once summer comes."

"That would be pretty dope," I tell her before she nods off.

When Knuck finally comes back we take the drive over to Tone's house to deliver his shit.

Walking in the house, I hand Tone the bags before walking down into his basement.

"That was foul man," I tell him referring to the additional drugs he made us smuggle.

"I knew y'all could handle it," he laughs and starts pulling the product out of the bag.

"Whateva, man," I mutter watching him weigh the bags.

"Y'all hungry?" Nina says coming down the stairs. "Tone, what the fuck?" She yells at him.

"I know babe. I'm almost done."

"You better be," she snaps disgusted walking back up the stairs.

"What's wrong?" Knuck asks.

"Same shit; different day. I'm not allowed to have drugs in the house," Tone laughs. "She's been givin' me shit lately about the whole drug thing all because I want to have another baby. She be trippin'."

"You gonna stop?" I ask.

"When the time and money's right. Soon. My heart ain't into this shit no more anyway. I've been doing this shit since I was twelve, man. Seen a lot of death in the process. I'm tired but more than anything, I'm tired of her naggin' me about it. She just doesn't get it and her not giving me another baby is fucked up. I've been beggin' her ass for two years now," Tone confesses. I walk up the stairs and into the kitchen. Nina hands me a sandwich.

"Never sacrifice you're Queen to appease the other pieces on the chess board," she says walking out the kitchen.

"She's right you know," Tone says coming behind me with Knuck. "Take this." Tone hands me the duffle bag.

"We already took our product," I tell him.

"I know. I need you to hit the block and make this delivery. That's part of your new job."

"WHAT?" Knuck and I blurt out.

"Shut up. Your cut," he says throwing stacks of money on the table and walking out the kitchen. Knuck and I grab the bag and our money and head to the car.

"Yo, we are doing this once and assigning somebody else to be the flunky," I tell him as we drive towards my old neighborhood.

"Agreed. Who do you trust?"

"Black or Mookie."

We arrive on the block and pull over in front of Tone's stash house. I look down the street at my old housing projects. I haven't set foot in that place since the day we left.

"Hold up," I tell Knuck while walking towards the building. The inside of the building is filthy and cold and the elevators aren't working.

"Miss Rachel?" I yell when I see her.

"Hey baby. Look at you and your fine self, looking just like your damn daddy," she laughs and gives me a hug.

"How are you?" I ask.

"I'm fine. Still here. Tryin' to find that damn Super. Do you know this whole building is without heat?" She says shaking her head.

"Here Miss Rachel. Go buy yourself some space heaters or something," I tell her handing her $200.00.

"Thanks baby." I turn to walk out the door.

"Jimmy," she calls my name.

"Yes."

"You come and see me when you become a man," she winks. I laugh and walk out the door.

"Memories," Knuck laughs patting me on the back. We walk back up the block and enter the stash house. Terry is sitting in a chair, looking like the bitch ass niggah he is.

"Here," I say tossing the bag at his feet.

"Niggah, pick that shit up and hand it to me," he says standing.

"You better get the fuck outta my face," I tell him.

"Or else what? Tone ain't here to save your ass."

"You still salty about that scar I left on your face?" I laugh. He swings cracking me in the jaw. Knuck springs to action.

"No. I got this," I tell him and charge at Terry. We exchange blows until I catch him in his jaw and watch him fall to the floor. I roll him over and put my foot on his chest.

"Didn't mean to knock out an old man," I taunt him. "I usually respect pussy," I laugh.

"Get your fuckin' foot off me," he yells.

"How you gonna be making demands from the ground bitch?" I ask as I hear the front door open.

"Nyce, let him up," Bo's voice bellows behind me. I remove my foot off of Terry's chest as Knuck, Bo, and other niggahs that came in with Bo back up.

"I should have fuckin' killed you when I had the chance pussy. Tone can't protect you forever," Terry threatens.

"If I don't kill you first and when that day comes, you will bow down to me," I warn before walking out the door.

"Yo, what the fuck was that?" Knuck asks cracking up.

"That niggah's a punk."

"Naw, I mean you fuckin' blacked the fuck out on him. I've never seen you like that and your little speech at the end; priceless. Shit. You had me scared," he laughs. I don't respond as I walk to the car pissed off.

After dropping Knuck off, I drive over to Grandma Norah's house to hide from Keisha's ass. After the day I had, I don't feel like dealing with her shit too. I know Keisha gonna be trippin so I decide to chill with my Grandma and let her stuff me with food.

"How's the roast, baby?" Grandma Norah asks.

"Great Grandma. Thank you," I tell her stuffing my face with pot roast, mashed potatoes, and glazed carrots. Grandma sits in the chair across from me, staring as she sips her tea.

"What?" I ask her as I wipe my mouth with a napkin. She smiles.

"You're so handsome," she laughs.

"Thanks Grandma," I chuckle.

"How are you?"

"I'm okay."

"How are you really?" She asks looking at me suspiciously.

"I'm stressed, Grandma. I don't think I'm a good person anymore," I admit to her.

"Why?" I don't respond to her question.

"Life is hard James. At some point we all have to make tough decisions that we may not be proud of."

"What if your decisions affect other people's lifestyle? What if you're stuck in a situation that you know is wrong but you can't get out of? I feel stuck Grandma," I confess. Though the drug money is fast and easy, I am bothered by the fact that I help contribute to destroying other people's lives.

"All you can do is pray, baby. Ask God to show you the way and ease your mind from the things that you cannot control."

I pray all the time but it never eases my mind or calms my soul. My fear is becoming someone that I no longer recognize and the worst part is, I am dragging my friends with me. If something ever happens to them, I am the one who would be responsible for introducing them to this lifestyle.

EIGHT
Senior Year 1994

It's finally, the first day of my senior year, and at the end of September, your boy finally is turning eighteen. School hasn't been the same since Knuck and Becky graduated. Despite that though, I still have my boys along with Wendy and Tobi who end up playing a crucial role in our little operation. That ride to Richmond was the first but by far was not the last. In fact, we've been going national. Smuggling drugs for Tone while being smart enough by having the girls take all the risk. Knuck and I pay them well to do it. So far, everything has been working in our favor. Becky works security at the airport so that helps out a lot for when Tobi and Wendy have to take flights and Knuck is attending Temple University fulltime majoring in biochemistry during the day and a boss "pharmaceutical representative" at night.

I've grown to love them all. Not on some type of romantic shit but as my extended family. We really do operate like pieces on a chess board.

"What up?" Mook greets when him and Black hop in my car before school.

"Nothin'. We back at this shit. Let's make this year memorable," I tell them.

"Did you do your schedule yet?" Black asks.

"Yeah," I reply and hand him my schedule.

"Oh, you're takin' Latin too? I heard Mrs. Wallace teaches that. She's such a bitch AND she's pregnant," Black points out shaking his head.

"Latin? What the hell you takin' Latin for?" Mook asks me.

"Because it looks good on my college applications."

"GEORGETOWN," Mookie chants. I laugh.

"That's the plan. I've been waiting for this moment since I can remember."

"Did you apply yet?"

"Not yet. Coach Rogers is having a scout sent here this year to see me but I have to wait for basketball season to start. I'm not even allowed to play football this year because he is too afraid that I might injure myself."

"Word. At least you don't have to do those damn drills he be killin' us wit'," Black points.

"Yeah right. That niggah got me on a whole work out plan after school." We pull up to the high school and park.

"Hey guys," Wendy greets us as her and Tobi approaches.

"What up mama?" Mookie replies.

"You didn't call me last night Mr.," Wendy says to me.

"I know, sorry. I got tied up."

"Whatever. I bet you will make time for me once homework kicks in," she rolls her eyes sounding annoyed.

"Don't be like that Wendy."

"Tell me what other girls smuggle your shit, cooks you food, and does your homework? Keisha sure ain't doing it," she pouts before storming away.

"What the hell is her problem?" I ask out loud to no one in particular.

"Her period just came on," Tobi laughs.

I'm haul-assin' to my Latin class because God knows I don't feel like hearing Mrs. Wallace's mouth for being late on the first day. She's mean as shit and I can only imagine how mean she is with her pregnancy hormones. As I'm turning the corner, I run into somebody.

"My bad," I apologize as I watch the papers scatter.

"It's alright," she answers in a sweet country accent. I help her pick up her papers.

"I'm Nyce by the way," I introduce myself while peeking down her shirt.

"Thank you, Nyce," she replies standing up. I stand up with her and hand her, her papers. She has to be at least 5'7; 150 pounds with round breast and a high ass. Her cinnamon skin is flawless.

"You better get on to class," she says when she realizes that I am staring.

"Only after you give me your number," I flirt displaying my best GQ pose and smile.

"I think not," she curves me rushing off. I watch her ass sway back and forth in her tight fitting skirt. She's kind of overdressed for school.

I rush down the hall to Mrs. Wallace's classroom. To my surprise, she is missing in action as everyone is sitting at their desks engaged in their own conversations.

"What up?" I say to Black sitting down next to him.

"Ain't shit homie," he says giving me a fist bump. "I'm out of pills though," he whispers.

"A'ight. I got you. I'll have someone stop by your crib later to drop some off," I tell him.

"Settle down please. I'm Miss Preston. I will be taking over for Mrs. Wallace," the girl in the hall announces. "Please take out your books and turn to page three," she instructs us while taking a seat at the teacher's desk. Holy shit. I am not about to look at this fine ass woman for the next 9 months.

When the bell for class to be dismissed rings, I patiently wait for everyone else to leave.

"So, you won't go out with me because I'm a student?" I ask Miss Preston.

"What young man?" She quizzes.

"I'll be 18 on the 28th. I'm legal," I smile.

"I think you better get going to your next class."

"It's my lunch period," I tell her. "So for my birthday, all I want is to take you out."

"And where will you be taking me little boy?"

"We can go out for some pizza and chocolate milk," I say sarcastically. She smiles before erupting with laughter.

"Oh look at that. I made you smile."

"You are being very inappropriate Mr. Hennessey."

"I'm sorry. I just think you're beautiful."

"Good day to you Mr. Hennessey," she dismisses me and exits the classroom.

"Yoooo, did you see the new teacher? She's bad as shit," I say to Black and Mookie when I join them at our table in the cafeteria.

"Hell yeah I seen her. I had a woody from the moment I sat down at my desk," Black laughs.

"Shit. I'm about to switch my class from Spanish to Latin fo' real," Mookie chuckles. I watch Miss Preston walk into the cafeteria. When I know she sees me, I wink my eye at her.

"Niggah, you always on some other shit. Ain't no way that woman is going to feed into your childish ass," Black says cracking up.

"Oh. You want to put a bet on this?" I challenge.

"What?"

"A bet. I bet I bag that before the school year is out."

"Fuck that. I want in on this bet too," Mookie chimes in.

"How much we talking about?" Black asks.

"Hmmm…your call."

"You and Knuck gotta give me my own territory."

"Not gonna happen," I tell him shaking my head.

"Come on Nyce. You'll be off to college and Knuck probably will quit the game when you leave. I'll be stuck working some bullshit job because my ass fucked up my academic career. My only option is community."

"I want in on this bet. Let Black and I work a territory," Mookie interjects.

"No y'all. After this summer, I'm out. This drug shit ain't a forever gig. Y'all better start thinking of shit to do when this is ova and no I am not putting you down with Tone," I tell them getting up from the table annoyed.

After school, we are all gathered inside Becky's garage. Mook, Black, and I are sitting on the couch watching *Demolition Man* as Becky is doing her thing in the kitchen and Tobi and Wendy are sitting at the table doing homework.

"Here," Wendy says throwing my math homework at me.

"What the hell is your problem?" I ask.

"YOU," she hisses walking away. Mook and Black laugh.

"Shut up y'all." I get up and walk over to Wendy.

"You want to tell me why you have such an attitude?"

"Because I've been waiting for you for almost 3 years and you still don't want to be with me."

"We are about to graduate. What difference does it make now?"

"I want to go to the prom with you," she reveals.

"Uh…"

"No uh. I know you bought Keisha that car. The least you can do is take me to the fucking prom."

"Hold up. I bought her a car but you're sitting here acting like I didn't just give you $500.00"

"You didn't give it to me, I earned it. Who else is gonna smuggle your shit?" She snaps and pushes me out of her way before walking out the garage.

"Women are headaches," I tell Black and Mook. They burst out laughing.

"Here y'all," Becky says handing over the crack rocks.

"Thanks Beck." I take the product out of her hands and pass it to Mookie.

"Well, that's my que," he says putting it in his book bag.

"We out homie," Black states.

"I'm leaving too," Tobi says packing up her stuff. Becky is sitting at the table doing a line. When she's done, she comes to join me on the couch.

"How's Knuck doing?" She asks laying her head in my lap.

"He's good."

"I barely see him anymore."

"I thought you guys talk all the time."

"We do but I don't see him," she sighs. She picks up a travel brochure. "You never want to just escape and get out of here?" She asks me.

"All the time."

"I hope you make it Nyce. I hope you get out of here and make it."

"Why you talkin' silly Beck like you're not coming with me?"

"I ain't Wendy. You don't have to tell me bullshit," she laughs.

"I'm not bullshitting you. You're like family."

"The thoughts nice," she smiles.

"I gotta go," I tell her nudging her head so she can get out of my lap.

"Alright," she says getting up. "Tell your boy to stop playin' me."

"For you two to always be in denial about being together, y'all sure be actin' weird."

"Whatever. Bye homie," she says kissing my cheek.

Later on that night, I drive over to Tone's house to chill.

"Yo, I got this bad ass teacher at school, man," I tell him.

"Oh yeah?"

"Yeah. My ass is gonna be in class every day."

"You're a mess," he laughs.

"Hey Uncle Nyce," Toni greets me.

"Hey Peanut. How was school?"

"Okay I guess."

"What's wrong Peanut?"

"The kids are mean to me," she discloses.

"People are always going to be mean to you. You just have to remember that you are loved," I remind her pinching her nose.

"Well how do I get them to stop pulling my hair?"

"You ain't say all that. Come on," I tell her picking her up and carrying her out into the backyard. I teach Toni how to box as Nina and Tone watch laughing. Her little fists hold no power but I pretend that she is the strongest person in the world. Now, if she were to fight another eight year old, she's set.

"You good?" I ask her once she's tired out.

"Yes. I'm not afraid. The only thing to fear is fear itself," she says repeating my words.

"Good. Never fear anybody. Every man bleeds," I tickle her.

School is coming along but I am struggling in my Latin class. It's harder than what I thought. Fuck the whole English language is the derivative to Latin. This shits hard.

"Not good Mr. Hennessey," Miss Preston scolds handing our papers back. Fuck. I got a D.

"Miss Preston, I think there has been a mistake," I tell her after class.

"No. No mistake. Your paper was rushed, lacked originality, and you had incomplete thoughts and sentences indicating that you are not comprehending the material."

"I comprehend."

"You sure?"

"My comprehension is fine. Something is wrong with your grading," I say pissed off. She laughs. It's already November and this is the third test in this class that I didn't do well on. If I don't pass this class, I won't get into Georgetown.

"I'm sorry. Can I do some extra credit or something?"

"I'm afraid not but if you need additional help, my office hours are posted on the door," she answers packing up her papers.

"You only have hours listed here for after school. Can I come on my lunch period or something?"

"What's so important to you that you can't meet after school?"

"I lift weights after school. It may sound stupid to you but my athleticism is my ticket out of here." She sits quiet for a minute.

"Fine. Meet me at this address tonight at seven. Don't be late," she instructs handing me a piece of paper with her address scribbled on it.

I pull up to Miss Preston's house at 7:55pm and knock on her door.

"You're late," she states.

"Sorry."

"I will see you tomorrow Mr. Hennessey," she says closing the door in my face. I knock again.

"Really Miss Preston?" I ask when she opens the door.

"Really. My time is valuable just like yours and I am not going to waste it on somebody who doesn't care about their future so we can try again tomorrow. Good night," she asserts closing the door in my face again. Bitch.

The next day I arrive at her house at 6:55.

"I'm early so there is no need for you to be rude," I tell her when she opens the door. She looks at me and then moves to the side for me to enter.

"You sure like red," I observe looking around her place.

"I'm a Delta."

"You don't have to explain. Red's my favorite color too," I smirk.

"Have a seat James so we can begin," she instructs escorting me to the dining room table.

"Thank you."

"So what seems to be troubling you?" She asks taking out her books.

"I guess everything."

"Have you made yourself some flashcards?"

"No. I haven't tried that."

"Well I suggest you get started," she says handing me a deck of blank index cards.

With Miss Preston tutoring me twice a week, my Latin grade does improve dramatically. By the end of the quarter, I managed to get a B- in her class and I'm finally all set to start applying to colleges. With my mom's help, I write the best damn essay of my life and mail off all my applications. The waiting game has just begun.

When February rolls around, it's game time as college scouts pack the stands to watch me play. I have all the support I need from Tone, Nina, Toni, Knuck and our little crew. Sometimes my mom and dad come too when their schedule allows them.

When I get my first acceptance letter in the mail from Michigan State, I'm happy as hell that my hard work is paying off. Of course Wendy has a lot to do with it as well since she's been doing my homework for the past 3 years. As the months roll by, the acceptance letters keep coming in but, as April nears and I still don't hear from Georgetown, I have a deep routed feeling of uneasiness. I can't seem to concentrate or relax.

"What's the problem Mr. Hennessey?" Miss Preston asks me during our tutoring session.

"Sorry. Just a little distracted," I admit.

"You want to talk about it?"

"Uh, is this like teacher/student confidentiality? Whatever I say you can't repeat?" She laughs.

"As long as you're not going to harm yourself or others," she jokes.

"I'm afraid," I tell her with all seriousness.

"Of?"

"I'm afraid that I didn't get accepted into Georgetown. My dad has been grooming me since birth. I don't want to disappoint him," I tell her letting out my truth.

"Have you applied to any other schools?"

"Yes. Got accepted to everyone I applied to so far but I still haven't heard from Georgetown."

"James, besides basketball, what are your goals?" I think about it for a moment.

"I don't have an answer Miss Preston."

"You need to think about that. I've seen you play and you are very talented, but you need to think about the *what if's*. What if you don't make it or get hurt? I'm not trying to be a downer but I have to be honest."

"It's fine. You're not saying anything that my mother hasn't said."

"It's getting late. Would you like something to eat?"

"No. I think I'm just gonna head home. Thanks for the offer."

I drive straight home after leaving Miss Preston's house with Georgetown and my dad heavily weighing on my mind. I walk into the house and straight into the kitchen.

"Baby, Georgetown is here," my mom says eagerly coming up behind me and handing me the letter.

"Mama, it's big," I smile as the feeling of excitement bursts through my body. I hold the letter in my hands.

"Open it," my mother encourages, snapping me out of my thoughts. She takes a seat at the table.

"I kind of want dad to be here when I open it. Do you know when he will be home?"

"A little later tonight. Do you want me to wake you up when he comes in?"

"Yes. I want you to wake up the whole house," I tell her giving her a kiss. I run up to the third floor and barge into Knuck's room.

"What up, niggah?" I greet him. Knuck is sitting in his chair playing *NBA Jam* on his Super Nintendo.

"I saw the package. Congratulations," he says pausing the game and giving me a hug.

"I didn't open it yet. I want my dad to do it. I might not have gotten in."

"Cut the bullshit. Them niggahs came to see you. You are the captain of the team with a 3.5 GPA and an 1120 on your SATs. You've been accepted to every college you applied to including the ones you didn't apply to. You got this."

"Thanks man. I'm scared as hell but I talked to Miss Preston about it."

"The fine ass teacher you was telling me about?"

"Yeah. Yo, she bad as shit," I laugh.

"Word? I gotta check her out 'cuz you been talking about her for months. I'm gonna have to make a little visit and say hi to all the teachers."

"Yeah right. They're glad that you are no longer a menace at that school," I laugh.

"Shut up. What you about to do?"

"I don't know man. Hide from Keisha's ass. She's wearing me out about prom and graduation. I just shelled out money for this damn prom. Her stupid gown was $1200 and now she talkin' about she needs shoes, and to get her hair and make-up done. Damn."

"Why you being cheap niggah like you ain't got it?"

"I ain't being cheap but I'm about to have to pay for living expenses for me and her. Not to mention pay for her tuition wherever she decides to go. Shit."

"Nobody told you to play husband at 18 my nig." Knuck says laughing and lighting up a blunt.

"Shut up. Black and Mook are on me too since they know that the cash is about to dry up."

"That's because them niggahs are small minded. I saved up $108,000.00. Not bad for 20."

"Damn. How the fuck you do that?"

"I don't have any women to support and I still live at home so my rent, food, and laundry is free, and I don't squander my money like your ass trying to be flyy."

"Whateva niggah. I'm out," I tell him getting up and walking out of his room. Knuck saved $108,000.00. I think I only have about $89,000.00. Okay I admit, I like nice things and the older you get, women be wanting more than just dick and time. All I know is if this money is to last me for the next 4 plus years while I'm in school, I definitely need to make some changes in my spending habits.

"Jimmy, Jimmy, wake up. Your father's home," my mom says waking me up out of my sleep. "Marquise and Morgan are already downstairs. I told Vi to get up but she hasn't yet," she says. I look over at my clock. It's after 2am.

"I'll get her," I tell my mom hopping out of bed. I go down to the second floor and knock on Vi's door.

"I'M COMIN'," she screams. I open the door to find Vi buried under her covers.

"Get up big head. I'm trying to celebrate with you," I say pulling the covers off of her. We play tug-of-war with the covers.

"STOP IT, NYCE. LEAVE ME THE FUCK ALONE," she yells at me. I laugh at her as she is trying to fight me. I finally get a good look at her face. Her eyes are bloodshot red and puffy. She actually looks miserable.

"What's wrong?" I ask her.

"Nothing, stupid," she answers before walking out the door and down the stairs. I join her along with the rest of my family at the kitchen table.

"Finally," Morgan yawns.

"Go ahead baby," my mom says to my dad. I look over at Knuck who looks just as nervous as I do.

"Dear Mr. James Hennessey. We are thrilled that you have chosen Georgetown University as your academic choice. Georgetown University has a history…"

"DAD, DID I GET IN?" I yell cutting him off. He laughs.

"See for yourself," he says handing me the letter.

"I'M A MOTHAFUCKIN' HOYA," I shout full of excitement as my mother slaps me in the back of my head for cursing. My father laughs and gives me a big hug.

"I knew you could do it son. I'm so proud of you," he says. Knuck and Morgan join in our group hug; followed by my mom and Vi. We are having a true Cosby moment.

"Okay. Off to bed everyone. Family dinner celebration this Saturday so no one make any plans," my mom announces dismissing us off to bed.

"James. I'm proud of you son," my dad says on the verge of tears. He gives me another tight hug.

"Dad, you crying?"

"No. I got something in my eye. Go to bed," he says pushing me. I laugh, run up the stairs and knock on Vi's door.

"Go away, Nyce," she screams. I open the door.

"What's wrong?"

"You don't fuckin' care. You're just like the rest of them," she cries.

"What are you talking about?"

"Men…you. All you care about is feeding girls false shit. Making us fall in love with you and then using and toying with our emotions. It's not fair and I hate you. I hate all men." I hold my baby sister and let her cry in my chest.

"Who did it?" I ask calmly.

"No. You're just gonna make it worse."

"Who did it, Viola?" I ask again.

"Just go away Nyce. You don't know him anyway."

154

"You don't know who I know. Now tell me who."

"I can't," she says looking at me terrified. The fact that I see fear in her eyes makes me press the issue.

"I'm going to ask you one last time before I get mad."

"Terry," she whispers.

"Yeah. I don't know no Terry. I only know one and I know we ain't talking about the same dude." Vi looks at me but doesn't say a word.

"That grown man, Viola? What the fuck are you thinking? He's twenty-six. You're only sixteen. I am going to kill him," I yell punching a hole in her wall. She jumps.

"It's not like that Nyce. We're in love."

"Love? Are you fuckin' stupid?"

"Just go away. You wouldn't understand and you and Knuck better not do nothing stupid."

"I am going to murder him."

"Please just leave it alone and let me handle this. If you do anything, he won't ever talk to me again."

"He's not fuckin' talking to you now dummy so what difference would it make?"

"You don't understand. You're just like him."

"I am not."

"You are. You don't know how many times I sat in this room consoling Keisha over you or how many times I had to fight defending Keisha making sure she didn't get jumped by jealous females. You don't care. You think playing with people's feelings is funny; a joke so why even bother? Just go away, Nyce," she says pulling the covers over her head. I leave my sisters room pissed the fuck off and ready for war.

The next day, I drive through the old block looking for Terry's punk ass. When I spot his car at the trap house, I jump out and enter.

"YOU'RE FUCKIN' MY SISTER?" I attack him on sight, jumping over the table he is sitting at to get to him. I punch him in his jaw and watch him fall out of the chair. I stand over top of him about to beat his ass when three of his idiots try to hold me back.

"FUCK OFF OF ME," I holler, throwing punches. Breaking free, I wrap my bare hands around Terry's throat.

"YOU WANT TO PREY ON MY LITTLE SISTER YOU PERVERT?" I yell squeezing tighter as his eyes bug out. I feel objects hitting me in my back but I don't let go.

"Nyce, let him go," Tone shouts grabbing my shoulder.

"Don't fuckin' touch me, Tone. Nobody fuckin' touch me," I warn them as I attempt to squeeze the life out of Terry.

"SNAP THE FUCK OUT OF IT. YOU MADE YOUR POINT," Tone yells. BANG a gunshot goes off but I still don't let go.

"Let him go," Bo says as I feel the metal press against my head. "Tone won't kill you but I will," he warns slapping me in the head with the barrel of his gun. I loosen my grip on Terry's neck before letting go.

"This ain't ova niggah," I threaten storming out the house.

"Nyce," Tone yells after me but I hop in my car and drive away.

Later while in my calculus class, Vi comes storming in.

"Shit," I curse hopping up and walking out the back exit.

"DON'T YOU FUCKIN' RUN FROM ME," she yells running after me. I honestly think this shit is funny; like the time when we were kids and my He-Man beheaded one of her Barbie's. Vi lost her temper and tried to fight me at nine years-old. I turn around to face her. She swings first as I duck out of her way.

"CHILL, VI," I yell at her as I block her flurry of punches.

"I HATE YOU. WHY WOULD YOU DO THAT?" She yells with tears coming down her face as she is still throwing punches at me. All the students and teachers file out into the hallway watching the altercation.

"OUCH...STOP...I'M SORRY," I tell her still blocking her punches.

"STAY THE FUCK OUT OF MY BUSINESS," she yells and swings. This one lands on my jaw. I laugh. Not because the shits funny but because she is startin' to piss me off. I grab her and hug her tight keeping her arms pinned to her sides.

"AH FUCK. WHAT THE HELL IS WRONG WITH YOU?" I yell pushing the shit out of Vi as I watch her stumble and fall to the floor. Crazy bitch bit me. I go to help her up off the floor. As I'm reaching down to grab her, she punches me in my dick. I instantly drop to my knees.

"TAKE THAT YOU ASSHOLE," she shouts while I am rolling around on the floor. I can hear people laughing at me; both the teachers and the students.

"Serves you right asshole," Ciara says kicking me in my back.

"BITCH. I WILL KICK YOUR ASS. THAT'S MY BROTHER," I hear Vi yell as she charges at Ciara. Mr. Thompson, the chemistry teacher stops Vi in her tracks. What an ass. Why didn't any of the fuckin' teachers help my ass when I needed it?

"Are you alright, babe?" Keisha asks helping me up off the floor.

"You get the fuck off of me because I know you knew about this shit."

"Mr. and Ms. Hennessey. My office NOW," Principal Brown yells. I limp to his office and sit in one of those hard ass wooden chairs. Vi comes in shortly after and takes a seat.

"You mind telling me what this is all about?" He asks. Neither one of us says a word.

"Do I have to call your mother?" He continues.

"It's just a misunderstanding; a sibling fight," Vi says. "That's all."

"Mr. Hennessey is there anything that you would like to add?"

"Yes. I'm going to kill my sister when I get home," I say through my teeth still recovering from when she punched me in my dick.

"Just because your sister beat you up, there is no need to make threats," Mr. Brown laughs. Oh, he finds this shit funny too? "Because you guys are siblings and I get that these things happen, I will let you off with a warning this time," he says writing us hall passes to go back to class. "Try to stay away from each other today."

"Thank you," Vi says grabbing her pass and walking out.

"Thanks," I tell him grabbing mine and limping out. In my rage, I walk down to the gym and into the athletic center where they hold all the equipment. I grab a baseball bat, go outside and look for Vi's car; a car that I bought her. I bang all her windows out and make dents in the body. When I'm done, I throw the bat, walk back inside, and go to class.

The rest of the school day is pretty quiet. Everyone decides to leave me alone; teachers included. As I have time to cool off and stop being angry with Vi, I start to feel bad about breaking up her whip. At lunch, I walk to her group table.

"Can I talk to you for a minute?" I ask her.

"Go away. I'm not talking to you."

"Let me talk to you for a minute Viola." She rolls her eyes and gets up from the table. I follow her out into the hall.

"Sorry about your eye," she says. I want to tell her to go fuck herself but I chill. My little black eye isn't shit. Apologize for punching me in the dick.

"You mean that?" I ask.

"Yeah. I'm sorry for everything but you had no right to do what you did. I am not a child. More importantly, I am not your child but I am sorry."

"You only hit me because you were mad, right?"

"Yes."

"So mad that you weren't thinking clearly?"

"Yeah Nyce," she says annoyed.

"Good." I grab and hug her. "Because I'm sorry about your car," I confess, holding her tightly.

"What did you do? You dumb ass," she says punching me in the back.

"I'm sorry. I'll buy you a new one," I tell her running away.

On Saturday, I am surrounded by all of my family and friends as they help me celebrate getting accepted into Georgetown.

"I'm so proud of you baby," Grandma Norah says giving me a kiss. I must have kissed and hug every damn relative in my family. Keisha's here but I'm still not talking to her. I know she knew about Terry and Vi.

Pastor Michaels says an awesome prayer that I feel in my soul. It puts me on an ultimate high to see how proud my parents are of me. Around 10pm, people start to leave with their bellies full.

I walk into the living room to say thank you to my Pop but he is passed out on the couch snoring. "Too much cognac old man?" I laugh covering him up with a blanket.

"Nyce," Keisha whispers. I shake my head no and walk into the kitchen.

"Did you have a good time?" I ask my mom.

"It wasn't about me baby. Did you have a good time?" She asks.

"The best," I tell her wrapping my arms around her.

"I'm going out for a little while. Thank you for today," I thank her kissing her cheek and walking out the back door. Had Keisha not been here, I would have stayed home but I don't feel like dealing with her tonight.

"Move ova, playa. We ain't done celebratin'," Knuck says hopping into the car.

"Where we goin'? I ask.

"Whereva you want."

"I'm not in a club mood."

"Cool. Neither am I."

"I had to get away from Keisha's ass."

"Yeah, about what you did to Terry's ass at the trap. Don't you eva leave me behind again."

"My bad homie. It was a spare of the moment thing."

"Dude, we in this shit together. I can't have your back if I don't know what the fuck is goin' on. If one of them niggahs would have tried you, I would have caught a case."

"You right. My bad homie," I tell him again. We end up driving to Tone's house.

"What up Georgetown?" He greets me at the door and gives me a hug.

"We good?" I ask referring to what happened at the stash house.

"Now you know I don't like Terry's bitch ass. That's Bo's boy so we're good."

"You're havin' a party?" I ask when I walk in.

"Something like that. Nina has her sorority sisters here for girl's night," he answers as I check out all the fine ass women walking around Tone's house.

"Miss Preston?" I call her name when I spot her across the room with a glass of wine in her hands.

"Hi James," she says cheerfully walking towards me.

"Y'all know each other?" Tone asks.

"Yeah, this is my teacher," I tell him.

"Oh shit. This is *thee* teacher?" Tone laughs.

"Shut up Tony," she says. "And why aren't you in the house studying young man?" She slurs.

"It's the weekend," I respond. She looks at me thoughtfully and then lustfully. Oh shit. Miss Preston wants to fuck ya boy.

"Stay out of trouble James," she teases placing her hand on my chest and then briskly walks away.

"Had I known that Jenna was the teacher you were talkin' about, I wouldn't have teased you. I understand why your ass was needing extra help now," Tone laughs handing me a beer.

I'm down in Tone's basement playing Spades with Tone, Bo and Knuck.

"That's fucked up what you did to my boy," Bo says slamming the Ace of Hearts on the table.

"It's fucked up that his bitch ass is fuckin' my sixteen-year-old sister."

"So. You don't touch nobody in the crew unless we ask you to."

"Bo, what the fuck did I ever do to you for you to be such a dick?" I ask tired of his shit.

"What you say to me?"

"You heard me," I tell him ready for a fight. Somebody suddenly starts banging on the cellar door.

"Y'all both shut the fuck up and cut the noise. That must be Chuck and Rob," Tone says getting up to answer. Two police officers walk inside as I check out their badges. Officer C. Boroughs is short, white, fat, and round. Officer R. Case is tall, and light-skin, with a slim athletic build.

"No invite to the party Tony?" Officers Boroughs asks.

"Not that type of party, Chuck," Tone replies walking over to the bar and pouring himself a drink.

"You know why we're here," Officer Case says.

"Yeah, yeah, yeah. You're here to rob the black man," Tone mocks. He pulls a duffle bag from behind the bar. Officer Case opens the bag and starts to pull money from it.

"It's all there," Tone says annoyed.

"It better be," Officer Boroughs snaps.

"Get your fat ass out of my house."

"Remember who runs this Tony boy. What you guys got going here?" Officer Boroughs asks walking over to the card table. No one speaks.

"You boys didn't hear me?" He says. Tone nods his head at us to speak.

"Cards. It's called playing cards," Knuck says venomously.

"I don't like your attitude boy," Officer Case smirks.

"You know Tony, $20,000.00 a month just doesn't seem worth it anymore if I can't get the respect I deserve from you boys. I did get an offer to take you guys out. What did Al's team offer us to take them out?" Officer Case asks Officer Boroughs.

"I believe your price tag is $50,000.00 Tony," Officer Boroughs responds.

"You got your money. I'll see you next month," Tone says walking to his cellar door and opening it for the officers to leave.

"Good day boys," Officer Boroughs says with a tilt of his hat. Officer Case grabs a slice of pizza, smiles, and walks out the door.

"Whose turn is it?" Tone asks taking his seat at the table.

"You want to tell me what that was about?" I ask.

"Sometimes Nyce, you gotta pay the piper," Tone answers and throws the King of Diamonds on the table.

About two hours later, we are all in a drunken haze and Knuck is passed out on the couch.

"I'm out." Bo gets up and gives Tone a pound.

"A'ight B. See you tomorrow," Tone says giving him a hug.

"You can sleep in one of the guest rooms," Tone advises plopping down next to me.

"You sure? I still here a whole bunch of females upstairs."

"It's after 3am. They should be leaving soon," he says lighting a blunt and taking a long drag. I am a little tipsy and tired.

"A'ight man. Thanks," I tell him and run upstairs to one of the spare guest rooms. I kick off my boots, strip down to my boxers, and am out cold as soon as my head hit the pillow.

"WHAT THE FUCK?" I yell snapping out of my sleep.

"Shhhh…relax," Miss Preston says on top of me trying to shimmy my boxers off.

"Miss Preston, you're drunk," I tell her trying to stop her.

"Shut up James," she says before sticking my man into her mouth and pinching my nipples with her fingertips. She gets no further objections from me as she slobs my knob like a fucking pro. I think my eyeballs actually rolled to the back of my mothafuckin' head, that's how good she is. Just as I am about to cum, she stops.

"Uh-ah. Don't you dare," she warns. I feel her bare breast press up against my chest. She licks my nipples and trails her tongue up to my neck while massaging my balls.

"Eighteen right?" She whispers in my ear.

"Yeah," I answer before she sits on my dick taking me all in.

"Fuuuckkkk," I exhale as she starts to ride my dick.

"Fuck. Damn," I say. Miss Preston is blowing my fuckin' mind as I desperately try not to cum. Her movements quicken and her moans become louder and longer. She finally cums as I feel her juices all over my midsection. When she's done, she lifts herself off of me.

"Wait. I didn't cum yet," I tell her when I see her feeling for her clothes in the dark.

"Mr. Hennessey, this wasn't about you," she says throwing her dress over her head, collecting her shoes and walking out the door.

"What the fuck?" I ask myself as I'm beating my dick to finish the job that Miss Preston started. "What the fuck?" I say again as I blast off in my hand. "What the fuck?" I repeat this time in total disbelief of what just happened. Miss Preston got that shit…that good shit. The kind of shit that niggahs write love songs about and start wars over.

In the morning, I take the sheets off the bed and go down to the laundry room to wash them. I walk into the kitchen and Nina is in there cooking breakfast.

"Good morning sunshine. I would have washed the sheets," she laughs. I smile.

"It's cool. I got it."

"Now Nyce, I told Jenna that you weren't the kind of young boy to go run and tell all your friends. Don't make me a liar and more importantly, don't cost Jenna to lose her job."

"It's not even like that. *Me and Miss Preston have a thing going on…we both know it's wrong but it's much too strong*," I sing to Nina while she burst out laughing.

"You just be careful," she says returning back to the stove to flip pancakes.

"Uncle Nyce," Toni says running into the kitchen and jumping in my lap.

"What's up Peanut?"

"You wanna have a tea party with me?"

"Sure. Set it up," I tell her.

I play tea time or whatever the hell girls call this game with Toni until Nina wakes everybody else up for breakfast. We eat and chill out for the majority of the day watching TV and politicking the way niggahs do. I call Miss Preston at least 20 times but she doesn't answer my calls so I end up making up and chilling with Keisha for the remainder of the night.

NINE

Monday at school, I wait for Miss Preston to dismiss class to talk to her. When the bell finally rings and all the students leave, I approach.

"So, you're not talking to me now?" I ask her.

"Look. I'm sorry about Saturday. It was totally unprofessional of me. Here is a list of tutors that are willing to help you. I can no longer continue to tutor you," she says not looking at me.

"What's the problem?"

"I have a boyfriend and you are my student. That's the problem."

"So. I have a girlfriend and I am 18. I still don't see a problem."

"You wouldn't. Listen, I think that you are a great kid..."

"Kid?" I cut her off. "Kid? Was I kid when you got on top of me? Did you enjoy the ride Miss Preston?" I taunt getting close to her.

"Please. Don't flatter yourself. I've had better, kid," she says. Bitch.

"Well let me redeem myself. I'll put in that work this time. You kind of raped me Miss Preston," I laugh.

She looks angry for a second but then she bursts out laughing.

"I'll stop by tonight," I tell her.

"James, no. I already told you."

"Well you're gonna have to get a restraining order then. I'll see you tonight," I tell her walking out of the classroom.

After practice, I end up in Becky's garage.

"What's up babe?" She says kissing me on the cheek. "You got something for me?"

"Just a little Becky. I think you have a problem," I tell her giving her a little bit of powdered heroin.

"Don't start your shit Nyce. I heard it from your fuckin' friend already," she barks referring to Knuck.

"He has a point."

"Whatever. Tell him just because I do what I do doesn't mean he has to avoid me."

"When's the last time you seen him?" I ask as I watch her do a line. She wipes her nose and then comes join me on the couch.

"He was here a few days ago," she says laying her head in my lap.

"Have you spoken to Wendy?" I ask her.

"Yes," she smiles with her eyes closed.

"Is she still mad?"

"No. Wendy has moved on and you better let her," she says opening her eyes and looking up at me.

"You act like I would stop her."

"Geez, men are such assholes. You don't care about her at all, do you?"

"Of course I care about her. She's family."

"You don't fuck family, Nyce."

"You know what I mean, Beck."

"Let's go to Paris," she says reaching for a brochure off the table.

"Can't get to Paris by train," I remind her about my fear of flying.

"Stop it. When you graduate, we should see the world together."

"You're high Becky," I laugh.

"So. It doesn't mean that I don't know what I'm talking about. We have all this money and barely enjoy it."

"You enjoy it. Nobody is stopping you." She closes her eyes.

"Shhh…close your eyes. We're in Paris Nyce, eating macaroons outside at a small café. We can see the Eifel Tower from where we are sitting."

"Becky, you're trippin'," I laugh.

"Shhh…just do it." I humor Becky and close my eyes as I hear her soft voice guide me through Paris. I must have been into what she was saying because the next thing I know, I am waking up off her couch.

"See. You liked my adventure," Becky says smiling.

"Damn Becky. What the hell did you do?" I laugh.

"Nothing. You were relaxed. That's what vacation and traveling does," she says. I look at my watch.

"I gotta jet," I tell her kissing her on her cheek and walking out the door.

I pull up to Miss Preston's house and walk around back into her backyard. I lie blankets down in her grass before running around front to knock on her door.

"I told you not to come," she says answering.

"I told you I would so put some shoes on. I want to take you somewhere."

"Where? I can't be seen with you."

"Trust me," I tell her. She puts her shoes on and I escort her to my car. I drive around the block and back to her house.

"I don't get it," she says.

"Wait here for a second," I instruct her as I proceed to the trunk of my car to remove the picnic basket that I had stashed. I walk to the passenger door and open it.

"James, you understand that this is not a date?" She asks when she sees the items in my hands.

"I know. You're like old and shit. I wouldn't want to date you anyway."

"You asshole," she laughs. I walk her around back and sit on the blankets while she remains standing. I open the picnic basket to remove the cheesesteaks and wine. She giggles.

"What's so funny?" I ask.

"I'm 29 years old and this is the first time that a man has taken me on a picnic; even if it is in my backyard. Pretty smooth kid," she winks and smiles.

"Well, shut your old ass up and come sit with me," I say sarcastically. She laughs and removes her shoes before sitting on the blanket. I open the bottle of wine.

"I'll take that," she says and pours herself a glass. I reach over to take the bottle from her to pour some for myself.

"Uh-uh, Mister. You're not old enough," she scolds taking the bottle out of my hands.

"Now Miss Preston…"

"Jenna," she says.

"Huh?"

"You can call me Jenna," she smiles. I pull her close to me and kiss her. She follows my lead and lies back on the blanket. I reach under her blouse and start to massage her breast before taking her shirt and bra off. She's so beautiful and mature looking. I suck on her breast a little as I try to unbutton her pants. She stops me.

"No. I am a woman. Women like it slow…teasingly. Make me squirm a little before completely undressing me," she whispers. I take my time and tend to her breast more engagingly. I pull, suck, and bite a little. She starts to squirm so I unbutton her pants and slowly pull them off. As I am taking a condom out of my pocket, she stops me again.

"There is no rush so take your time. Four play is a necessary art when it comes to sex."

"Tell me what you want me to do," I whisper half annoyed and yet half intrigued.

"Open my legs. Kiss in between my thighs using your tongue. Get into a rhythm and when it looks like I am lost, you lick in between my lips."

"Um Miss Preston…Jenna, I don't eat pussy," I inform her.

"Well James, I think our business here is done," she says gathering her clothes.

"Wait," I tell her grabbing her clothes from her. Shit. I grab the wine and start drinking that shit right out of the bottle like it's a Pepsi. She starts to giggle.

"What the hell is so funny?" I ask.

"You. Eating pussy isn't so bad. You might enjoy it," she laughs.

"Easy for you to say. I know the shit that comes out of it."

"It has flavor and mine is sweet. Come on, you owe me one."

"I ain't ask you to suck me off."

"I know but I wanted to because that's what adults do."

"So, what you're really trying to say is that if I don't eat the box, our little relationship is over?"

"We don't have a relationship but yeah, in a nutshell, so hurry up and make up your mind. You're soft now anyway," she says pointing out my limp dick. She sits up and gently pushes me back. I'm loving how controlling she is. Getting on her hands and knees she starts to give me head. Shiiiiitttt. Miss Preston is a pro. Fuck the pussy. I'll be straight if she just gave me head every day. It doesn't take long before my man is rock hard again.

"Stop," I tell her.

"Now why would you want me to do that?" She asks, not stopping and looking up at me all sexy and shit. Fuck. I'm about to nut up.

"Stop Miss Preston...I mean Jenna. Damn," I beg trying to think about something that would stop me from cumming.

"You know you really don't want me to," she says seductively still working. My toes curl and my eyes roll into the back of my head. ABCDEFG…shit. Get it together man. 123…7…12…don't cum…don't cum…don't…

"FUUUUCK," I let out as I blast off in her mouth. She doesn't even stop. She just keeps sucking making sure that she gets every damn drop.

"FUCK," I say again when I can't take anymore. She got my whole fuckin' body convulsing and I almost want to punch her in her head to make her stop. When she finally does stop she wipes her mouth with her fingertips and laughs.

"What's so funny? You're always laughing at me and shit," I say to her.

"Nothing," she responds looking amused.

"Just give me a second. I'll get up again."

"Oh yeah? So that's how you're working?" She asks, and lays her head on my chest. "It's pretty chilly out," she says shivering in my arms. I grab the extra blanket to cover us up.

"Thank you," she says. I close my eyes and hold her tight for a second before I realize what I'm doing. I want to tell her to get off of me and yet I want to tell her to stay where she is as I inhale the scent of her hair.

"What's your story Jenna?" I ask her.

"What do you mean?"

"Your story?"

"Well for starters, I'm a teacher," she laughs. "I was born and raised in Savannah, Georgia, attended Morris Brown, lived in Atlanta for a while and then accepted a job in Philadelphia."

"Where's your man?" I ask.

"He's the reason why I'm here."

"What do you mean?"

"His job transferred to Philly and I came with him."

"So where is he?"

"Let's just say we are having our differences at the moment."

"So why are you with me?" I ask out of curiosity.

"Why are you with me and me being fine isn't an answer," she throws back. I laugh.

"I'm with you because I like you," I tell her truthfully.

"I like you too," she says pecking my lips before fully engaging into a kiss. She glides her tongue down to my chest, sucking and biting my nipples as she massages my balls. My dick slowly comes back to life as I entwine my fingers in her hair pulling her up to kiss me. Using her tongue, she plays with mine, sucking on it and it's turning me the fuck on. We switch positions so now I'm on top. I start kissing on her neck before sucking on her breast. Inserting a finger in her, I check to see if she's wet. The warmth and wetness of her pussy has my dick's full attention as he stands fully erect while her pussy pulsates around my fingers. She lets out a soft moan and closes her eyes. I grab the condom off the blanket.

"Don't you dare," she says. I laugh.

"Alright…alright…alright…yooooo," is all I can say as I shift my body and am now face-to-face with her pussy. I pause and stare at it.

"It isn't going to eat itself," she laughs.

"Alright," I say one last time before spreading her legs and lips apart. I stick out my tongue and start licking, darting my tongue in and out of her.

"What…the fuck…are you doing?" She says slowly while popping her head up.

"I don't fuckin' know."

"Forget it. Stop. Eating pussy isn't for you. Luckily you're working with 9inches, a nice body and a fine ass face," she laughs sitting up and trying to kiss me.

"Hold up. You just fuckin' insulted me and my manhood."

"So. What are you going to do about it?"

"Fuck you, Miss Preston," I tell her and gently shove her down to lay back. I start to glide my tongue in between her thighs. I part her lips and lick slowly. She moans.

"Now use your tongue to play with my pearl."

"Your what?"

"My pearl. My clit. It's right here," she points showing me her clit. I start to lick her swollen clit and she arches her back some.

"Be a little aggressive James," she says while feeding my face. "It's like a sloppy French kiss". I lick a little harder and gently bite down on her swollen clit. She screams.

"SHIT. I'm sorry," I tell her.

"No. That's it. Do that shit again," she orders pushing my head back down. I do it again causing her to really moan. Oh shit. I think I just found my signature move.

"Use your fingers," she tells me in a breathless whisper. I stick my finger in her slowly; one and then two.

"I meant eat my pussy and finger me at the same damn time," she says annoyed. I do what she asks and her moans becomes louder and longer. Her moaning and the smell of her pussy is not only feeding my ego but it's got me all the way turned the fuck on. The more turned on I get, the more in to it I become until she finally blasts off in my mouth. She tastes sweet and tangy. Not the best thing I ever tasted but not the worst, I think as I keep going.

"Now you can stop," she says as she starts to squirm.

"No. All that shit you just talked," I tell her holding her down. She uses her feet to try to push me off of her but I keep going until she screams. I mean, really screams as she makes a puddle on the blanket.

"Can I fuck you now Miss Preston?" I ask.

"Now would be a great time," she answers handing me the condom. I grab the condom, roll it on and do what I know I'm good at except I take my time. Normally, I let a girl cum and then cum shortly after but I actually care about what Miss Preston thinks, so I take my time and cater to her needs, making sure that no body part is left unattended. She seems to be loving it. I let her cum two more times before I finally allow myself to.

"Four," I tell her rolling onto my back.

"Four what?" She asks, snuggling up to me.

"You came four times so no more talking that kid shit."

"Uh…almost kid. Not quite yet but I love that you are willing to learn," she smiles and kisses me on my chest. I check the time on my watch.

"I know you are not going to play me like I am some little school girl? You are not going to come up in my house, fuck me and then leave," she scorns.

"Miss Preston, it's a school night and I have curfew," I laugh. It's already 11:30.

"I thought you said that you were 18," she says looking worried.

"I am 18 but I am still in high school living under my mother's roof. My mom's crazy when it comes to grades and school," I laugh. "I'll be back though," I tell her pulling her into my arms and kissing her softly.

"It's all good James. I understand." I kiss her goodbye and rush home. I sleep like a mothafuckin' king that night.

As the months pass, I kick it with Jenna almost every night when she allows it. We talk a lot about my future and goals in life and she schools me on making investments and how to save and spend money. Being with her ends up being one of my favorite things to do within my day. When I visit her, she always has a meal waiting for me and helps me study for her class as well as others. We talk and joke around for hours and end the night with intense sex. How can she not be my favorite part of the day?

I'm chilling in Becky's garage while she cooks up. Knuck and I are playing on her Sega Genesis while Tobi and Wendy are sitting at the table doing homework.

"Geez. I can't wait until high school is finally over. Homework sucks," Wendy whines.

"Well, homework is still going to be there when we go away to college," Tobi reminds her. "Did you put all of your applications in?" She asks Wendy.

"Yeah. I'm going to NYU. You?"

"USC," Tobi answers.

"We will be out of this hell hole finally," Wendy says throwing her pencil. She walks over to the weed table and rolls a joint before coming over to me and sits on my lap.

"How come you are the only one who doesn't smoke?" She asks.

"Cuz I'm an athlete," I remind her

"So. What does that mean?"

"It means I need my lungs," I tell her trying to stand up to get her off my lap. She gives me a funny look.

"You okay?" She asks.

"I'm good." Truth is that ever since me and Miss Preston started kickin' it, I really don't want to be bothered with other females.

"Is my English paper ready?" I ask her.

"Yeah. It's on the table," she answers.

"Homie, you got this? I got a tutoring session," I say to Knuck.

"Yeah, you good. Go do your thing." I peck Wendy's lips and grab my paper off the table.

"Will I see you later?" She asks.

"I'll call you," I tell her kissing her on the cheek.

I pull up to Miss Prestons's house, run up the stairs and knock on her door.

"You're late," she says answering the door. She jumps up on me, wraps her legs around my waist, and kisses me.

"I'm sorry. I had something to do. I got you something though," I tell her handing her a single rose.

"That's really sweet. Are you hungry? I made dinner."

"I could eat," I answer. She disappears into the kitchen and comes back with a plate in hand serving me steak, a baked potato, and broccoli.

"Thanks babe," I tell her as she hands me the plate of food.

"Beer, juice, or water?" She asks.

"Water please." She comes back with a glass of water.

"Are you ready for your test tomorrow?" She asks, sitting the water down in front of me.

"Yeah. I have a great tutor," I smile.

"Where are your index cards? Let me quiz you." I point to my book bag while pouring more A1 sauce on my steak.

"Qui ambulavit in via," she says.

"The man walked down the street," I reply with a mouth full of food.

"Mulieres in habitu est rufus," she continues.

"The woman's dress is red."

"Now how do you say the dog won't stop barking?"

"Canis...latrat...non prohibere," I slowly respond.

"You forgot the verb."

"Man, shit."

"You need some motivation. Hmmm…," she says putting down the flash cards and walking towards me.

"Let's see," she ponders to herself. "If you get a 90 or better, I will give you some classroom head," she promises pulling my chair out and climbing into my lap.

"If I get a 100, can I get some classroom head and ass too?"

"Hmmmm…I think I can accommodate that," she agrees while licking behind my ear and gliding her tongue down my neck. I'm suddenly full. I lift her up, carry her up the stairs to start working on extra credit.

When I return home, Vi is at the kitchen table doing homework.

"What's up dork?" I greet her.

"Your hoes been calling here all damn night," she says with an attitude.

"I ain't got no hoes. Where's mom?" I ask.

"She had something to do at the school and dad is at work as usual."

"Did you cook and feed Morgan?"

"Of course. I burnt the rolls though because Shelby called for you and we got into it. I don't know what you see in that mutt anyway."

"Whose says I'm talking to Shelby?"

"Fine. I'll pretend that you are not cheating on my best friend as long as you stop trying to insult my intelligence. Tell those bitches you got office hours or something or make them call you on your line. What's the point of having a line if you never use it?"

"Only important people get that number. Everybody else has this number. Don't be mad 'cuz nobody is checkin' for you," I tease, rustling her hair.

"Stop, stupid." She punches me in my arm. "If the phone isn't ringing for you, it's ringing for that other fool," she says referring to Knuck. "How is Terry supposed to call me if the damn phone lines are always tied up?" She utters and quickly coves her mouth when she realizes she slipped up. I just stare at her.

"Nyce, he treats me good. Can't you just be happy that I'm happy?"

"Fuck no. He's a grown ass man raping a sixteen-year-old girl," I snap.

"He's not raping me and like I said, he treats me right."

"What is your definition of being treated right? Because he buys you shit and takes you out on cheap dates?"

"He does more for me than how you treat the women you cheat on Keisha wit'."

"He is using you, Vi. You don't see that? That man has a girl and kids, remember?"

"Him and his girl only live together for the kids."

"Are you really that fuckin' stupid?"

"You don't know shit, Nyce," she snaps. The phone rings and she quickly pops up to answer it. I softly mug her in her face and grab the phone out of her hands.

"Hello," I answer. Silence.

"Niggah, I know it's you. Speak," I bark.

"Let me talk to Vi man," Terry says.

"I told you to stay away from my fuckin' sister," I snap as Vi fights me for the phone.

"I'll stay away from her when she starts staying away from me. What can I say? Your sister has a thing for my dick," Terry laughs. I hang up on him.

"Why would you do that?" Vi screams at me.

"You need to end it. End it NOW," I tell her.

"Or else what? What the fuck you gonna do?"

"I'm gonna tell mom and dad and have that man arrested for statutory rape."

"Oh, you snitching now? Does Tone know he's workin' wit' a snitch?" She laughs.

"You heard what the fuck I said," I snap walking out the kitchen before I accidentally hit her. Yes, I am that pissed off.

"Yeah, and if you tell mom and dad, I'm gonna tell Keisha about all the females that be calling here," she yells behind me.

"Go ahead. You do that shit already," I shout back while running up the stairs. I enter Knuck's room and see him and Morgan sitting in the middle of the floor playing *Mortal Kombat*.

"Hey James," Morgan greets putting the game on pause and giving me a hug.

"Hey baby girl. Is your homework done?"'

"Yes and already checked by this one," she explains pointing at Knuck.

"How was school?"

"Okay. The usual. Nothing much to tell. How was your day?"

"Same here kid."

"Come on girl so I can finish beating your ass on this game," Knuck says.

"He's so bossy," Morgan laughs.

"Aye Ock, we good?" I ask Knuck referring to the product.

"Yeah. We straight wit' it. Jeff and Rick already did a pick-up. Mookie and Black just have to get theirs tomorrow."

"Cool. Morgan, don't stay up too late. It's already 8:30. Did you take your bath?"

"Yes James," she replies annoyed.

"Alright. You better be in that bed by 9 o'clock."

"Can you read me a story?" She asks.

"Yeah but it has to be now."

"Okay. Night Knuck," she says kissing him on the cheek. Grabbing my hand, she leads me to her bedroom.

"What shall it be?" I ask thumbing through her books.

"I don't know. Surprise me," she answers jumping in her bed.

"Here. This used to be one of my favorites. Throwback classic," I say pulling *Where the Wild Things Are* off the shelf. "How about you read it to me," I tell her.

"Okay," she agrees grabbing the book. Morgan reads the book to me as I pretend to be interested.

"Okay kiddo. Bedtime," I tell her once we finish.

"James. What am I going to do without you?" She asks as I'm tucking her in.

"What do you mean?"

"You're leaving for college. I heard that Georgetown is in Washington, DC. Isn't that far?"

"Not really. You act like you are never going to see me again."

"You promise to come home at least once a month?"

"I promise Organ."

"Morgan," she corrects me.

"I love you," I tell her kissing her forehead.

"I love you Yimmy," she smiles.

"You better. Now go to bed," I smile and wink at her before turning out her lights and shutting her door. When I turn around, Keisha is standing there.

"You're really good with her," she compliments. I give her a peck on the lips.

"Thanks babe. What are you doing here?"

"I've been calling your phone but you weren't answering so I decided to stop by. Problem?"

"No babe, there is no problem. I'm glad you're here."

"You better be," she says walking towards the third floor stairs. I follow behind her. As soon as we get inside my room, she starts taking off her clothes.

"Wait baby. I have to take a shower."

"Why? Who was you wit'?" She asks with an attitude.

"I was wit' nobody but I worked out and didn't get a chance to shower yet," I lie.

"Hurry up. She's waiting," she says winking. I take my time in the shower hoping that Keisha somehow loses her urge. The truth is, Miss Preston wore me out. When I return to my room, Keisha is lying in my bed naked. Shit. Hopefully my dick cooperates. I take my towel off to join her. I climb on top of her and start kissing her.

"Miss Preston called," she says in between kisses. "Why is she calling?"

"She's my tutor remember?" I tell her thinking that if I hurry with Keisha, I can get her out and return Miss Preston's call to see what she wanted.

"Yeah, I know but didn't you see her already after school? So why is she calling?"

"You really want to talk about my teacher?" I ask annoyed hoping she drops it. This talk about Miss Preston is fuckin' my head up.

"I'm sorry babe," she says placing her hands on my man to insert inside of her but it is too late. Every thought I am having at this moment is about Miss Preston so I close my eyes and envision me fucking her.

"Damn baby," Keisha says moaning in my ear.

"Turn over," I command.

"What?"

"Turn over. Let me hit it from the back."

"No. Do I look like a dog to you?" She refuses. What the fuck? Keisha is boring in bed sometimes. I don't want to press the issue so I continue to please her in missionary position while thinking about Miss Preston and all the freaky things we do with and to each other. I let Keisha cum three times before I finally cum.

"Wow," she moans breathless. "You've been practicing," she laughs. I laugh too.

"So who the fuck you been practicing with?" She yells, slapping the shit out of me.

"What the fuck, girl?"

"All of a sudden you are some Don Juan Casanova. I've been fuckin' you for damn near four years. Did you think I wouldn't notice?"

"Keisha, why do you always have to ruin the mood?" I ask calmly.

"Because I am tired of these bitches laughing behind my back."

"Nobody is laughing at you. You are being paranoid," I tell her looking over at the clock. "You have to go before my mom comes home."

"Fine," she says kicking the covers off.

"Mom's home," Vi says barging in my room.

"What the fuck girl?" I yell at her pulling the covers over me.

"My bad. Mom's home and I think I just heard dad pull up," she says as Keisha is finding her clothes.

"Girl, hurry up," Vi quietly yells picking up Keisha's shoes.

"I'll be downstairs babe," Keisha says kissing me and running out the door with Vi. I pick up my phone to call Miss Preston.

"Hello," she answers.

"Miss me?" I ask.

"You're funny. Your little girlfriend answered the phone earlier."

"She told me."

"I guess I didn't do my job right if you went home still wanting some sex."

"Lady, your pussy is the only one I want to be in," I attest.

"Don't bullshit a bullshitter," she laughs. "I was just calling to see if you made it home safely. I will talk to you tomorrow," she says hanging up on me. Damn. I wanted to talk to her some more; to hear her voice some more; to be with her some more. Hold the fuck up. What the fuck is happening to me?

School is school for the remainder of the week. Friday is finally here and I am looking forward to the weekend. I'm sitting in my Latin class as Miss Preston is handing back our test papers. Fuck. I got a B.

"Miss Preston, you gave me an 87," I complain to her after class.

"I'm sorry James but at least it's not a D," she smiles.

"But Miss Preston," I damn near whine thinking about my reward. *Snap the fuck out of it*, I tell myself.

"Why don't you stop by tomorrow for some extra credit," she suggests packing up her things. "I'll see you then," she confirms grabbing my dick on the sly. I have a game tonight and then I promised Keisha that I would spend some time with her so this shit actually works out in my favor.

I dominate the game scoring 35 points for my team. I celebrate a little with them before showering and running outside to meet up with Keisha.

"Hey baby," she says kissing me when I get to the car.

"Hey you. Did you check what time *Sugar Hill* starts?" I ask her.

"Yeah. It starts at 10 o'clock," she responds. I look at my watch. It's only 8:30. "I guess we can go out to get something to eat."

"Yes please 'cause I am starving." We go to eat at a local Chinese Restaurant before heading down

Delaware Ave to catch the movie. I'm holding Keisha's hand while standing in line to buy the tickets.

"James…Keisha…hello. Funny running into you here," I hear Miss Preston's voice. Without thinking, I let go of Keisha's hand before turning to face Jenna.

"Hey Miss Preston," I greet her.

"Hi Miss Preston," Keisha smiles.

"Baby, I got the popcorn," some guy says walking up behind Miss Preston.

"Derrick, this is one of my students," she says introducing me to dude.

"Hi," we greet each other.

"Well you kids enjoy your movie," Miss Preston says grabbing Derrick's arm and walking away. I pay for our tickets, wait in line with Keisha at the concession stand, and walk into the theater. I'll be damn. Miss Preston and her bitch ass dude are in the same theater.

"Come on babe," Keisha says walking towards the back. I hear her but my eyes are fixated on Miss Preston, watching her kiss dude.

"Naw. Let's sit up here," I tell Keisha. Fuck that. I'm at least gonna sit a couple of rows in front of them so I don't have to watch their bullshit love affair. I find two seats, four rows ahead of Miss Preston and punk ass Derrick.

"You usually like to sit in the back," Keisha states while handing me my drink.

"I know but you know, trying something new," I tell her. She looks at me funny.

"Anyway, prom is coming. We have to rent the limo and stuff now," she reminds me.

"Go ahead and get it. Just let me know how much," I let her know and put a handful of popcorn into my mouth. I get cozy with Keisha as the movie starts.

After the movie, I chill with Keisha at my house but my mind is heavily on Miss Preston and her punk ass dude. I don't even know why it's bothering me.

The next day, I wake up early, run some product and make it to Jenna's house by the afternoon.

"So, that was your man?" I ask Jenna when she answers the door.

"Yup. That was him," she replies as I follow her to the kitchen. She opens the fridge and hands me a beer.

"Y'all workin' it out?"

"Trying," she casually answers. We walk into her living room and sit on the couch. Jenna turns the TV on.

"So where is he now?"

"Really? If we are going to talk about Derrick then maybe you should leave," she says annoyed.

"Damn. I can't ask you any questions?"

"Do I ask you questions about your relationship?" She snaps.

"Fine," I back down pissed off.

I chill at Jenna's house for the rest of the night and into the morning; waking up early to cook her breakfast.

"You cook?" She smiles, walking into the kitchen.

"I do what I do," I tell her putting a piece of turkey bacon into her mouth.

"So what are you about to do?" She asks me as we're sitting at the table eating.

"You're looking at it."

"Uh, I have work to do James."

"Is that your way of telling me that I have to leave?"

"Don't be like that. You've been here since last night," she states as if I am bugging her.

"It's cool Jenna. I'll go." I'm not feeling this shit. When did I become a bitch?

After breakfast, I knock Miss Preston off one last time before she kicks me out.

"Knuck man, she fuckin' kicked me out this morning," I tell him sitting in his room.

"Little homie, sounds to me that you done got pussy whipped," Knuck laughs.

"Fuck you niggah. No I'm not," I object.

"Yeah, a'ight Marcus Graham. You straight got boomeranged," he laughs. "How often do you think about her?"

"All the fuckin' time" I admit. "Shit. What do I do?"

"You better find some better pussy," he laughs.

<u>TEN</u>
June 1995

Do I find some better pussy? Fuck no. It's so bad that I cut all the females that I'm fucking off to the point that the only women I am fucking is Miss. Preston and Keisha. To be completely real, half of the time, I don't even want to fuck Keisha's ass.

As the school year winds down, I'm glad to be getting up out of here. With graduation being next week, I just have to make it through this summer and then me and Keish are off to Georgetown. She didn't get a full scholarship so I got stuck paying her tuition. We're not able to get an off campus apartment that I had hoped for. Being a freshman on an athletic scholarship, the school doesn't allow it but I am still looking forward to it.

I just finished a last minute flunky delivery for Tone and am headed to Becky's to drop off a little bit of blow for her when Miss Preston pages me CODE: 123 indicating that she misses me. I quickly forget about Becky and head to Miss Preston's house.

"You miss me, huh?" I ask her walking inside.

"I always miss you," she says giving me a kiss.

"Whatever big head," I joke before mugging her in the face. "What you been up to?"

"Grading finals," she replies, stretching.

"Let me take care of you," I tell her lifting her up and carrying her up the stairs. I give her a massage before dicking her down.

"There's less than two weeks left of school. Are you ready for graduation?" She asks me while cuddled up in my arms.

"Of course. I can't wait to start this new chapter of my life."

"When do you leave for Georgetown?"

"July 12th."

"Isn't that a little early?"

"It's for basketball camp."

"Oh. Did I ever tell you how proud I am of you?"

"No," I smile kissing her on top of her forehead.

"I am. I am extremely proud of you."

"Thank you."

"I'm moving back to Atlanta," she blurts out.

"Why?"

"Derrick and I are working on our relationship and he has been offered a better job."

"Are you just going to follow that man wherever he goes?"

"Like Keisha does with you?" She sarcastically spits back. "That's my man James. Yeah we have our ups and downs but what relationship doesn't?"

"When are you leaving?"

"Right after graduation."

"So that's it?" I ask referring to us.

"Is there supposed to be more? You're leaving to go to school."

"That doesn't mean I was going to stop seeing you." She sits quietly for a moment.

"Can you at least wait until I leave to go to school before moving back?" I ask her. She looks at me and smiles.

"I will do that for you," she assures, kissing me and then climbs on top.

After an entire afternoon of having sex with Miss Preston, I'm hungry as shit. I watch her sleep for a moment before tickling her.

"Wake up," I whisper in her ear. She laughs.

"Stop boy," she giggles.

"You hungry?"

"Yup but I don't feel like cooking."

"Want to go out to dinner?"

"How about some fast food?"

"Still don't want to be seen with me in public?"

"Come on. I just don't want to chance it."

"It's cool," I tell her getting out the bed and putting on my clothes. We drive to the nearby Burger King. On our way back, I see a cop tailing behind me.

"Babe, stash this on you," I tell her in a panic handing her the blow I had for Becky.

"What?"

"Please? They won't search you. Put it in your pants."

"No. I'm not doing shit," she snaps, pissed off.

"Please?" I beg. The cop's sirens go off. "Babe, please?" She slaps the shit out of my face before grabbing the baggie out of my hands and stuffing it into her pants.

"License and registration," the officer asks when he approaches my window. "Do you know why I pulled you over?"

"No."

"You forgot your turn signal back there," he says. I know damn well I ain't forget my fuckin' turn signal. I look at Jenna who is looking like she is about to kill me.

"Here you go Mr. Hennessey. I will let you off with a warning," the officer says.

"That's because I didn't do anything wrong," I mumble under my breath.

"What?" the officer asks.

"I said thank you," I lie with a fake smile. I pull off and head back to Jenna's house.

"I CAN'T BELIEVE YOU FUCKIN' HAD ME PLANT THAT SHIT," she yells throwing it at me. "YOU'RE ON DRUGS?"

"No. Why would you think some shit like that?"

"Then what the fuck is that?"

"I sell them. I don't do the shit."

"You're a fuckin' drug dealer?"

"Yeah. I thought you knew."

"How the fuck am I supposed to know some shit like that?"

"Because of Tone."

"Tone sells drugs?" Fuck. I spoke too much.

"Tone sells drugs?" She asks again. I don't say anything.

"Get out of my house James," she says calmly.

"Babe…"

"OUT," she shouts pointing towards the door. I grab my shit and leave. Throughout the day, I try to call Miss Preston but she's ignoring my calls.

On Monday, I rush to my Latin class in hopes to finally talk to her about what happened. To my surprise, we have a substitute teacher. The school day couldn't end fast enough. As soon as the final bell rings, I ditch my boys and drive straight to Jenna's house. She doesn't answer her door and I don't see her car parked anywhere. Defeated, I leave in hopes to talk to her the following day but Jenna never comes back to the school. She is straight missing and avoiding me as I continuously call and do drive-by's, by her house.

"I fucked up, Knuck," I tell him while getting ready for graduation.

"Stop thinking about it. This is your day man," he says fixing my tie.

"You don't understand homie."

"Nah, I get it but what can you do? You're leaving for school soon. Just let it be."

After the graduation ceremony, I spot Miss Preston congratulating other students and greeting their parents. I try to hurry my parents up who are caught up in the moment of taking photos of me and Keisha.

"Dad, hold up," I tell him before walking towards Jenna. Locking eyes, she looks at me and shakes her head no. Ignoring her, I keep walking towards her until I see her bitch ass dude pop up out of nowhere, wrapping his arms around her. He whispers in her ear. Whatever he said makes her laugh and blush right before he kisses her. My blood is boiling as I watch him throw his arm around her and leads her away.

"Homie, don't let her mess up your day. You just graduated," Knuck says throwing his heavy arm around me and walking me back to my parents for more pictures. Keisha looks at me pissed off but I don't fuckin' care. I finish taking pictures with my people and then group photos with other students before heading back home.

"SURPRISE!" my family shouts when I enter my house.

My parents throw me a surprise graduation barbecue and all of my relatives swing through. Black and Mookie are also here with their parents and Becky, Wendy, and Tobi stop by to join the festivities.

"Why the fuck is she here?" Keisha asks me referring to Wendy.

"Don't start your shit right now Keisha. I'm not in the fuckin' mood," I snap at her.

"What the hell is wrong with you? You've been acting shitty all week."

"You," I spit back walking away. I run upstairs to my room and try to call Jenna again. No answer.

"FUCK," I yell.

"Nyce," Knuck calls my name, barging in my room.

"What?"

"You need to snap the fuck out of it and come the fuck downstairs to be with your family."

"Fuck you, Knuck. I didn't even ask for this bullshit party."

"A bullshit party that your parents spent their time and money throwing."

"So."

"You ungrateful asshole. I would kill to fuckin' have parents," he snaps slamming my door.

"FUCK," I yell again picking up the phone and calling her one last time. When she doesn't answer, I get myself together and go back downstairs.

The next evening, I drive over to Tone's house.

"What up graduate?" He greets.

"Uncle Nyce," Toni screams, running towards me.

"Hey Peanut," I say picking her up.

"We saw you yesterday graduating. I wanted to say hi but daddy said I couldn't."

"We was there homie but your parents," Tone shrugs knowing that he has to keep his distance from me when I am around my folks.

"It's all good homie. Thanks for coming."

"We got you a gift. I picked it out," Toni tells me wiggling out of my arms and running to get my gift.

"Ain't no we. I got you a gift. It cost some bread too," Tone says smiling. "What's wrong homie?" He asks.

"Nothing man. I'm good."

"Here," Toni giggles running back to me and handing me my gift. It's an iced out Peter Philippe watch.

"You picked this out Peanut?" I ask her.

"Uh-huh. You like it?"

"Yup. It's dope," I tell her putting it on.

"Hey suga," Nina says coming down the stairs. "Congratulations." She walks over to me and gives me a tight hug and kiss on the cheek. "You looked so handsome yesterday."

"Thank you." Nina looks at me thoughtfully for a moment before handing me an envelope. She smiles and winks at me before disappearing into the kitchen. I look at the envelope and recognize Jenna's handwriting written on the front.

James,
Congratulations. I am very proud of you and wish you well with whatever you decide to do in life. I'm sorry for the way things ended between us and please forgive me for leaving the way that I did. I left for Atlanta right after graduation. I know I told you that I would wait until after you left for Georgetown but I feel that this was the best solution. I urge you to leave the drug game behind you. You are far too intelligent to waste your potential on being something you are not. I see the good in you and it breaks my heart to watch you go down this path. Don't let this game turn you into somebody you are not. Anyway, continue to make me proud and I will always be cheering for you from a distance.

The letter is written on her custom pink stationary paper that has her name *Miss Jenna Preston* engraved in gold lettering. I stuff the letter into my jeans, walk into the basement and pour myself a drink. As I'm sitting on the couch watching ESPN, Nina comes down and sits next to me.

"I'm sorry kid," she says.

"I'm not a kid," I snap.

"You're right Mr. Grown Man," she jokes putting her hands up.

"Sorry."

"It's cool. We've all been there."

"Where?"

"There," she says pointing at my heart.

"I don't want to talk about it."

"You do know that it was never going to work, don't you?"

"I don't want to talk about it," I sternly repeat. She leaves me alone.

After drinking a shit load of alcohol at Tone's house, I somehow make it back to my house safely in the wee hours of the morning. I stagger up the stairs into my room and pass out fully dressed.

"WHAT THE FUCK IS THIS?" My father yells at me waking me out of my drunken slumber. It takes me a minute to get my eyes open to see what the fuck he's talking about.

"JIMMY, WAKE THE FUCK UP AND ANSWER ME," he yells kicking my bed frame. I'm finally able to pry my eyes open; head pounding.

"What are you talking about dad?" I ask as I adjust my eyes to the light. My dad is standing at the foot of my bed holding one of my shoe boxes with stacks of money and my ledger.

"You're going through my stuff?" I ask hopping out of bed.

"You're selling drugs, James?" He asks ignoring my question. God, not today.

"Answer me boy," he shouts getting in my face.

"No. I am," Knuck interrupts walking into my room and tries to take the shoe box and ledger out of my father's hands. "I'm sorry Mr. Leonard."

"Are y'all trying to play me for a fuckin' fool? I know my sons got damn handwriting. I am going to ask you again, what is this?" He yells at me. I don't know what to say as I stare at my father.

"You two, get the fuck out of my house," he says.

"What?" I ask in disbelief.

"I SAID GET THE FUCK OUT OF MY HOUSE. NOW!"

"YOU WOULDN'T HAVE THIS FUCKIN' HOUSE IF IT WASN'T FOR ME," I snap.

"What boy?"

"I'M A FUCKIN' MAN AND I DID WHAT I HAD TO DO TO PUT FOOD ON THE FUCKIN' TABLE WHEN *YOU* COULDN'T; STARTED PAYING *YOUR* BILLS AT THE AGE OF TWELVE WHEN *YOU* COULDN'T; PROTECTED THIS FAMILY WHEN *YOU* COULDN'T. ME. I DID THAT SHIT. I TOOK CARE OF MOM AND MY SISTERS BETTER THAN *YOU* EVER COULD. I RAISED MYSELF SO DON'T SIT HERE AND PREACH TO ME ABOUT BEING A FUCKIN' MAN BECAUSE I AM MORE OF A MAN THAN *YOU* EVER WERE." My dad looks at me with shocked, hurt eyes.

"You think you're a man? You are just another black bum tearing the community down selling the devils poison. That don't make you a man, that makes you an enemy to man."

"SHUT THE FUCK UP, NYCE," Knuck yells at me before I get the chance to respond.

"Go be a man out on your own. I want you out of my house within an hour," my dad orders shoving the shoe box into my hands.

"What the fucks wrong with you?" Knuck says shaking his head in disgust before walking out of my room. I pack my shit and head back over to Tone's house.

"What the fuck is wrong with you?" Tone asks as I am searching the newspaper for an apartment.

"Don't start, Tone. I'm in this shit because of you."

"I never told you to disrespect your father. You need to be thankful that you actually have a father that is there and cares about your punk ass. Where's Knuck?"

"I don't fuckin' know," I reply, annoyed as hell. I lost Jenna and my family in less than 24 hours. I just want to be left alone.

The following week I find an apartment in Wynnefield and move in. I apologize to my mom who is more concerned about me and my father's relationship rather than the whole drug thing. She preaches to me about how wrong I am and prays over me but I'm really not trying to hear it. I reach out to Knuck a few times who is shacking up at Becky's house. For the most part, if it's about business, Knuck will talk to me but if it's on a personal level, he has no rap. I really miss my brother.

I'm in the kitchen frying chicken when someone starts banging on my door.

"Who is it?" I yell from behind the door.

"Me," Keisha says. I open the door to let her in.

"Remember me?" She asks. Damn, she's looking really pretty. Once she steps in, I grab her and pull her into me for a kiss. I hold her tight vowing to never let her go.

"You okay baby?" she asks once she catches her breath.

"Let me make it up to you for acting like a dick. Let's go away."

"Anywhere?" She shrieks. I see the excitement in her eyes.

"Not anywhere. I'm not getting on a plane," I laugh.

Keisha and I go to Martha's Vineyard the following week.

"This is so nice baby," she says as we're lying on the beach.

"I'm glad you're having fun," I tell her pulling her into my arms.

"I always have fun with you," she assures looking into my eyes.

"I love you. You know that right?" I ask her.

"Sometimes, it's hard to tell."

"I know. I've been an ass but let me make it up to you."

"If you can," she challenges kissing me.

I take Keisha shopping later that day. We are in a little boutique trying to find something for her to wear to dinner tonight. She comes out of the dressing room and models a tight fitting black dress for me. Her ass looks amazing and her nipples are hard in the thin material.

"What do you think?" She asks me with a bright smile.

"I think you look beautiful, amazing," I answer. She blushes.

"Good 'cuz the dress is $600," she giggles before walking back into the dressing room.

We're back at the house I rented for the week getting ready for dinner. While Keisha is getting dressed, I run out to get her some roses to go with the diamond studded earrings I bought to surprise her at dinner. When I get back we head straight out. At the restaurant, I had to pay our waiter $100.00 in advance just so he would serve us wine.

"My flowers are beautiful babe," she beams.

"Not as beautiful as you," I tell her winking my eye. She smiles.

"I got you something," I say digging in my pocket to get the earrings.

"Oh my God," she screams, excited when I pull out the box. She opens it.

"You asshole. I thought it was a ring," she laughs "But thank you. They are very beautiful."

"One day babe there will be a ring."

We walk along the beach before heading back to the house. Once we arrive at the house, I open a bottle of wine as she is changing out of her clothes. When she returns, she is dressed in a sexy black teddy and heels.

"You ready for me daddy?" She seductively purrs, walking her sexy ass towards me. I smile.

"I'm always ready," I whisper in her ear before biting her earlobe. From her earlobe, I go in to kiss her, sucking on her tongue while effortlessly moving her thong to the side to slide my finger into her.

"I missed you," she whispers in my ear.

"I missed you too," I say picking her up and carrying her to the bedroom. I lie her down and slowly undress her; sucking her toes and then gliding my tongue up to her inner thigh before blowing on her pussy.

"Shiiiitttt," she moans as I insert my fingers back inside of her. She arches her back before I put my face in it and attack her pussy with my mouth and fingers.

"Fuck...Nyce...Shiiiit," she purrs.

"You like that?" I whisper.

"Fuck, yes," she says in a breathless whisper as she begins to feed my face.

"Nyce...shit...fuck," she says again, confirming that I am doing my job right in making her feel good.

"Come sit on my face," I whisper to her while rolling onto my back. She climbs onto my face and grinds as I suck and lick on her pussy.

"AHHHH FUCK," she screams as she grinds faster and harder.

"OH SHIT. I'M CUMMING," she screams again before wetting my face. We change positions so I am now on top. I shower her face with kisses.

"I love you," she says looking up at me.

"I love you," I tell her kissing her sweet lips. I move my tongue down and suck on her nipples while inserting a finger into her to get her juices flowing again. When she's nice and wet, I slide into her as she lets out a soft moan. I stroke her deep and slow at first until her walls start to open up and I increase my speed.

"FUCK BOY," she moans as she grinds her hips. She makes another puddle in the bed before her legs collapse.

"You're giving up on me?" I whisper in her ear.

"I'm trying not to," she laughs.

"I'll cum."

"You better. I'm tapped out," she giggles. I move in and out of her slow to get her juices flowing before increasing my speed. She's moaning and screaming and then starts clawing my back. Fuck, her scratching up my back hurts like shit but her pussy is too good for me to stop.

"Am I hurting you?" I ask as I increase my speed.

"No...no...ah...no," she says trying to keep up with me. "I'm cumming again," she says making the ugly face.

"Cum on," I tell her tonguing her down as she blasts off for a third time.

"You ready for me to cum now?" I whisper and suck on her ear. She nods her head up and down.

"Naw. I ain't ready. I'm gonna be here all night," I tell her increasing my speed some more. She can't hang anymore as her legs begin to quake and she drops them in defeat. I laugh and throw her legs over my shoulders, stroke deep for a good thirty seconds before blasting off in her.

"Punk," she says when I collapse on her.

"What's that for?" I ask staring into her face.

"Because I hate when you do that. I hate when you make me tap out first," she says playfully slapping me in the face.

"Move in with me."

"Of course," she smiles and kisses me.

We spend a week in the Vineyard exploring and loving each other. It was something that we needed to get our relationship back onto the right track.

The following week, we return home and Keisha moves her things in. It's pretty cool to come home to somebody waiting for you. I honestly can say that I like having her here.

Knuck slowly starts to come around and before we know it our friendship is back on track. Right now, we still are grinding to get this money before quitting the game completely prior to me leaving for Georgetown. I still haven't made up with my dad yet but I talk and sit with my mother and Morgan every day while he's at work.

ELEVEN
July 1995

It's Friday and I just left off the block picking money up for Tone and am now headed home. I leave for Georgetown next week and can't wait to be done with this shit. Entering my apartment I walk into the bedroom to greet Keisha.

"Hey baby," I lean in to kiss her.

"YOU WERE FUCKIN' MISS PRESTON THIS WHOLE TIME?" She yells at me throwing the letter Jenna wrote in my face.

"I don't know what the fuck you're talking about," I lie trying to grab her.

"NO...NO...I'M DONE. FUCK YOU," she screams packing her shit. I grab the bag out of her hands.

"Babe, we have plans. What are you doing?"

"I'M LEAVING YOUR ASS FOR GOOD THIS TIME. I AM SO FUCKIN' TIRED OF YOU," she shouts with tears coming down her face.

"Keish man, this is not what you think." She storms out of the room and runs into the bathroom throwing her soaps and shit in her duffle bag.

"Babe, for real?" I ask her.

"I loved you," she says tearfully.

"I love you too and I'm not lying to you. It's not what you think and she's gone anyway. Baby come on. Please don't do this."

"YOU did this. OH MY GOD. A fucking TEACHER? You have no respect for me or this relationship. Four years and I don't think you have ever been fuckin' faithful. You had bitches laughing in my face. I fought for you and now you just stabbed me in the heart by fuckin' our teacher. Really, Nyce? Who else are you fuckin' that I don't know about; my mother?" She carries on crying hysterically. The house phone rings. I glance at the Caller ID on the nightstand and see Knuck's name flash across the screen. I ignore the phone. I got to fix this with Keisha.

"Babe, you're coming to join me at the end of the summer; we live together. If I were cheating, I wouldn't be here. I would have my own place. Come on, think about it. I'm not cheating."

"I'm not listening to you anymore Nyce. All you do is lie. I'm not going with you to Georgetown. I am going to call LaSalle to see if they still have room for me. I don't want to do this anymore," she tells me still crying. The phone rings again and again. It's Knuck calling.

"So, this is it? You're breaking up with me?"

"You can't break up with someone who was never in the relationship. You left me a long time ago," she says as I see Knuck's name flash across the Caller ID again. It must be something important.

"HELLO," I yell into the phone annoyed. I don't have time to be dealing wit' the bullshit right now.

"Yo. 911. Come to the house. It's your sister," he says.

"What?" I ask confused.

"Vi's in trouble, man. She needs us."

"Be right there," I tell him hanging up.

"Did you talk to Vi?" I ask Keisha.

"No."

"Can you ride with me to my mom's?" I ask her afraid if I leave she won't be here when I get back.

"I have to pick up my mom from work," she says.

"Keisha, will you be here when I get back so we can finish talking? I really have to go."

"I'll be here, Nyce," she nonchalantly answers.

"Promise?" I ask sticking out my pinky finger. She still has tears falling from her eyes but she does smile.

"I promise." I grab and kiss her. If I didn't have to go, I would seriously be fucking her right now to make up for the bullshit. I grab my keys and run out the door.

"What's up?" I ask Knuck when I walk into the house.

"I don't know what happened but Vi came home with a black eye and locked herself in her room. Black called talking about he seen Terry hit her. I rode around for a minute looking for him but I can't find his punk ass," he tells me. I say nothing. I'm trying to calm myself down before I do something stupid but it's too late; my mind has already snapped as I bang on Vi's door demanding that she let me in.

"GO AWAY, NYCE," she yells.

"OPEN THIS FUCKIN' DOOR BEFORE I KICK IT DOWN," I yell back.

"YOU AIN'T GONNA DO SHIT; NOW GO AWAY." It takes 3 good kicks for me to break down Vi's door. I am inside her room but she's not in here.

"What the fuck?" I say as I run over to the window to see if she is crazy enough to jump. I check under the bed, nothing. I go to the closet and find Vi balled up in fetal position trying to blend in with her clothes. I grab her.

"STOP...STOP," she says fighting me. "IT WAS AN ACCIDENT. STOP NYCE. LET GO." I grab her face and force her to look at me. Her left eye is swollen shut and she has tissue up her nose. I let her go and start to walk out her room.

"Nyce...please don't...DON'T. You're gonna make it worst," she says following behind me. "NYCE," she screams crying. "I will never forgive you if you do something to him," is the last thing I hear her say to me before walking out the front door.

I jump in my car. Knuck is already in the passenger seat.

"What the fuck took you so long?" He asks as I pull off. I drive to North Philly and park my car at Tone's stash house. Knuck and I jump out and start to walk around the neighborhood trying to find Terry.

"You strapped?" I ask Knuck.

"You know it," he says lifting his shirt displaying two guns. "Here," he says trying to hand me one.

"Nah, I'm good. Gonna handle this shit the old fashioned way. You just make sure that nobody interferes."

"Can I at least hit him first? That's my sister too."

"I got this homie." We walk around in silence for a moment before seeing Terry posted up on the corner by Mr. Paul's store across the street from the schoolyard.

His small crew is with him along with Tone. I see Knuck take his gun out from his waistband.

"Only shoot if you have to," I tell him.

"I got this," he says. Terry never saw my fist coming when it landed on the bridge of his nose. He didn't have time to recoup when I punched him in his jaw and watched him hit the concrete. I hear the gun shots in the background but my focus is on Terry, his face, and my size thirteen Timbs.

Y'ALL NIGGAHS CHILL," Tone yells as I hear two more gun shots and the sounds of people scattering.

"Nyce, stop," Tone shouts but I don't stop. I can't stop. I continue kicking and punching Terry determined to beat his ass to death.

"Knuck, grab your boy," Tone says to him.

"He's gone Tone. He'll snap out of it when he's ready."

"He's goin' to kill him."

"So be it," Knuck says before I hear sirens in the distance.

"A'ight…a'ight…that's enough," Knuck yells trying to grab me. I push Knuck off of me as he stumbles back into Tone and I turn back to continue to beat on Terry.

"NYCE…THE COPS," I hear both Tone and Knuck yell at me.

"HE'S NOT WORTH YOU GOING TO JAIL FOR," Knuck shouts grabbing me again. I swiftly grab the gun out of Knuck's hand and point it at him.

"DON'T FUCKIN' TOUCH ME. GET THE FUCK OUT OF HERE," I tell him before turning back around and continue to beat Terry's ass in the head with the butt of the gun.

"LET'S GO," I hear Tone tell Knuck.

"I can't just leave him," Knuck says to Tone.

"Then y'all both goin' to jail," Tone says. I feel Knuck's powerful hands lift me and slam me to the ground. That's all I remember before everything goes black.

"FREEZE," the cop yells when I come to my senses. The cop and his partners are pointing their guns at me. "YOU HAVE THE RIGHT TO REMAIN SILENT," he continues as they lift me up off the ground, roughly turning me around and slapping handcuffs on. I watch the paramedics work on Terry. He has a brace around his neck and they are pumping air into his lungs as they lift him onto the stretcher and into the ambulance.

Shit. I didn't fuckin' kill his ass, are my final thoughts when I climb inside the squad car.

It's been two days and I am still sitting in a jail cell. I've talked to Tone and Knuck and through them, I found out that I cracked Terry's skull, broke his jaw and nose, punctured a lung, cracked 3 of his ribs, swelling on his brain and my footprints are up and down his body. Out of shame, I refuse to call my parents, and Keisha isn't accepting my calls.

I'm currently waiting in line for my turn to use the phone. When I make it to the front, I pick up the phone, dial the operator and give her Knuck's number.

"What's up man?" He asks once he accepts the call.

"What's good?" I ask. "You hear from Keisha?"

"Black said he stopped by the apartment. All of her stuff is gone," he replies. I'm quiet for a moment. "When are you going to call your mom? I can't keep making excuses for you as to why she hasn't seen or heard from you."

"You didn't tell her I was locked up did you?"

"No, but she's going to find out sooner or later."

"I go to court tomorrow to hear my charges. I want to hear what the judge says first before I get them involved."

"Have you spoke to your lawyer?"

"Yeah. Tone sent one up yesterday; Jake Bell. He's supposed to be good. They're charging me with child endangerment, assault and drug possession. Apparently Terry had drugs on him and now they are trying to pin that shit on me."

"Child endangerment?"

"Yeah. For fighting near a school. That's bullshit."

"You have 3 minutes left," the operator chimes in.

"I'll be at the courthouse tomorrow. No worries homie. I got you."

"Thanks man." I know that Knuck didn't mean for my head to hit the pavement as hard as it did when he body slammed me but I'm glad he did. Instead of assault charges, I might have been looking at murder charges and because of Knuck, I am safe from catching a gun charge on top of that.

"You have to find Keisha," I tell Knuck before the operator ends our call. Keisha knows where my money is to pay for a lawyer. The fact that no one can find her has me worried. Is she alright? Did one of Terry's goons get to her? I am straight stressed the fuck out. Stressed in a way that I haven't been since I was a child stressing over food and bills; stressed because I have no idea what my fate is now. What about my scholarship? Where the fuck is Keisha? Is Vi okay? How disappointed my parents will be when they find out I am locked up. FUCK. And on top of all this shit, my life is now being fucking dictated by pigs in blue.

I go out in the yard to shoot some ball but the courts are being monopolized. It's cool though. I probably shouldn't play anyway. Niggahs are always fighting up in here and I don't need that shit added to my jacket; not that anyone would try me though. Tone has set that up already where the old heads pretty much take me under their wing. People know that I'm not to be fucked with but still. There is always gonna be that one punk ass niggah that ain't got shit to lose. Instead of ball, I walk over to the gym equipment to lift some weights, trying to clear my head.

"HENNESSEY," the C.O. shouts the next day as I jump up eager for my day in court. He opens up the cell and cuffs me. I walk into the interview room to speak with my lawyer before we take the ride downtown to the courthouse.

"What are we looking at?" I ask him when I take my seat. I rub my wrist to get the feeling back in them because the dickhead C.O. put the cuffs on too tight.

"Well, you have aggravated assault and drug possession charges. You are looking at 5 years."

"I'm not doing 5 years up in here."

"You can take a plea deal. That will reduce your sentence down to 3 years."

"No. That mothafucka hit my sister. I was protecting her."

"Will your sister testify?"

"I think so. I don't know."

"If you get her to testify, I may be able to spin it but that doesn't excuse the drug charges."

"They weren't my drugs."

"I'll see what I can do. If the judge offers bail, will you be able to post?"

"I don't know. I can't find my girl. She has my money."

"Well this is just the bail hearing and how you are going to plead your case. Again, I would suggest you take the 3 years."

"No. I'm not doing that."

"Well I guess I'll see you in court," he says standing from the table. He knocks on the door for the officer to let him out. The officers come back into the room and shackle me like I'm a fuckin' slave before escorting me outside to the van that is driving me to the courthouse.

I take my seat next to my lawyer, anxiously waiting for the judge to arrive.

"All rise," the bailiff announces as an old, wrinkly, white man in a black robe takes his seat on the bench.

"The Commonwealth of Pennsylvania VS James Hennessey. How do you plead?" The judge asks.

"Not guilty, Sir."

"Proceed," the judge says to the DA.

"Your honor, we are asking that bail be denied. Mr. Hennessey is a public menace. I have witnesses who can attest that Mr. Terrence Rhodes did nothing wrong when Mr. Hennessey attacked him," the DA begins.

"Your honor, I ask that my client be given a chance to testify. Mr. Hennessey is a good kid with a 3.5 GPA and has an athletic scholarship to Georgetown University. He is not a flight risk, attends church every Sunday, and this is his first offense."

"That may be but I've seen the pictures of Mr. Rhodes. Mr. Hennessey, are you aware that if the cops hadn't come when they did, you would have killed him? That man is in a hospital bed fighting for his life. Bail denied," the judge says hitting his gravel.

"Fuck. What am I going to do now?" I ask my lawyer.

"You let me do my job and find your sister. We need her to testify," he says as the cops cuff me.

Two months have gone by and I am still stuck in this shit hole.

"I found Keisha and your sister," Knuck says through the glass during his visit. "They moved to Mount Airy somewhere."

"My parents allowed that?"

"Vi's pregnant with Terry's baby. That's why he beat her ass. Your dad pretty much threw her out."

"So where's my money?"

"Gone I assume. It looks like Keisha bought a house with it for her and Vi."

"That bitch left me in here to rot? Burn her shit down."

"I tried to talk to her, man. She's a woman scorned. There is no reasoning with her. She pretty much told me that you need a time out to sit in here and think about all the wrong you've done to her."

"Really, is that so?" I sarcastically ask feeling myself getting pissed. I've never hit a woman before but at this moment, I swear I could choke the life out of Keisha's ass.

"She's fuckin' Brian."

"That dick from the football team?"

"Yeah. Apparently they have a few classes together at LaSalle. You want me to take care of it?" Knuck asks.

"Nah. Let the bitch live. Bitches ain't shit."

"There's more. Vi won't testify for you and she's keeping the baby."

"So you're telling me that my girl and my own fuckin' sister are working against me? Are you fuckin' serious? After all I've done for those bitches," I yell. The guard looks at me with his baton in his hands. I take a deep breath.

"Your parents know. Vi finally told them. I'm glad she did because I was running out of lies. They've been trying to get up here but they aren't on your visitors list. You need to add them to it."

"No," I respond quietly.

"Nyce, man. They're worried about you."

"I said no." I can't let my parents see me like this. I can't watch my mama cry over this shit.

"I paid Jake again. He's a greedy bastard."

"Just get me a public defender. No need for you to go broke too," I tell him feeling defeated.

"I would never. You're my dude. We in this together. If I go broke so be it. Besides, Tone and I take turns paying him. On a positive note, Tone is still looking for Terry. I think Bo's protecting him though. I promise you we will find him."

"Thanks man."

"TIME," the C.O. yells out. Knuck places his fist on the glass. I do the same before turning around to head out. I walk to the payphone to call Jake.

"James. How's it going?" He asks.

"Court date?" I ask annoyed. I don't know if this mothafucka is trying to hustle me for money or if he is really on my side.

"I told you James, it takes time."

"I've been doing some reading. It takes 30 days for me to get a fuckin' court date. We are at day forty-seven. What kind of shit are you pulling?"

"I pushed the date back?"

"Without consulting with me? Why?"

"Without your sister, you have no case. I can hire a Private Investigator to find her but that is going to be another $10,000.00 on top of my fee."

"You're fuckin' fired. Don't take any more money from my people," I tell him slamming the phone down.

I internally go into isolation. By day 134, I stop calling Tone and Knuck and remove Knuck's name off my visitors list. The only person I see is my shitty ass Public Defender who is clearly overworked because half of the time he forgets my name but I no longer care. I am alone. Keisha left me, my sister has no loyalty and I lost my scholarship to Georgetown. I no longer have a plan for my future.

I receive letters from Becky, Wendy, Jenna, and my mother at least once a week but I never open them. I just toss them into my footlocker and continue to shield myself from the outside world. I stick to myself and work out like crazy. It becomes a ritual for me as the homies in the yard line up for me to train them. Working out helps me keep my mind off of things and burns off the pint up aggression that I feel in my soul.

"HENNESSEY," the guard yells. I jump off my bed and retrieve the three letters out of his hands. I shuffle through them. Jenna, Becky, and a letter from my dad. I sit on the edge of my bed and pull out my footlocker from underneath to toss the letters inside but my dad's letter stops me. It smells like him; Old Spice and cognac. I miss my dad and haven't spoken to him since the day he kicked me out.

James (Hoya),

I'm sorry I failed you son to the point where you felt that you didn't have any options or choices. I'm sorry that I kicked you out and said hurtful things to you. I still remember the day that the doctor placed you in my arms and how proud I was to be a Father. How proud I am to be your Father. I am still proud of you son. Please let me come see you. You can't do this alone. Please call the house so your Mom and I know that you are alright.

Your Mom and Morgan cry themselves to sleep almost every night worried about you. Please let us see you or at least hear your voice. We love you son. I love you.

Dad

"I'm sorry dad and I love you too," I say hopping off the bed to make my way to the payphone. I give the operator my house number.

"JIMMY," Morgan screams through the phone hysterically crying. "Jimmy, are you okay? When are you coming home?" She asks as I hear her pain through the phone. My heart breaks.

"I'm okay," I tell her getting choked up. This is a mistake. I shouldn't have called.

"I'm going to get mom. Please talk to me when you're done, okay? I miss and love you Yimmy," she says.

"I love you and miss you too Organ."

"I know. Hold on," she responds and places me on hold. I wait for approximately 30 seconds before my mom's voice comes thru the receiver.

"James," she says with stress in her voice. I hang up on my mother. I can't. All the sacrifices that her and my father made and I still ended up here; their loser son who went to jail. I return to my cell and open the box of letters. I decide to open one of Becky's letters thinking that it would be harmless.

Hey big head, we miss you out here. I think it's fucked up that you won't call or put us on the visitors list. Knuck is going crazy without you; he won't admit it though. Tobi sends her love from Cali and Wendy is Wendy but she sends her love too. Anyway Nyce, when you are feeling caged in, I want you to close your eyes and get lost on an adventure like we used to do just sitting on my couch. Picture us all being there with you walking the canal in Paris or horseback riding on the beach. Keep your head up and please, please call me.

I Love You,
Becky

I close my box and stick it back under the bed. Becky letter does makes me feel a little better. I smile, close my eyes and wander to a far-off place just like we used to do in her garage.

"HENNESSEY. YOU HAVE A VISITOR," the guard yells out to me on day 147. I have no idea who's visiting because I have no one on my list who is allowed to visit.

"Who is it?" I ask confused.

"Your lawyer," he says as he slaps the handcuffs on my wrists.

"Mr. Hennessey?" the lawyer questions when I walk into the interview room. She is a middle aged white woman with blond hair and green eyes. She's either very attractive or I am attracted to her because I haven't busted a nut in almost six months.

"Who are you?" I ask taking a seat.

"I'm Casey Decker. I have been hired to take over your case. We have a lot of prepping to do. Your trial is in two weeks," she tells me as she looks over her papers.

"Who hired you?"

"Your parents."

"No. I can't. Please give my parents their money back. They don't have it to be spending it on an expensive attorney," I tell her standing up from the table.

"Too late Mr. Hennessey. They already refinanced their home and paid me so please take a seat and let me do my job," she says.

"I'd rather stay in here than to see the disappointment in their eyes," I tell her.

"Sure, stay in here. Not only will your parents lose the $25,000.00 they paid me to get you out but you will be wasting your life away at 19. Are you prepared to stay in here until you are 25? That's only the minimum amount of time that they are trying to give you," she tells me. I pull out my chair and take a seat.

"I've been working with your friends Anthony Middlebrooks and Marquise McMillian. Do you know them?" She asks referring to Tone and Knuck.

"Yes."

"Good. They brought Mr. Rhoades to my office. He is willing to testify to state that the drugs that they found that day belong to him. Apparently he has an addiction and is seeking help to overcome it so that looks really good for you. You no longer have a drug charge pending against you. He also stated that he no longer wishes to press charges against you for the assault."

"That's good. That means I can get out of here," I say with some excitement.

"Not so fast. Just because he dropped the charges doesn't mean that the state will. It does however hurt their case because they no longer have their star witness. The good news is, is that we have some of your teachers willing to testify on your behalf. Your coach, Mr. Rogers and your Latin teacher, Miss Jenna Preston are both willing to testify that you are a bright young man with a bright future. Mr. Paul Wilson, the owner of the store that you were fighting in front of and Pastor Eugene Michaels are also willing to testify as character witnesses on your behalf.

"In addition, I have a written statement from your sister, Viola Hennessey, who admitted that you were only trying to protect her. She asked not to testify on the stand so I am hoping that the judge allows the written statement. If not, I will have her subpoenaed."

"Don't bother. I will win this without her," I tell her still pissed off that Vi left me in here.

"Very well," she says unfazed. "So, that will take care of the assault and drug charges; that's the two charges that are hurting you primarily. You are now just faced with Public Nuisance, Disturbing the Peace, Disorderly Conduct, and Child Endangerment. The Child Endangerment charges; don't worry about that. I will have that dismissed. The rest of the charges are 90 days in jail max with fines associated. I will have the fines dismissed as well since you have been here for a little over 6 months and the 90 days, well we will consider that as time served. Any questions?" She asks with much confidence as if she has already won the case.

"No. I'm good," I tell her putting all my trust and faith in her.

"Well Mr. Hennessey, see you on the other side," she says standing up and giving me her hand to shake.

Two weeks later, I am back inside the court room. I spot my parents and quickly turn my head, too ashamed to look at them. Miss Decker rips the DA a new asshole in her opening argument. When she is done, she takes her seat next to me, pats my leg and winks. The DA stands to plead his case.

"Your honor, the State no longer wishes to pursue charges against Mr. Hennessey. The State rests and asks the case to be dismissed," the DA says and takes his seat.

I'm free. I'm fuckin' free. I don't know what the hell the judge is saying and I don't fucking care. I'm free. I stand and hug Miss Decker and then kiss her right on the lips. I didn't mean to. I'm just that damn happy. I hear my mom yell out "Thank you Jesus," at least 99 times before I finally let go of Miss Decker.

"Sorry," I tell her a little embarrassed. She smiles and starts to pack her papers up; sliding them into her briefcase.

"My niggah," Knuck says grabbing me and giving me a big bear hug. Tone is next.

"Thank y'all, man," I tell them with tears building up threatening to spill over. I hold on to Knuck until I am able to get my emotions in check before I face my parents.

"My baby," my mom shouts grabbing me away from Knuck and giving me a giant hug.

"Hey Ma," I say inhaling her scent. Damn I missed this woman. My mom lets go of me and slaps me across the face.

"Don't you ever..." she starts with tears rolling down her face.

"I'm sorry Ma," I cut her off while trying to hold her again. She puts her hand up to stop me.

"Don't you ever turn your back on me again. You hear me? You are my child. I don't care how mad or disappointed you think I am, don't you ever go six months without talking or looking at me. You understand?" She says sternly with tears falling from her eyes.

"Yes Ma'am. I understand," I tell her softly.

"Son," I hear my dad call out to me but I can't look at him. I don't want to look at him as I hold on to my mother tighter.

"Son," he says again putting his hand on my shoulder. I turn around to face my dad. He embraces me.

"I lost Georgetown, Pop," I tell him as tears spill out of my eyes. My dad holds me tighter as I cry silently into his shoulder.

"It's okay, James. It will be okay, James," he says holding me.

"I'm sorry I disappointed you."

"I am proud of you, son. Never forget that. I know that you were only protecting your sister. That's what a man is supposed to do; protect the women they love. That's what I taught you."

<u>TWELEVE</u>

I've been home for a little over a month now, laying low trying to stay away from the drama. Tone wants me to pick-up where I left off but I've been avoiding that whole situation. I didn't want to do it to begin with. He eventually stops pressing the issue and allows me to have my space. I need time to think. Morgan stays by my side not leaving me alone. Prior to me going to jail, this would have annoyed the fuck out of me but since I barely leave the house anymore, she and Knuck seem to be the only people I want to be around.

Black, Mook, and Beck visit me too and try to keep me company but I am never in the mood to be around them. Don't get me wrong, I love them but I'm broke, penniless, with no job, skillset, or a plan for my future.

Jenna calls me almost every day but I refuse to talk to her. I really don't have much to say to her anyway. She said all she had to say that day she left for Atlanta.

I am sitting on the couch in the living room playing *Tekken* when I hear the back door open and close. Both of my parents are at work and Morgan and

Knuck are in school so who in the hell is coming into the house. I get up and walk into the kitchen.

"Nyce," she says looking at me as if she is seeing a ghost. "When did you come home?" Viola asks me. I look at her rounding belly and shake my head. "I'm sorry, Nyce," she says with tears in her eyes as she takes a step towards me. "Say something. Please James. I'm sorry," she says again.

"Fuck you, Viola," I tell her with venom in my voice. If she wasn't pregnant, I probably would have choked her. I turn to leave.

"James, please. I'm pregnant and scared. Daddy won't talk to me and Terry abandoned me. You are all I have," she cries running after me. I grab my coat, walk out the front door and end up at Becky's garage.

"BABY," Becky squeals when I walk in. She runs and jumps into my arms.

"Hey Beck."

"Good thing I took off today. Nice to see you out of the house," she says plopping down next to me. "What's wrong Nyce?"

"Just shit on my mind."

"Want to talk about it?"

"Not really."

"I am about to get high so…," she says pulling out a little baggie. She puts the powder on a spoon.

"What the hell, Becky?" She looks at me puzzled.

"You can leave," she tells me annoyed. I watch Becky melt the heroin in a spoon, take a syringe and inject herself in between her toes.

"Did we do this to you?" I ask in shock that she has graduated to shooting up.

"Don't be stupid Nyce," she replies swaying before she lies down and puts her head in my lap.

"I'm sorry, Becky," I tell her feeling guilty for helping to feed her habit all these years.

"Nyce, I've been getting high since I was fifteen after one of my mother's boyfriends raped me, so stop making this about you and know that this is my decision," she discloses with her eyes closed.

"I'm not going to sit here and watch this. I'm out," I tell her but she's already passed out. I remove her head out of my lap and leave to drive to Tone's house.

"UNCLE NYCE," Toni squeals. "I missed you," she says jumping into my arms and squeezing me tight.

"Hey Peanut. I missed you too," I tell her walking into the kitchen.

"Hey Nina," I greet her kissing her cheek.

"Hey sweetie. How are you?"

"I'm good."

"How are you really?" She presses. When I don't say anything, she makes Toni go upstairs.

"We're worried about you. Jenna's worried about you."

"Jenna's gone," I remind her.

"So. Does that mean she is exempt from worry?"

"No. That means she ain't supposed to be worried about me. She left, remember?"

"Don't be stupid and hard headed. You know why she left."

"Where's your husband?" I ask changing the subject.

"Running the streets. Do you want me to page him?"

"No. I was just stopping by to say hello."

"Nyce, you may not be in the game anymore but don't be a stranger, okay? Toni loves you; I love you and Tone loves you too even if you're not working for him."

"I know and I love y'all," I tell her kissing her cheek and walking out the door.

I'm lying in my bed staring up at the ceiling. It's been two weeks since I've seen Vi and this whole situation between me and her is bothering me. We use to be close but somewhere we lost our bond and what she did to me is unforgivable. I close my eyes and drift off.

"Nyce," Keisha whispers.

"Where the fucks my money, bitch?" I ask hopping out the bed and standing on my feet towering over her.

"Why are you talking to me like that?" She asks stunned with a hint of fear in her eyes.

"Because you are the bitch who stole my money."

"Baby, it's not what you think."

"No? So you tell me what the fuck I think."

"I bought a house with the money to raise our child," she cries.

"What child Keisha? If you're pregnant, it surly ain't mine. In case you forgot, I was in jail for six months."

"I was pregnant before you got locked up. That is why I was so angry with you that day. It was more than Miss Preston. I was pregnant and the father of my child can't even keep his dick in his pants."

"So where's the baby, Keisha?" I ask half believing her.

"I lost it," she says crying harder.

"And you lost me so get the fuck out."

"I WAS ANGRY," she yells. "For 4 years I allowed you to mistreat me. I loved you and clearly you didn't love me enough to respect me. You fucked half the school AND were fucking one of the teachers. How the fuck do you think that makes me feel? You had all those bitches laughing at me behind my back," she yells as tears continue to roll down her face.

"WHAT THE FUCK YOU CRYIN' FOR. YOU ABANDONED ME WHEN I NEEDED YOU THE MOST?" I bark at her.

"YOU ABANDONED ME A LONG TIME AGO, NYCE."

"I heard about you and Brian by the way." She doesn't say anything.

"I was mad," she whispers. "I was angry. You left me no choice. I wanted to hurt you. What was I supposed to do?"

"YOU DON'T FUCKIN' LEAVE ME TO ROT AND THEN TAKE ALL MY FUCKIN' MONEY."

"I know, I know, I'm sorry. Baby please. We can fix this. I will sell the house and give you your money back. I just want us to go back to the way things used to be with us. Baby please?" she begs.

"I will never trust you again. It's over. Forever." She comes closer.

"You don't mean that," she says with tears falling. "It's me and I fucked up but I forgave you every single time you did me wrong. You have to forgive me. I can't live without you."

230

"You've been living well without me so I'm not trying to hear your bullshit."

"Make love to me, Nyce," she says seductively, slowly unbuttoning her shirt.

"What? Get the fuck out of my house."

"You don't mean that," she says taking her shirt off and then her bra. My dick slowly stands at attention.

"Get out," I tell her fully erect.

"You don't mean that," she says again with her clothes fully off. She walks over to me and tries to kiss me.

"I love you, baby. Give me a chance to prove it," she says dropping to her knees.

"Stand up," I demand. "You want me to fuck you?" I ask her coldly.

"No. I want you to make love to me."

"Ain't no love here but I will fuck you if you want me to," I tell her. I know that I should be done with her but I ain't get none in almost 8 months and a niggahs past due.

"Then fuck me then," she says seductively. "You will see that it's supposed to be me and you forever, just like you promised."

"Situation has change," I tell her kissing her roughly. "You're a scheming bitch to me and that is all you will ever be," I say forcefully turning her around and taking off my sweatpants. I insert myself inside her.

"I know you love me," she whispers moaning softly.

"Shut the fuck up. No talking," I tell her slapping her hard on her ass before ramming myself inside of her. I start to fuck her. I mean, really fuck her. She's screaming but she doesn't tell me to stop as I roughly man handle her, getting my frustrations out.

"STOP," she finally yells.

"Shut the fuck up," I tell her as I keep going.

"Nyce please, you're hurting me," she cries as I feel her pussy walls dry up.

"You wanted this remember?" I tell her ramming myself inside her and slapping her on her ass as hard as I can.

"STOP," she yells again. I can hear her tears in her voice.

"Fuck you," I bark at her pushing her down on the floor and squirting my cum at her. She looks at me horrified as I stare down at her. Am I sorry? Yes. I'm 100% wrong for treating her like this. Was I going to apologize? Fuck no. Bitch deserved it. I enjoy watching her cry in the middle of my floor until I snap out of my vengeful trance. *Fuck. I am not this type of dude.*

"Keish, I'm sorry," I apologize lifting her off the floor.

"Babe, I'm sorry," I say again feeling like a piece of shit. I lay her gently on my bed and watch her bundle up and cry softly not looking at me. I walk down the hall and into the bathroom to run her a hot bath. I return to my room, lift her up, and carry her to the bathroom and gently place her into the tub.

"Why would you do that to me?" She whimpers.

"I'm sorry. I was trippin'. I didn't mean to hurt you," I tell her kissing her softly. She sits in the tub silently crying to herself. I grab a washcloth and soap and gently start to bathe her.

"I'm sorry," I tell her again kissing her shoulders.

"Get out," she whispers snatching the washcloth out of my hands.

"I'm sorry," I say standing up.

"GET OUT," she screams. I walk out of the bathroom and back into my room. I throw some sweatpants on and wait for her to come back. Fifteen minutes later, she enters my bedroom wrapped inside of a towel.

"Are you okay?" I ask her as she sits on my bed.

"I can't shut my legs," she says softly. I walk over to her, gently lay her back and open her legs. *Fuck!* Her lips are swollen and she's bleeding.

"Keisha, I am so fucking sorry," I tell her lying down next to her.

"I forgive you if you forgive me," she says caressing my face while tears roll down her face. I pull her into my arms.

"I forgive you," I whisper to her more out of guilt for what I had just done.

There is a soft knock at my door waking me out of my sleep. I look down at Keisha who is still sleeping peacefully. I creep out of my bed to open the door.

"Miss me?" Morgan says beaming from ear to ear. This has become our everyday routine after school.

"I always miss you," I tell her stepping out into the hall. "Keisha is sleeping."

"Keisha? What is she doing here?"

"She stopped by."

"I don't like her anymore, Jimmy," Morgan whines.

"Why?" I ask her. Her and Keisha have always been close. She shrugs her shoulders.

"I just don't," she says. "Is she your girlfriend again?"

"For now," I tell her. Morgan huffs and then walks back down the stairs. I go inside my room and lie back down next to Keisha. I pull her into my arms and gently kiss her forehead.

"I'm hungry baby. Let's go get something to eat," she says.

"Can't. I'm broke. Somebody stole all of my money," I laugh.

"Well, that's temporary isn't it? I'm sure if you call Tone you can get your old job back."

"I don't want it back," I tell her.

"Then what are we going to do for money?"

"I'll get a job."

"You're not going to find a job that is paying what Tone was paying you, Nyce," she says sounding annoyed.

"Don't you worry about it. I will find a way. I always do."

"I'm just saying, you should go back. The money is fast and easy."

"So I was about to be a father, huh?" I ask her changing the subject. She's starting to get on my nerves with this Tone shit.

"Yes," she smiles brightly. "Until I lost it," she whispers. She hops up and digs into her purse.

"She was a girl," she says handing me an ultra sound picture.

"Do my parents know?" I ask looking at my daughter.

"No. I asked Vi not to tell until I figured everything out."

"What happened?"

"I just lost her. No rhyme or reason. I guess God has other plans for me," she says crying.

"I'm sorry babe. I wish I was there for you," I tell her pulling her into my arms.

"It's okay. We have time to do it right. Are you coming home?"

"I guess it is my house huh since I paid for it," I say tickling her.

"It's our house babe and I'm sorry. I was just so mad at you and felt that I was owed something for my pain and suffering due to you dogging me out all these years. Are you done with that Nyce?" She asks, looking into my eyes.

"Yeah baby. I'm done. I'll be good," I laugh. "What's the mortgage payment on the house?"

"No mortgage. I own it. We just have to pay the taxes and insurance. It's $323 per month."

"How did you buy it? I mean, you paid for it in cash?"

"No. You promise not to get mad?" She asks.

"Never mind. I don't want to know."

"There's one more thing," she says.

"What?"

"Vi lives with me."

"She has to go."

"Don't be like that Nyce. That is your sister and she has nowhere to go."

"That's not my problem."

"Maybe not but she is carrying your nephew. At least let her stay until she finishes school. It's her last year and she's almost done. Are you just going to abandon them?"

"Vi's having a boy?" I smile.

"Yeah. She is."

"Where is Terry?"

"We don't know. He wants nothing to do with her or the baby. She really needs you. Your dad is still pissed and she doesn't feel like hearing your mom's shit either. That's why she moved out."

"I have to think about it."

"You forgave me so you have to forgive her too."

"This is different. Vi is my blood. She betrayed me-her brother."

"She knows and she's sorry. Believe me, she is. I can't just throw her out, Nyce."

I think about it for a moment.

"I guess Uncle Nyce is to the rescue," I tell her. It's going to be hard for me to forgive my sister but on the strength of my nephew, I have to step up since his bitch ass dad won't.

I stay at Keisha's house a few nights out of the week but haven't officially moved in yet. I refuse to until I have a steady paycheck. Looking for a job is hard. Becky tries to help me but there isn't that many jobs that I actually qualify for. I have no work experience, and no real education. For the past two weeks, I have unsuccessfully been filling out applications. My dad said that he is waiting for a position at SEPTA to open up to get me in but I'm not even gonna lie, ain't nobody trying to be a damn bus driver. Ain't nobody really trying to work for the man either.

To occupy my time when I'm not busy filling out applications, I lift weights and play a little basketball. I can't let my skills dry up just in case.

I'm driving through the block to go visit Mr. Paul. I never thanked him for stepping up to be a character witness on my behalf.

"Hey Old Man," I greet him when I walk into his store.

"Well, well, well. You finally remembered me," he says coming from behind the counter to give me a hug.

"I can never forget you," I tell him wrapping my arms around his large frame. "Thank you for trying to help me out."

"No thanks required. I did what was right. I never liked Terry's ass anyway."

"Me neither and now my sister is about to have his baby on some stupid shit. Sorry. No disrespect," I tell him apologizing for cursing.

"Well, you ain't a kid any more that's for damn sure," Mr. Paul jokes feeling the muscles in my arm.

"You crazy Mr. Paul. Listen, I was wondering if you needed help around the store."

"Are you serious? I thought that you were one of Tone's boys," he whispers.

"Mr. Paul, have you ever seen me on the block? Why would you have that impression of me?" I ask taking a page out of Tone's book. Mr. Paul chuckles.

"I see that Tony has taught you well," he laughs. "I am working on a business venture. It's going to be illegal but it's not drugs," he tells me. I stare at him in shock. I always thought Mr. Paul was a straight laced dude.

"I'm not stealing either," I tell him.

"No, no. I just could use some muscle. It's a speakeasy; a place where we can gamble and drink without having to drive all the way down Atlantic City."

"Oh. I like that idea Mr. Paul. I think I can help you out with that."

"Good. Stop by this address sometime this week and we will discuss," he says scribbling the address on a piece of paper.

"Cool. Thanks Mr. Paul," I tell him. I drive home to my parents' house to grab a change of clothes before heading over to Keisha's.

"What up little Organ?" I greet her when I walk in the back door into the kitchen.

"Stop calling me that," she says rolling her eyes and focusing her attention back to her homework. I laugh and run up the stairs.

"Vi's having a girl," Morgan says in my doorway. I hadn't even heard her come up the stairs behind me.

"You sure? They seem pretty adamant that she's having a boy," I tell her folding up my clothes and putting them in a duffel bag.

"She's having a girl. She's going to name her Destiny."

"You just found out?" I ask her still packing my bag.

"No. I found out a couple of weeks ago when I was eavesdropping on her and Keisha," she answers quietly, looking at me. She stares blankly at me for a second.

"Are you still leaving?" She asks.

"Awww…you don't want me to go?" I tease.

"But Vi's having a girl," she says again in a more serious tone. I look at my 10 year-old sister for a second.

"Okay." I look at her, confused. I know she's not jealous that she is not the baby anymore.

"Keisha was never pregnant. She said that to get you back. The ultrasound photo that you have sitting on your dresser is Vi's baby; not Keisha's," she blurts out with tears rolling down her face. I pause and look at her.

"How do you know?" I ask.

"I overheard them talking," she says quietly. "Please don't tell Vi I told you. I don't want her to be mad at me," she begs.

"I won't," I tell her sitting down on my bed. Those fuckin' bitches. They played me for the last fuckin' time. The worst part is, I already knew. I just wanted to be wrong.

"Yo. Come with me to Radio Shack," I say to Knuck when I enter his room.

"What for?" He asks.

"I need to buy some bugs."

"Bugs? Who we spying on?"

"Keisha," I tell him walking out his room. Knuck and I drive to Radio Shack and then to Keisha's crib to bug her whole house while her and Vi are at school.

"Homie, what are we doing this for?" Knuck asks me.

"Keisha was never pregnant."

"Niggah, I could have told you that shit. She's sneaky as hell. Vi's ass too though. Love her to death but if she wasn't like a sister to me, I would never fuck with a chick like her," he says placing a bug underneath the coffee table.

For the remainder of the week, I act normal around both Keisha and Vi not letting on to the fact that every room in the house is bugged. On day 5, I remove the bugs, sit at the kitchen table, and press play to hear what they are talking about when I'm not around. I sit at the table for an hour listening to their conversations. The tapes are boring and they don't say much. When I'm about to give up, I find what I'm looking for.

"Nyce still hasn't returned to Tone yet?" Vi asks.

"No. He's on some self-righteous shit and his little $300 that Mr. Paul is going to pay him ain't shit," Keisha says.

"Bitch, you got to get pregnant. Nyce doesn't know how to struggle. He's been like that since we were kids. He feels that he has to take care of everyone. Right now, there is no pressure on him to make money since my parents are good. You getting pregnant is the only way he is going to return to Tone. Man, I'm not working a fuckin' dead end job tryin' to support me and this baby," Vi says.

"You think I haven't tried to get pregnant? Shit. I even gave him head last week and let him bust in my mouth. I ran into the bathroom after, spit his cum into my hands and tried to use that shit to insert inside me."

"Did it work?"

"I don't think so. For real, for real, I am tired of broke Nyce. I am so tempted to leave him and be with

Brian. At least Brian comes from money and doesn't mind taking care of me."

"You can always fuck Brian and let him get you pregnant and blame it on Nyce," Vi suggests.

"Nah. Your brother is way too smart for that. I've been on birth control since we were 15 and he rarely busts in me and we don't use condoms so I can't even trap his sperm."

"You do love him though, right? I mean, he's still my brother."

"Of course I love him but what does love got to do with it? At the end of the day, love doesn't pay my bills nor does it keep me flyy." I cut the tape off and sit quietly at the table for a moment. I walk over to the fridge and take out the steak, peppers, and onions to cook dinner. An hour later, I have the radio blasting and the house smelling good with the aroma of pepper steak and rice. I hear the front door open and shut.

"Hey baby," Keisha says walking in and kissing my cheek.

"What up boo?" I greet her. "Where's Vi?" I ask.

"She should be right behind me. You got the house smelling so good. What did you make?" She asks, lifting the lid off the pot.

"Your favorite; pepper steak and rice. As soon as Vi gets here, we can eat."

"She better hurry up because I'm starving," she says taking a seat at the kitchen table.

"So how was your day?" I ask.

"Long. I had two tests today. One in my chemistry class and another in my philosophy class."

"How do you think you did?" I ask taking off her shoes and massaging her feet.

"I think I did alright. Damn baby, that feels goooood," she purrs, slouching down in the chair and closing her eyes. I hear the front door open and shut.

"About time," Keisha yells from the kitchen.

"What?" Vi asks waddling in.

"Nyce made dinner so sit your fat ass down so we can eat. I'm starving."

I get up from the table to fix them a plate. I place their food in front of them and walk back to the stove to fix mine. Afterwards, I join them at the table.

"How's my niece Vi?" I ask putting a fork full of food into my mouth.

"What? I'm having a boy," Vi answers and cracks a nervous smile.

"Oh yeah, silly me," I say putting another fork full into my mouth. "Do y'all like the food?" I ask.

"Yeah baby, it's so good. Thanks for cooking," Keisha says but Vi stops eating.

"What's the matter? You don't like it?" I ask.

"Did you poison this?" She asks me.

"What? Why would I do some dumb shit like that?" I answer, staring into her eyes. She stares back at me looking like she's in deep thought.

"What's going on?" Keisha asks when she notices that Vi and I are in the middle of having a staring contest.

"Nothin'. Vi's trippin'," I answer still staring at Vi as she is staring back at me. Keisha stops eating and looks at us confused.

"Finish your food Keish," I tell her calmly picking up my fork to eat but Vi still doesn't move as she watches me.

"So, how was your day, Vi?" I ask her.

"Cool," she answers curtly.

"Keish, has Vi ever told you that she used to pee the bed when we were little? I would have to get up in the middle of the night and help her wash the sheets out in the tub before my parents woke up so she wouldn't get in trouble. I even stole sheets for her from the store so when she had her accidents, we would flip the mattress, change the sheets and then hide the other sheets from my parents," I laugh. Keisha laughs too.

"You remember that time you cried because you wanted a Cabbage Patch Doll but mom and dad couldn't afford to buy you one so I went to the toy store and stole one for you? What did you name the doll again? Jalisa?"

"Jamesha," she replies.

"Oh yeah. You named it after me for being the best brother in the world," I laugh putting another fork full into my mouth.

"What's the matter? Eat your food," I tell her.

"I'm not hungry," she says staring at me.

"Ironic right? How many times did I go hungry when we were kids just so you wouldn't? Even bought you your first car and made sure that you had the nicest clothes and jewelry; paid for you to keep your hair and nails done too. You was a little ghetto princess. Even spent 6 months in jail for you."

"Nyce, stop," Keisha says as Viola sits quietly on the verge of tears.

"Stop what? All I'm doing is talking to MY sister. MY flesh and blood," I reply looking into Viola's eyes.

"Nyce," Keisha calls my name again.

"Babe, I kept you flossin' too, right?"

"Yes baby, you did."

"Paid for this fucking house that ain't even in my name."

"It's our house."

"Nah, this is all you. Call it your parting gift."

"What?"

"That whole suckin' my dick so I can nut in ya mouth and use it to get pregnant, that's some genius shit right there. Wait till I tell the homies that we ain't safe from gettin' head. Bitches still scheme."

"W-what?" Keisha stutters. I place the recorder on the table, push play, and then continue to eat my food. When I look up, both of them are sitting with tears coming down their faces.

"I don't know what the fuck y'all cryin' for. I ain't even mad. You's a skank bitch, you skunk. I should have known better," I say to Keisha.

"Nyce," she whispers. "I was just joking; venting. I didn't mean …," Keisha says but I put my hand up to cut her off.

"Don't worry Keish; we good. When I want some pussy from you, I promise to call you, but you," I say pointing at Vi. "If it wasn't for my NIECE, I swear on my life I would never talk to you again. You have no sense of loyalty but hell, even Cain killed Abel. I like the name Destiny by the way," I tell her standing up from the table, grabbing my jacket, and walking out the door.

I'm home sitting in Knuck's room playing *Street Fighter* on his Playstation with him.

"I'm thinking about selling the house," I say to Knuck.

"Why?" He asks.

"Because it's just sitting there. I only bought it so we had a place to stash product but since neither one of us is doing it, what's the point of keepin' it?"

"Because that shits collateral. Don't sell yet. Fix it up and see if someone will rent it from you."

"Man, I have no money. My pockets are busted. I appreciate Mr. Paul giving me a job bouncing at his club but shit, $300.00 a week ain't even worth it."

"Well, what are you going to do?"

"I don't know. I am still tryin' to figure it all out."

"I hear you. I just paid next year's tuition and now I'm tapped out. I don't even know how I am going to get through my senior year," Knuck tells me.

"You can't get any grants or something?" I ask.

"I'm gonna try. My grades are pretty decent. What about you? Have you applied to any schools?"

"No. I'll be a twenty-year-old freshman. Maybe I'll take some classes at Community or something."

"Why are you limiting yourself?"

"I'm not but like you, I'm broke. Keisha taking all my money really hurt my pockets."

"Tell me about it," he says.

"I'm sorry. I'll figure out how to pay you back," I tell him thinking about the $15,000.00 he put up to pay my attorney fees. Had he not paid it, he would have the money to finish his senior year.

"We good. Don't ever think I regret it or want my money back," he assures me while lighting up an L.

THIRTEEN
Summer of '96

"What's up man?" I say to Tone when he answers his phone.

"Nothing much. You should swing through. I got something to tell you and I'm about to throw some steaks on the grill. Toni is asking for her Uncle Nyce too," he says.

"A'ight. I guess I can swing by for a little while. It's not like I got shit else to do."

"Cool. You know where I live and you might as well bring your swim trunks wit' you."

"You sure you want me parading my body around your chick? She might leave your ass for me," I laugh.

"Whatever dude. Just for that, I'm gonna make sure that your steak is extra rare," he laughs before hanging up. I throw on my trunks and a t-shirt and drive over to Tone's house.

"What's up, man?" He says greeting me at the door and giving me a giant bear hug.

"What up."

"Nina's pregnant," he announces full of excitement.

"That's what's up, homie. Congratulations."

"Yup so get prepared to be a Godfather," he tells me. "Come on out back, that's where Nina and Toni are. I'll be out in a minute," he says running up the stairs.

I exit out the patio doors and the first person I run into is Jenna looking like heaven in a white bikini. She looks good; hella good. She does look a little heavier than the last time I saw her but her weight went into her ass and thighs so she is still sexy as fuck for a woman of thirty-one.

"Why haven't you returned any of my calls?" Is the first thing out of her mouth when she sees me.

"Why are you calling me? Don't you have a boyfriend to talk to?"

"Don't act like an ass, James."

"You first," I spit back trying to step around her.

"No. You are not going to play these little childish games wit' me."

"What do you want, Jenna?" I ask her.

"I want you to make love to me," she whispers in my ear. My dick automatically goes up in the air.

"Where's your boyfriend?" I ask her.

"Where's Keisha?" She replies.

"That relationship is dead," I tell her.

"Oh, pity," she mocks, grinning. "So you won't feel guilty when you cum all down my throat," she says stepping into my zone and touching my erect penis. "Come upstairs with me," she whispers in my ear.

"Fuck it. Let's go." I grab her hand and lead her inside the house. As soon as we make it inside one of the guest rooms, it's on. Without hesitation, Jenna drops to her knees.

"Shiiittt," is all I can say as she begins to attack my dick with her mouth. When I am on the verge of cumming, I make her stand up and then throw her on the bed.

"I missed you," she smiles up at me.

"Yeah, whatever," I tell her while inserting myself inside of her. Damn, she feels fuckin' amazing.

"Yes, baby. I've missed you soooo much," she purrs in my ear, turning me on even more.

"Show me how much," I say to her. She gently pushes me off of her, gives me head for a few moments before mounting my dick.

"Damn. I forgot how good you feel," she moans riding me like she is auditioning for a rodeo.

"Come here," I tell her making her bend down to kiss me. I break the kiss and begin sucking on her nipples as she continues to ride.

"Fuck daddy. I'm cumming," she screams as her juices makes a mess all over my pelvis and stomach.

"Turn over," I tell her flipping her onto her stomach. I insert myself back inside of her and gently stroke her from behind.

"Uh...Damn baby," she purrs as she bites on the sheets. I grab a chunk of her hair as I increase my speed.

"Oh fuck," she says taking the words out of my mouth. "Fuck," she repeats. With every moan I increase my speed and slap her on her ass.

"Damn, shiiiittttt" are my final words as I blast off inside her. We lay for a moment holding each other.

"That was good baby. I taught you well," she laughs planting kisses on my face. "You've been practicing," she giggles.

"Shut up girl," I tell her playfully.

"Did you miss me?" She asks.

"A little something."

"Just a little something?" She says, climbing back on top of me.

"Give me a minute," I tell her laughing hoping that my man cooperates.

"No," she says slinking down under the sheets and initiating round two.

A half-hour later, she is resting in my arms while I gently stroke her hair.

"I really did miss you James and I was worried about you. You should have called me. You could have at least responded to my letters."

"I know, I'm sorry. I was in a fucked up place. I didn't want to be bothered with anybody."

"But it's me. I thought we were better than that."

"If we were better than that then why did you leave the way you did? You wrote me a letter. You didn't even give me the respect to talk to me face to face."

"I know but I didn't know what to do. I'm thirty-one years old. My biological clock is ticking and I want to get married. You're not there yet so I made the decision to leave and put us behind."

"I understand," I tell her.

"Do you?"

"Yes."

"Good," she says reaching up to kiss me.

"Are you ready to get married?" I ask her. She sighs.

"Yeah, I am. I am ready to pop some babies out," she giggles.

"Do you want to have my baby?" I ask her.

"What?"

"You heard me."

"If the circumstances were different. You're just a kid. You're not on that level of marriage and kids yet."

"So if I got you pregnant, you wouldn't keep it?" I ask inserting myself back inside of her.

"Mmmmmm," she moans closing her eyes as I start to make love to her nice and slow.

"Will you?" I whisper in her ear.

"No but we can pretend that we are making a baby now," she responds whispering in my ear and grinding her hips. "I never want you to leave me," she moans. I look at her as she pops her eyes open realizing her mistake.

"Do you love me, Jenna?" I ask her while on the verge of busting my fourth nut of the day. She stares at me.

"Do you love me?" She throws back. I slow down my stroke some so now we're staring into each other's eyes.

"I will if you let me," I tell her.

"I'm old, James. You're not going to want me in a few years," she smiles.

"I am always going to want you," I tell her as I cum inside of her.

"Liar," she says kissing my face. We lie in silence for a moment.

"I really did miss you," she says again locking her fingers into mine.

"I missed you too," I tell her kissing her forehead.

"Uncle Nyce; Aunt Jenna," Toni calls us banging on the door.

"We'll be right out Peanut," I yell. Jenna looks up at me.

"Really wished you were older," she says getting out the bed. I pull her back to me.

"Wherever you are and whomever you're married to, when I'm ready, can I come ruin your marriage?" I tickle her.

"Depends," she says laughing. "But I wouldn't mind you being my boy toy on the side," she giggles.

"Nah. I don't share. Besides, I busted enough in you to make sure your ass is pregnant. You ain't goin' nowhere," I laugh kissing her. We get dressed and join Tone, Nina, and Toni in the backyard.

"About time," Toni yells running into my arms. I scoop her up.

"You have all of my attention now, Princess."

"Good," she says wiggling out of my arms.

"Yo, Knuck just called. You feel like going to get him? He said that he let Becky hold his car," Tone asks as he flips burgers on the grill.

"Yeah. I'll go scoop him up," I tell him.

"Are you coming back?" Jenna whispers in my ear. "I'm not done with you yet."

"You know I'm coming back," I promise her with a kiss. I hop in my car and drive to pick up Knuck.

"What up, son?" Knuck says when he gets in the car.

"Ain't shit. Jenna's back," I tell him smiling.

"Word. Oh shit. You about to be that pussy whipped dickhead again," he laughs.

"Shut up," I say cracking up.

"So what you gonna do?"

"You mean what haven't I did. I've been waxing her ass down all afternoon. I guess we can just be on our creep for now. I'll go down there to see her and what not. Let's see how this goes. Right woman; wrong decade," I say shaking my head.

"I hear that." We stop by the liquor store to pick up more beer before heading back to Tone's house. I pull up in Tone's driveway and park.

"I hope Tone got the chess board set up 'cuz I'm about to bust his ass," Knuck says while hopping out the car.

"The food smells good as shit, right?" I say to Knuck shouting over the music.

"Hell yeah. I can't wait to bite into a greasy ass burger. I'm starving."

We walk around back to an empty back yard. I dump the beers into the cooler and grab one for myself before walking inside the house. When I open the back door, I stop in my tracks and drop my beer out of my hands. I hear the glass shatter on the kitchen floor as my body goes into shock and I think my heart actually stops beating as my mind races in hysteria. Tone is lying in the middle of his kitchen floor in a pool of blood.

"KNUCK," I yell once I snap out of my trance. I run over to Tone to try to help him. He's been shot in the back and is barely breathing.

"FUCK," Knuck shouts when he walks inside. He runs over to the kitchen phone.

"I need an ambulance. NOW!" he screams into the phone. Tone is trying to say something to me as I kneel down beside him.

"T-T-Toni…upstairs," he whispers. I run out of the kitchen and trip over Nina whose brains are scattered all over the carpet and walls.

"FUCK," I yell as I spring to my feet trying to hold down the food that is rapidly rising up my throat. I run up the stairs two at a time and bust inside Toni's room. It's empty. I check under the bed and then run to her closet.

"OH GOD," I yell as tears immediately start falling from my eyes. Jenna's lifeless body is cradling Toni's body. I fall to my knees not knowing what to do.

"Uncle Nyce," Toni whispers with tears coming down her face.

"Peanut. You're alive," I laugh with my tears still falling as I struggle to peel Jenna's dead arms off of her.

"Uncle Nyce," Toni says again in distress and that's when I notice that she's been shot too.

"Shhhh…don't talk Peanut," I tell her trying to grab her gently. There is blood everywhere. After a couple moments, I am finally able to free her from Jenna's grip. I lift her up and gently place her down in the middle of the floor.

"I knew you would come back," she says smiling as I examine her. She's been shot in her stomach.

"Save your strength, Peanut," I tell her as my tears fall while trying apply pressure to her wound.

"It's okay Uncle Nyce. It doesn't hurt anymore. I'm just cold," she says. I run over to her bed and grab the blankets.

"Peanut, I need you to be strong for me, okay. I need you to hold on until the ambulance gets here."

"Okay. There's nothing to fear but fear itself. Right, Uncle Nyce?" She smiles at me before shutting her eyes.

"No, no, no, you have to keep your eyes open. Please Toni, can you do that for me? Peanut, please open your eyes," I beg her but she doesn't respond.

When the ambulance finally arrives, I am still sitting in the middle of the floor holding Toni's lifeless body in my lap and Jenna's lifeless hand.

"Sir, sir, are you okay? Can you hear me, sir?" The paramedic asks as he shines a light in my eyes. "Sir, you have to let go," he says to me while trying to pry my hand off of Jenna and take Toni out of my arms.

"SIR," he yells.

"We got shit to do. Snap out of it homie," I hear Knuck's voice.

"I'm okay. I'm okay," I tell the paramedic as I let them take Toni away from me and reluctantly let go of Jenna's hand. I stand covered in blood.

"We have to get to the hospital. Tone is still alive," Knuck informs me. I follow him down the stairs and into the car. Tone had to be choppered to Temple University Hospital while Knuck and I rip through the streets trying to hurry up and get there. Once at the hospital, we're informed that Tone is in surgery and in critical condition. I look at my hands covered in blood.

"You alright, homie?" Knuck asks quickly wiping his tears away.

"They killed her, man," I tell him talking about Jenna, Nina, and Toni.

"What kind of monster kills a child?" I ask with flashbacks of Toni's body trying to cling on to her life.

"A man that has to be put down," Knuck affirms.

The cops show up at the hospital to question me and Knuck. We tell them everything we know, which is nothing, and wait to hear something about Tone's status. Three hours later, a nurse comes out to give us an update.

"Is he alright?" I ask her.

"He's stable. He's resting. Does he have any family we can call?" She asks.

"I've called them all. They should be on their way. Is everything alright?" I repeat, asking her again.

"It's just better when he wakes up that he has a support group."

"Why? What's wrong?" Knuck asks.

She smiles and walks away.

"Fuck man. What are we going to do?" Knuck asks. I stare at Knuck who is covered in blood and look down at my blood stained hands.

"Let's get out of here," I tell him. I just want to wash this day away.

Knuck and I pretty much stay shacked up at my parents' house too afraid to be left alone. Not afraid that someone is after us but afraid to see the haunting images of a dead Nina, Toni, and Jenna. Either Knuck is sitting up under me or I am sitting up under him. We even start sleeping in each other's rooms, too afraid to shut our eyes as the images haunt our dreams. I haven't slept in four days and Knuck tosses and turns when he is finally awarded fifteen minutes worth of sleep.

We visit Tone daily who is still in ICU. They still won't let us in to see him so we sit in the waiting room hoping for our friend to come around.

"They finally shipped Jenna's body," I inform Knuck. We are sitting in my room watching videos with the TV on mute. Knuck is sitting in the middle of my floor rolling a blunt.

"Do you want to drive to Savannah? I'll go with you," he offers putting the blunt to his lips.

"Yes," I reply, watching smoke clouds come out of his mouth. "Let me get that," I tell him referring to the blunt. He passes it to me and I hold it in my hands and stare at it.

"Fuck it," I say as I inhale the smoke. I cough before passing it back. Me and Knuck smoke in silence not saying a word to each other. I'm feeling the effects of the weed and shut my eyes. I must have finally dozed off because the ringing of my phone scares the shit out of me causing me to jump out of the chair. Knuck laughs.

"It's the hospital," I say after checking the Caller ID. "Hello."

"Hi. Is Mr. Hennessey available?" A woman asks.

"Speaking."

"Hi. This is Nurse Carla from Temple University Hospital. Your friend, Anthony Middlebrooks is up and requesting to see you."

"I'll be right there," I tell her hanging up the phone. Knuck is already on his feet putting on his boots. We make it to the hospital and enter Tone's room. He's sleeping so I take a seat on the couch.

"Nyce," Tone whispers. I jump up and walk over to the bed.

"What's up?" I ask trying not to look at him. It's hard for me to see him this way.

"Tell me I'm dreaming, man. Tell me that they didn't kill Nina and my baby girl. Please tell me that shit didn't happen," he begs with tears pouring down his face. I don't know what to say to him as I feel the grief he's feeling in his heart.

"They killed my family, man," he cries while I hold his hand.

"Who? Who did this Tone?" I ask fighting my own tears.

"They tell me I'm paralyzed. I'll never walk again."

"You don't know that. We can get some great doctors. This isn't it, Tone."

"This is it, Nyce. She told me. She told me all the time to stop. I wouldn't listen. I didn't listen. I killed my wife; I killed my daughter. My greed killed them," he cries, blaming himself before passing out. I stay at the hospital with Tone until visiting hours are over. With all the drugs they are pumping into him, Tone slept for most of the day but when he did wake up, he would mumble "I killed them," and fall right back to sleep.

The following week, Knuck and I attend Nina and Toni's funeral. Right after their funeral, we hit the road and drive down to Savannah to attend Jenna's. Mentally, I am exhausted and I know that Knuck is too as we both become habitual smokers trying to escape the reality of what we saw that day.

<u>FOURTEEN</u>

"AHHH," I hear Knuck yell. I pop my eyes open.

"I'm sorry, Marquise. I didn't mean to step on you," Morgan giggles turning on the lights.

"What's up, Morgan?" I ask looking over at the clock. It's 3:26am.

"Mom and dad just left to go to the hospital. Vi's in labor," she says. I sit up in my bed and look down at Knuck who's lying in the middle of my floor staring up at the ceiling.

"Well are you guys gonna get up so we can go?" Morgan asks. I haven't talked to Vi since that day at Keisha's house.

"She's still family, Nyce," Knuck says.

"Let us get dressed Morgan. We'll meet you downstairs." We dress quickly and drive to the hospital. When we walk into the waiting room, Keisha and my dad are sitting in the chairs reading a magazine. I walk over to my dad.

"Hey. How is she?" I ask him.

"She's fine. The baby is fine; 6 pounds 9 ounces," he announces with joy. "The nurses and your mom are in there with her trying to nurse the baby," he says.

"So your good now, Pop?" I ask him.

"What can I say? I did my best by you kids but ultimately you are going to make your own decisions." Morgan comes over and climbs into his lap.

"You have one more left, dad. She's good; nothing like me and Vi. She won't be a disappointment."

"James, you are not a disappointment. Yes I wished things went a different way for you but I am still very proud of the man that stands before me today," he says. Yeah right. How could he not be disappointed in me when I'm disappointed in myself?

"Hey," my mom greets me with a hug and kiss.

"Hey Mama. How's Vi?" I ask.

"She's alright. Baby has a full head of hair. You can go and see her if you like," she says as Knuck, my dad, and Morgan stands up.

"I need a minute," I tell her.

"Jimmy, don't keep your niece waiting," my mother says softly. I watch her walk up the hall with my dad, Knuck, and Morgan and disappear into the maternity ward.

"I'm sorry to hear about Miss Preston," Keisha whispers. I hadn't even noticed that she was still sitting in the waiting room with me.

"Thanks."

"Are you okay Nyce? Seriously. Are you okay?" She asks with a look of concern.

"I don't want to talk about it," I tell her standing up to go see my niece.

In the weeks that follow, I find myself spending more and more time over at Vi and Keisha's house to spend time with my niece. Something about how sweet and innocent she is, is making me gravitate towards her, helping to numb the pain I feel in my soul for losing Jenna, Nina, and Toni. I am still bouncing at Mr. Paul's spot at night but during the day, I sit up under Vi, Destiny, and Keisha trying to forget. I am cordial with Vi and Keisha. To them, they think that I forgave and moved on but to me, I know that I will always have to watch my back and not trust a word that comes out of their mouths.

"Hello," I answer the phone.

"What's up?" Tone says on the other end.

"Hey. How's it going?" I ask.

"I'm leaving this place. I can't take it anymore."

"Tone, do the recovery. Don't be hard headed," I tell him. Tone's been in a rehab facility for over a month now.

"Fuck that. I am not going to walk again and I am fine with that. I have other issues I need to take care of," he says. "I'm signing myself out of here tomorrow. I would really appreciate it if you and Knuck came through and got me."

"Say no more. We'll be there," I tell him getting up. I spend the remainder of the morning calling around different places to make Tone's house handicap accessible for him. I jump in my car and drive over to meet the installers. As soon as I pull up, my stomach immediately starts feeling uneasy. I haven't set foot in his place since that day. Knuck is the one who went to meet the cleaners once the cops gave us the greenlight. He said he sat in his car smoking until they were done. He didn't have the heart to go inside.

Smoking inside my car, I sit and wait for the installers. Ten minutes later, they pull up in the driveway. I unlock the front door to let them in.

"Right this way," I tell them escorting them inside. I freeze in the hallway and stare at the spot where I tripped over Nina's dead body. I stare at the paint job on the walls that helps conceal her splattered brains. I excuse myself from the installers and go outside to wait on the stairs until they are completed. About an hour later, the house is handicapped accessible for Tone. I lock up and leave with urgency to get out of here.

The next day, Knuck and I drive over to the rehab facility to pick up Tone.

"You good?" I ask Tone as we are riding through the city. It was weird having to help him in the car. Hell, it's weird to see him in that chair.

"Yeah. I'm good," he says flatly. "Knuck, did you have Becky hook me up?" He asks.

"Yeah. She got you a room at the Four Seasons," Knuck answers.

"You're not going back to the house?" I ask.

"I'm stopping by to get some things but no. That is no longer my home." I wish he told me that shit yesterday prior to me spending all my money I had saved. I pull up to Tone's house and sit in the driveway. Nobody gets out the car. We sit in silence staring at the house.

"Well, can one of y'all help me out the car please?" Tone asks breaking the silence. Knuck hops out of the backseat and walks to the trunk to get Tone's wheelchair. He opens the passenger side door and helps him out the car.

"Nyce, you comin'?" Tone asks. I reluctantly get out of the car and follow Tone and Knuck to the back of the house and into the shed.

"Why are we in here?" I ask.

"I need to put y'all to work," Tone responds. "See those sledgehammers over there? I need y'all to grab those and get to work."

"What?" Knuck and I ask in confusion.

"X marks the spot," Tone says wheeling himself to the far right corner. "I have 5 million dollars in this spot. I need y'all to get it for me."

Knuck and I grab the sledge hammers and get to swinging at the concrete. By the time we finish, both of our hands are blistering from the impact. We pull the chest out of the ground and sit it in front of Tone.

"Sit down you two. I need you to grab all of my pictures and Toni's blanket. I miss her smell," he says reminiscing. "I need you to gut out my basement. Remove all the furniture and install a long beam with hooks," he says handing me a piece of paper with drawings as to how this beam is supposed to look. "The beam and hooks should be strong enough to hold four grown men. I need you to find Officer Boroughs, Officer Case, Bo and Terry. You need to get them here. I don't care how you do it, just get them here," he says.

"Bo and Terry did this?" I ask.

"No. Just the two officers but I know that they had something to do with it. Anyway, I can't stay here. They know I'm not dead and it's just a matter of time before they come to finish the job."

I am at a loss for words. I don't even know what to say as I feel my rage building. My biggest regret is not killing Terry a long time ago.

"Take this number," Tone says trying to hand me a piece of paper. When I don't respond, he hands it to Knuck. "Only call him when y'all are ready. Call him if you decide to get back into the game; not as a worker but as a boss; the King on a Chess Board."

After packing up all the things Tone wants to keep, we drive him downtown to the Four Seasons. Becky is in the lobby waiting for us since the room is booked in her name.

"Hey guys," she says giving Knuck a kiss and hugging me and Tone.

"Hey Beck," I greet her while wheeling Tone over to the elevator. We ride up and help Tone get settled in.

"You going to be alright?" I ask. Tone is sitting by the window holding a photo of him, Nina, and Toni.

"I'm good. Let me know when y'all capture those fools. I'll be here waitin'," he replies.

The next day, me, Knuck, Black, and Mookie go to Tone's place and start to clean out his basement to install the beams.

"What does he plan on doing?" Mook asks as he is hammering the hooks into the beam.

"Man, I'm afraid to ask," I admit.

"Well here. Let's test this thing out," he says when he finishes installing the hooks.

"How?" Black asks. I grab the rope and look at each guy.

"Knuck, you're the heaviest," I tell him.

"Fuck outta here. You're not tying me up," he refuses.

"Don't be like that. Five seconds tops," I assure him.

"Fuck, man. I'm always being dragged into some dumb shit," he says holding out his wrists. I tie his wrists up.

"Can you get out?" I ask.

"No," he says trying to get out.

"Uh, I have to lift you up there," I tell him pointing up at the beam and hooks. Knuck looks up and then shakes his head.

"This some bullshit," he says stepping onto the chair. He places his wrists in the hooks.

"I'm going to remove the chair," Mook says. Knuck is now dangling in midair with his feet barely touching the ground.

"A'ight. Get me down," he says.

"Y'all hungry? We should go get something to eat," I say walking towards the door. Black and Mook laugh and follow.

"I swear if y'all leave me hanging like this. This shit hurts. Let me the fuck down," he fusses as we walk out the door. We stand in the driveway laughing and watch Knuck through the window struggling to get out.

"A'ight, whose lettin' him out?" I laugh knowing that Knuck will probably try to swing on us as soon as we let him down.

"Man, I ain't fuckin' wit' him. He ain't knocking me the fuck out," Black says. Mook is still cracking up, peeking through the window.

"A'ight, we all gonna go back in there, cut the rope and run. Black, start the car," I tell him as me and Mook go back inside.

"Y'all niggahs ain't shit. Wait till I get the fuck down from here," Knuck says when we walk back inside.

"Chill homie. It was just a joke," I tell him pulling the chair to him. Mook places my car keys on the table so Knuck can drive himself home. I look at Mook who's looking at me.

"1...2...3," I count. I cut the rope, watch Knuck dramatically fall to the floor then bolt for the door. Mookie and I hop in the car and drive away with Black. We are hysterically laughing as Black speeds through the street. I haven't laughed like this in a minute. I needed this. It feels good.

"We can't find Terry or Bo's ass. We've been lookin'; trust me. Terry hasn't even been by the house to see Vi and the baby and I've followed Vi a few times to make sure her ass isn't lying but nothing; them niggahs disappeared." I tell Tone sitting in his hotel room.

"What about the officers?" He asks.

"Every evening after their shift, them and some other officers go to the same bar for happy hour- 5:15 on the dot...every day," Knuck says.

"And you really can't find Bo or Terry?" Tone asks. He wheels over to his dresser and picks up his photo of Nina and Toni.

"No," I tell him.

"That's going to be your job to finish," he says putting the photo down. "I know they set me up but the officers pulled the trigger. I'm ready," he says looking at us.

"Now what?" Knuck asks.

"Have them at my house by ten tonight," Tone responds. Knuck and I get up to leave.

"Nyce," Tone calls me.

"What up?"

"I'm sorry about Jenna," he apologizes.

"I know," I tell him walking out the door.

Knuck and I pull up to the bar around 5:30.

"You remember the plan?" I ask.

"Yeah. You?"

"Yeah. You got the roofies?" I ask Knuck.

"Yup. Beck even turned them into a liquid," he says handing me a vile.

"Becky is like a mad scientist," I laugh putting the vile in my pocket. I walk into the bar and take a seat in the far corner, waiting. About an hour and a half later, Officer Boroughs stumbles into the men's room. I follow him.

This is easier than I thought I think as he is in the stall taking a shit. He left his beer sitting on the counter so I dump some of the liquid in. I wash my hands and quickly leave out of the bathroom before being spotted. Fifteen minutes later, Officer Case is carrying Officer Boroughs to his car.

"Geez Charlie. What the hell did you drink?" He asks putting his partner in the passenger side of his car. I run and jump into the rental car that is waiting parked across the street. Officer Case pulls off as I trail behind him. As planned, Officer Case pulls into an empty lot. I hop out of my car and jump in his back seat.

"What up?" I say to Knuck who is in the back seat already holding a gun to Officer Case's head. Officer Boroughs is still knocked out in the passenger seat.

"You fucking thugs will not get away with this. I'm a cop and…," his words are cut short when Knuck hits him in the head with his gun.

"Shut the fuck up Robert. Nobody cares," Knuck says to Officer Case as blood starts to drip from his head. "Drive to Tone's house."

"Who is Tone?" He asks.

"Are we really going to play this game or do I need to hit you again to refresh your memory?"

"Fuck you. Kill me."

"Cool. And then when I'm done, we will kill your wife Carol, your daughter Tatyana and your son Matthew while we're at it. Eye for an eye, right?" I threaten.

"Don't hurt my family."

"Why not? You killed mine."

"I didn't. I swear…," his words are cut short again from Knuck's hit.

"DRIVE," Knuck commands.

We pull up to Tone's house. I struggle to get Officer fat ass out the car.

"Look boys. I don't know…," Officer Case's words are cut short again as Knuck knocks him out cold and throws him over his shoulder.

"Shit. I should have made you carry his fat ass," I say to Knuck carrying Officer Borough's body.

"You go to the gym. You good," Knuck jokes as we enter through the back door. We throw the 2 officers down the basement stairs. When we reach the bottom step, Tone is already down there with Mookie and Black.

"Take their clothes off and hang them up," Tone instructs. We do as we're told and hang the Officers up like the pigs they are.

"Y'all can leave," Tone says to us.

"What?" I ask.

"Leave. I got this."

"I'm not leaving," I tell him.

"Neither am I. They were our family too," Knuck says walking over to the hanging bodies and stuffing socks into their mouths. We sit and wait. When Officer Case comes to his senses, Tone wheels himself to him.

"Remember me, pig?" Tone asks putting a silencer on his gun. Officer Case looks terrified and starts pissing himself.

"Remove the sock out of his mouth, Black," Tone orders. Black gets up and removes the sock.

"Tony, man. I had nothing to do...," BAM. Tone shoots him in his knee. It looks like his knee just exploded as Officer Case screams in agony.

"Tone, man. Somebody will hear," Black warns.

"I don't care," Tone says. "Was it Bo and Terry who set me up?" Tone asks. Officer Case begins to cry and nods his head up and down.

"Hmmm...," Tone says wheeling himself behind him. He pulls out a Swiss army knife.

"I'm paralyzed you dick," he says.

"Tone...please..."

"I remember asking to let my family go but you executed them anyway."

"I...I...I didn't."

"You shot me and didn't stop this asshole for shooting my wife, my child, and my child's Godmother."

"It went too far, man. I didn't mean...AHHH," Officer Case screams as Tone stabs him in the back.

"I'm not exactly sure what angle I need to stab you for you to become paralyzed and not die," Tone says taking the knife out of his back and examining it. "I guess it doesn't really matter. You're dying tonight anyway," he says wiping the knife on his pants.

"How long before this asshole wakes up?" Tone asks referring to Officer Boroughs.

"Should be any minute now," Knuck answers.

"I've never watched anybody bleed out before," Tone declares wheeling himself in front of Officer Case to get a better look. Officer Case looks woozy as his blood seeps out making a puddle on the carpet.

"Fuck. I wasn't ready to kill him yet," Tone snaps looking up at Officer Case who looks like he is going to kick the bucket any moment. I run over to the fireplace to start a fire.

"What the hell are you doing?" Mookie asks me.

"About to stop this fool from bleeding," I answer as they watch me stick a metal poker into the flames.

"Now this may hurt a little, Robert," I say to Officer Case before placing the hot poker on the exact location where Tone stabbed him. I can smell his flesh burning as he screams in agony.

"I think it worked. He's not bleeding anymore," Mook informs me sticking his finger in the spot. Officer Case screams again.

"We can't wait for this fool to wake up," Tone says. I walk over to Officer Boroughs and remove the chair from under his feet. Within a matter of minutes, he finally wakes up.

"What the fuck?" He groggily mumbles.

"Hey Chuck. How are you?" Tone sarcastically greets. Tone motions me to hand him the hot poker.

"Fuck you, Tony," Officer Boroughs says.

"Hmmm…I can't really reach you in this chair but," Tone says as he places the hot poker on one of Officer Boroughs nipples. He screams.

"Can you please stop screaming, Chuck? You are going to wake my neighbors."

"Fuck you, you nigger. I should have fucking killed you with everybody else. HELP," Officer Boroughs screams.

"I wouldn't do that if I were you," Tone sings.

"HELP," he screams again. I stand in the chair to cut Officer Boroughs down.

"What the fuck are you doing?" Black asks.

"Just make sure his ass doesn't run," I tell them as they form a small circle. I cut Officer Boroughs down and Knuck is the one who instantly knocks him out so he wouldn't run. We pull him to a chair and tie him up. Five minutes later he wakes up to me patiently waiting sitting across from him.

"Nyce, is it?" Officer Boroughs questions.

"That's me."

"You had a thing for that black bitch teacher didn't you?" He asks with a smirk smeared across his face.

"Her name was Jenna," I calmly correct him.

"Black bitch," he laughs.

"No. Jenna."

"She looked like fun. Considered raping her before I shot her."

I jump out of the chair and punch him in his mouth and then grab Tone's army knife. Knuck holds Officer Boroughs head back as I pry his mouth open and cut out his tongue.

"Say something else now bitch," I taunt as blood oozes out of his mouth and sprays all over the place. He is now groaning and making weird gargling noises.

"You know somethin', Chuck?" Tone says wheeling himself over to him. "My dick doesn't work anymore. You know what that does to a man? I don't think I've ever been faithful to my wife. Fucked so many bitches; disrespected our marriage but I would give anything to make love to her one last time. You took the love of my life from me." I can see the hurt and pain in Tone's eyes as he speaks to Officer Boroughs.

"You took my daughter away from me and my unborn child," Tone continues. "My fucking dick don't work," he snaps and swiftly pulls out his gun, shooting Officer Boroughs in the dick. Black, Mook, Knuck and I jump and reflexively use our hands to shield our dicks, feeling Officer Boroughs pain.

"I guess we're done here. They're gonna bleed out," Tone says wheeling himself to the bar and pouring himself a glass of whiskey. I watch Tone closely and I'm startled when I hear Officer Boroughs making more weird noises.

"What the fuck are you doing?" I ask Knuck who is examining one of Officer's Boroughs eyeballs in between his fingers.

"What? I've always wanted to pluck a niggahs eyeball out ever since I saw the *Terminator*," he laughs.

"You're a sick bastard," Black says cracking up. Tone chuckles and pours himself another drink.

"Y'all want some?" He asks. When nobody answers, he wheels himself back over to us with two bottles of whiskey in his lap. He crashes one of the bottles over Officer Boroughs head. He then wheels himself over to Officer Case and pours the whiskey out onto the carpet under Officer Case's feet.

"Grab y'all shit and get out. Let me honor my family and finish this shit myself," Tone orders. We give Tone that respect and walk out the cellar door.

"What the fuck was the whiskey about?" Mook asks once we are in the driveway about to get in to the car.

"I don't know. That was weird," Black says.

"Shit. Isn't whiskey flammable?" Knuck asks. Without another word we bolt back up the driveway. We find Tone in the middle of the floor laughing as the two men are screaming as their flesh burns. Knuck and I grab Tone.

"LEAVE ME YOU IDIOTS. LEAVE ME," Tone cries trying to fight me and Knuck. I throw Tone over my shoulder as Knuck grabs his chair. We make it outside and into the street. I place Tone back into his chair.

"LEAVE ME," he shouts. "NINA," he cries as we watch his house go up in flames. "TONI," he cries in agony. Black starts honking the horn. I grab Tone again and throw him over my shoulder.

"GET AWAY FROM ME, DUMMY. GET AWAY. DON'T YOU GET IT? I WAS SUPPOSED TO DIE IN THAT HOUSE. I WAS SUPPOSED TO DIE WITH MY FAMILY. PUT ME THE FUCK DOWN," he yells hitting me in my head. When Tone realizes that I'm not going to grant him his wish, he stops fighting.

"Nyce, put me down please," he says calmly. "Someone has to take the rap. Put me down or the heat will be on all of you for killing two cops."

"But…," I start to say.

"No buts. This was always the plan. I die tonight so put me down. I had the 5 million dollars delivered to your mom's house earlier now go before the cops get here." I don't know what to do. This is my brother and I don't want to leave him like this. I don't want him to take the rap for this. I sit Tone back in his wheelchair and look him in the eyes.

"Tone…," I start to say before he puts his hand up and cuts me off.

"I love you. Remember everything I've taught you. Now go," are his final words to me before I hop in the car.

"I love you too, Tone," I yell out the window before Black speeds off. We can hear the sirens in the distance as we drive through the streets.

FIFTEEN

That summer of mayhem is the summer I will never forget. It's the summer that made me the man that I am today at the age of 26. The first mistake I made was trying to justify my actions and do God's work. My second mistake was calling the number that Tone gave me.

If you would have told me that my life would have ended up like this, I would have laughed as I replay the events that happened that night. In a matter of minutes, all four of us had helped commit murder and became instant millionaires in the process. I want to say that night hasn't changed us but it did. People think that revenge by murder is rewarding but they never tell you about the aftermath; the nightmares; the fear of getting caught or worse, the piece of your soul that dies killing your human compassion for others. Killing is the easy part; it's the aftermath that eats at your soul until there is no soul left; that moment where you really don't give a fuck. It didn't take us long to get there.

Helping to kill Officer Boroughs and Officer Case was the first murder I committed at the age of twenty. I wish I could say it was the last. After Tone's arrest, his team was so divided and even though he gave me the keys to reign, it didn't sit well with others that were already playing the game. We were children; not yet twenty-five and we were given the keys to an empire. The more niggahs tried us, the more bodies we collected which led people to fear and respect us.

At first we took it slow, reclaiming the territories that we had originally with Jeff, Rick, and Becky reworking the suburbs. Knuck and I set up Mook and Black to put pawns back on the streets, taking over territories and reclaiming what was once Tone's. Slowly, the niggahs who broke away after Tone's arrest came back to work for us once they realized that Tone has prepped me for this job since the age of fourteen. Those who didn't come back escaped all together or sided with Terry and Bo which sparked a never ending war between us. Those niggahs are like roaches. No matter how many hits and set ups Knuck and I put out on them, they seem indestructible and out of reach but their days are numbered. Six years may have gone by but as long as I'm breathing, they will always have to watch their backs especially Terry's ass for dogging out my sister and not being there for my niece.

With the help of Tone's nephew Lamar, we expanded to Camden, NJ. I am officially the King on the chess board, with Knuck being my right hand. If you ask me if I liked my job, no. I fuckin' hate it but the money…the money…whoa.

Tone's arrest weighs heavy on my heart as well. In the beginning, Knuck and I had to beg him to plead guilty to avoid the death penalty. It wasn't that he thought he could beat the case; he simply didn't want to. Tone had lost everything therefore trying to destroy the last piece that binds him to this world; himself. Tone wanted to die. After on-going psyche evaluations during the first few months of his trial, they ended up giving him life in prison without the possibility of parole. I don't know if they did that to torture him or if they really thought he was mentally insane. He's good now though. We write at least once a week and I always keep money on his books. Since I took over his role, me visiting him isn't wise; a rule that he taught me when I was fourteen.

Black and Mookie found women crazy enough to marry them. I on the other hand am still me, and still dealing with a few random chicks including Keisha. Yeah, I know but I am finally at a good place with her. Keisha will never be my girl again but we are friends who occasionally fuck each other, nothing serious. I'm not really interested in getting serious with a chick anyway so I finally grew up and stopped lying. Not that it helped any though. Bitches be crazy but Tone told me a long time ago if you find a girl that silences your demons, she's the one. I guess a piece of me has been looking for that girl and maybe that's why I seem to have an insatiable appetite for women. I haven't found the one that is able to make my world stand still.

After I sneakily bought my parents' house for them when I was twenty-two, Knuck bought a house in Wynnefield to stay close to my parents and I moved out to Cherry Hill, NJ. I've been out there close to four years now. I needed to get out of Philly and escape to a place where no one knows me; a place where I can run and hide from my demons and the sins I've committed. Staying true to form and abiding by the rules that Tone has left me, nobody knows I live there besides my boys and a few random chicks including Keisha and Vi. I also make some pretty good investments to help turn my money legit. It's not working though. I make way more drug money than plausible so after Grandma Norah passed away and left me her house, I turned her basement into a vault to hold all my dirty money.

July 2001

"What up Beck?" I ask answering my phone.

"Hey you. I called Knuck but he's not picking up," she says.

"Yeah, he's takin' care of some business but I'll be over in a few," I tell her grabbing my keys. I drive over to Becky's garage.

"What's up baby girl?" I greet her with a hug.

"Nothing much. I figured I call you before heading out of town," she says grabbing her "cooking utensils". I unload the packages and sit them on the table.

"You think I can get $200.00," she asks me.

"For what? How are you broke already?" I ask throwing $200.00 on the table.

"Who said I was broke? I just want to spend yo' money," she laughs.

"You lucky we go way back. Where you going anyway?"

"Down the shore for a few days. Jeff and I rented a house to go party. You should come."

"Nah, I'm straight. Y'all are takin' product with you too, right?"

"Of course. I will be greasing your pockets next week Big Daddy," she giggles. I sit down on the couch, turn on ESPN and roll up a blunt. I'm smoking and watching *Pardon the Interruption* when Becky comes waltzing over and sits on the table in front of me.

"Can I have this?" She asks with a small amount of heroin in her hand.

"When you gonna cut that shit out, Beck?"

"Hey, you have your vice and I have mine," she answers. I shake my head at her.

"Don't do that Nyce. I am not some flunky addict."

"Yeah, but it's only a matter of time."

"I do it every now and then, Nyce. I don't do it every day. I'm fine."

"You're not fine, Becky. You look like your damn near 35-years-old at 28."

"Are you going to give it to me or not?" She snaps frustrated.

"Whatever Becky," I reply getting up and walking over to the fridge to grab a beer. I watch Becky cook up the powder in a spoon until it's liquefied, grab her needle and insert it in between her toes. She lays back on the couch to enjoy her high with her head slumped. I open the kitchen drawer and remove the Naloxone that Knuck had stored there in case she ever overdosed.

"You guys really get on my nerves wit' that," she slurs. "I am fine," she says. I walk back over to the couch and sit next to her. She lays her head in my lap as I light up my blunt.

"Knuck's worried about you," I tell her.

"I know. In another life, if I wasn't screwed up, maybe we could have been together," she sighs.

"Why not this life?"

"Because he doesn't look at me the same anymore," she says softly.

"He just wants you to get your shit together."

"What about you Nyce? Are you happy?" She asks, changing the subject.

"I'm okay."

"That wasn't the question. Are you happy?"

"I don't know what that means. I'm surviving."

"You're a millionaire, Nyce. You should be happy and traveling the world and shit like that," she says with her eyes closed.

"You still afraid to fly?" She giggles.

"Yeah. I ain't fuckin' wit' no airplane."

"The likelihood of you being in a plane crash is slim. You have a higher risk of getting into a car accident than an airplane crashing."

"The likelihood of me surviving a car accident is higher too."

"What if you meet someone and she wants to travel the world with you?"

"If it can't get me there by car then I ain't goin'."

"You're going to fall in love one day and I bet you she is going to be the one to get your ass on a plane."

"Love don't live here, Beck."

"Love is great. What you and Keisha had, that was puppy love but wait until you have a taste of the real thing. There's nothing like it."

"Are you done being high and talking about love?" I laugh.

"No. When I'm high, that's the only time I feel love," she says.

"You're crazy. I have to go."

"Promise me something first. Promise me that next year, we will get on that plane and take a trip for my birthday."

"February, right?" I ask referring to her birthday month. She hits me because she knows I'm just fucking with her by pretending that I don't know when her birthday is.

"Yes. You, me, and the whole crew will hop on a plane and get the fuck out of here and take a real vacation with white beaches and blue seas. Can you do that for me?" She asks, looking up at me. I laugh and gently nudge her to get up and grab the rest of the powder off the table.

"What are you doing? I thought you were giving me that," she whines.

"I'm leaving and no one is here to supervise you."

"The fuckin' Naloxone is in the drawer."

"Yeah but if you're overdosing, you can't save yourself."

"God I hate you guys sometimes," she says annoyed.

"I love you too Becky," I tell her kissing her on the cheek.

"Nyce?"

"What's up?"

"Don't be afraid to open your eyes, fall in love and see the world."

"I won't Becky. Have fun on your trip. I'll see you when you get back," I tell her packing up my bag and walking out the door.

"What up, homie?" I greet Knuck when I walk into his crib.

"What's up," he says grabbing the bag out of my hands.

"Just seen Beck," I tell him.

"Yeah, I know. I just got off the phone wit' her."

"What's up wit' you two?"

"Man Nyce, if I could save her, I would."

"You love her, man?" Knuck cracks a smile.

"She's my friend. She held me down before your parents took me in and for a long time, she was my only friend that I trusted so of course I love her. I'm not in love with her if that's what you mean."

"Even if she cleaned herself up?"

"Nah. My Mama would be rolling around in her grave if I brought home a Becky," he laughs. I laugh too.

"No one can dictate your happiness," I tell him.

"You was talking to Becky wasn't you? Beck be on some love shit every time she's high."

"Yeah," I laugh. "She got me thinking though. I'm 26 and you're 28. We can't do this shit forever. I want kids someday."

"I feel you," he says unpacking the bag. I sit at the table and light a blunt. We share the blunt as we divide and break down the bags.

"I wish I was mature enough for Jenna when I had her," I confess breaking the silence.

"I know brotha, shit. I'm still surprised that Mook and Black are married with kids before us but Sabrina and Gia are cool. They got them two niggahs in check though," he laughs.

"Don't they though?" I laugh.

"You ever wanna give this shit up?" Knuck asks me.

"You?"

"I ride when you ride my niggah."

"Then we gonna be ridin' for a long time because money over bitches."

"Word," Knuck says leaning over the table to give me dap. I help Knuck pack up the bags so he can make his deliveries.

"What you getting in to tonight?" He asks.

"I don't know. Keisha is buggin' me to spend some time with her."

"Spend time?" Knuck questions.

"You know what I mean."

"I'm just surprised her ass is still holding on considering you have a bitch for every damn day of the week," he jokes.

"Shut up. My dick game is intoxicating," I laugh.

"I don't need to know all that niggah but I ain't gonna front. You doin' something right because you be havin' bitches trippin'."

"Why you act like you don't be having your fair share?"

"Not like you do," he laughs.

Knuck and I finish bagging our shit before parting ways. I head back to my condo in Jersey thinking about Knuck,

Becky and the conversations I had with the both of them for the remainder of the night.

"I do want a family someday," are my final thoughts before going to bed.

A week later, I am back at Becky's garage waiting for her. She said that she was coming back today so she should be here by now.

"Yo. You heard from Beck?" I ask Knuck over the phone.

"Nah. Not since last night."

"What about Jeff?"

"I haven't called him. You good?"

"Yeah, I'm straight. I've just been calling her phone but she's not picking up," I tell him a bit worried about her.

"You know her. I'm sure she will pop up soon." I hang up with Knuck and get comfortable. I'm watching TV when my red cellphone rings.

"Fuck," I say out loud looking at Jeff's number flash across the screen. When the red cell rings, it means that someone got locked up.

"Hello," I answer disguising my voice.

"Hey. Becky got locked up but they won't tell me anything."

"Is there bail?" I ask.

"So far no."

"When you comin' back?"

"Tonight. Around 5 or so."

"I'll see you later." I tell him hanging up.

At 6:30, Knuck and I pull up at Jeff's house and beep the horn for him to come out. Knuck steps out of the car as Jeff approaches. I watch Knuck pat Jeff down to make sure he isn't wearing a wire and then he tells Jeff to get in the backseat. Jeff knows not to say anything once inside the car. I pull off and drive for 20 minutes to make sure that we are not being followed before saying anything.

"What happened?" I ask when I'm sure Knuck and I are safe.

"They came up in the house. One of the neighbors complained about noise. We all bolted out the back door but Becky was high as fuck and was passed out upstairs so they got her."

"Drugs?"

"They didn't get much. About $2500.00 worth but I'm sure they have whatever stashed cash Becky had around the house. I have mine though. It's back at the house."

"How much?" I ask.

"Six-thousand," he answers.

"Keep it," I tell him. Yeah, I'm pissed that I just lost ten-thousand dollars between him and Becky but there is no way I am taking Jeff's money not knowing if the bills have been switched out by the cops.

"You good right here?" I ask Jeff pulling up at the train station.

"Yeah. I'm good."

"You remember the rules?" I ask.

"Yes. Thank you for the advance. I guess I'll see you next year," Jeff answers disappointed while stepping out of the car. The rule is once you hit the red phone, you have to lay low for some time so I can make sure you are not fucking with the cops. During your "downtime", you are not allowed to talk to anyone within our network; both customer and employee.

"Here," Knuck says passing me a new red phone. "I already text the number to everybody."

"Cool, thanks. I left the other phone back at Becky's."

"You're violating your own rules," Knuck reminds me.

"I didn't want to break the phone in case she calls me. I left it at her house so if they trace it, it will lead them there."

"She hasn't called me either," Knuck informs checking his phone. I look at Knuck.

"She wouldn't. Just give her time. She'll call," he says.

Three days pass by and still no calls from Becky. Mookie is on Jeff but so far so good. He assures me that Jeff basically goes to work at the record store he owns, goes to the gym and then returns home. Nothing out of the ordinary and Jeff isn't talking to any suspicious characters.

"What's up?" I say walking into Keisha's house.

"Oh, now you have time for me?" Keisha asks with much attitude.

"I can leave," I tell her turning to go.

"No, please don't go," she whines.

"You're looking beautiful today. Come give me a kiss." She slowly walks over to me.

"Why do we have to play these games, Nyce?" She asks me.

"What games?"

"The game of complimenting me, making love to me, telling me shit I want to hear and yet you won't be with me."

"I tell you that you are beautiful because you are," I whisper in her ear.

"You make me feel low and used."

"You're using me too."

"What am I using you for?" She asks.

"Who bought you this outfit you're wearing?"

"I did."

"With whose money?" She smiles.

"I want to look good for you. You are all that I want."

"You use me for dick and money so stop playing," I tell her backing away.

"With all the females you have, why do you need me, Nyce? Why do you continue to play with my feelings knowing that I am in love with you?"

"Keisha, I don't want to talk about this. You don't need permission from me to see other people because we are not together. We will never be together."

"But do you love me?" She asks. Fuck. I can see the tears building in her eyes. I only stopped by here to bust a quick nut and now I am caught up in one of her soap opera episodes. It seems like we go through this every couple of months.

"I love you but not the way you want me to," I answer honestly.

"But...," she starts to say something before I cut her off.

"If you can't handle this, then maybe we should just be friends; no sex and if that's still not enough, I will leave you alone completely if you want me to. I hate seeing you miserable over me. I really do but I am never going to give you what you want," I tell her truthfully.

"Excuse me," she says running up the stairs. I tolerate this from Keisha because we have history but when other females act like this, I usually cut them off and let them go but Keisha's different. I do love her, I'm just not in love with her.

"Fuck man," I say out loud before following her up the stairs to make sure she's okay.

"I'm fine. Please go away," she yells through her locked door.

"Come here. Let's go out for a little while."

"Only if you're buying me the Gucci bag I want." I laugh because I know that this is what really keeps her around. Don't get me wrong, I believe she loves me but I also know that if I were an honest working man like my father, she wouldn't be with me.

"Why should I?" I ask through the door.

"Because if I can't have your heart, I can at least benefit my pockets. It's for my pain and suffering," she giggles.

"You have five seconds to get in the car."
She yanks the door open and smiles brightly.

"I'm ready," she sings.

While Keisha is ripping through the mall spending my money, I text Knuck to see if he has heard anything from Becky. He texts me back no and my mind begins to race. What the fuck happened to her?

Keish and I go out to lunch and then to the movies to see *The Fast & The Furious*. My phone vibrates in the middle of the movie and Becky's number flashes across my screen. I jump up and answer it as I walk out into the hall.

"What's up?" I answer.

"Hey. I'm back," she says cheerfully.

"Why the hell haven't you called?"

"I lost my phone. I just bought one today."

"So is everything okay?"

"Yeah. Why do you ask?"

"Just checking on you."

"Cool. When will you be stopping by?"

"Soon. I'll let you know," I tell her hanging up. I walk back inside the theater with my thoughts running wild. Why didn't Becky tell me she got locked up and who bailed her out?

After the movies, Keisha and I drive across the bridge over to Jersey. I keep calling Knuck but his phone keeps going straight to voicemail. I pull into the Lukoil to get some gas before heading to my crib.

"Do you feel like getting me a bottle of Cranberry juice?" Keisha asks me as I pay the gas attendant.

"Sure," I tell her jumping out of my truck. I try Knuck again, and again his phone goes straight to voicemail. I'm about to leave a message but someone keeps interrupting my fuckin' thoughts.

"WHAT?" I bark turning around. The girl takes a step back from me as I feel my lips part up into an involuntary smile as I stand stuck staring at her. My stomach feels funny. *What the hell is this?* I think to myself as I stare, starting at her beautiful toes and working my way up. She's beautiful. I mean, I've had bad bitches before but she's polished; a different kind of beautiful; an angelic innocent type of beautiful. She's beautiful without even trying in her brown fitted t-shirt, jean shorts and sunglasses. Her legs though, damn, I can't wait to feel them wrapped around me.

"Nyce, are you just going to stand there or are you going to get me some juice?" Keisha snaps breaking me out of whatever the fuck this is that has me standing here like a love-struck twelve-year-old little boy.

"Ah, yeah. Can I help you?" I ask in a voice that isn't mine. What the fuck is my problem?

"Um, yes. Can you tell me where the Park Place Condos are?" She asks me. Her voice is intoxicating. She sings when she speaks in a soft rhythmic tone.

"No," I respond. She says nothing more and slowly turns away from me to walk back to her car.

"I CAN SHOW YOU," I yell out to her while checking out her booty. Yeah, shorty's stacked. She definitely can get it.

"What?" She hesitantly asks.

"I live there. You can just follow me. What's your name?" I've never seen her before and if she's living or has a friend staying in my complex, I should at least know her name, right?

"Aneesah," she replies.

"Nyce." I introduce myself to her and extend my hand. She grabs on to my hand and I can hear and feel my heart beat. Her hands are so soft like I just grabbed a handful of feathers. My stomach starts to dance and that's when I know that whatever this shit is, isn't natural so I fling her hand out of mine.

"Well come on," I bark at her making a mental note to stay the fuck away from her.

"Who the fuck is that? What the fuck was that about? You're just gonna disrespect me right in front of my face?" Keisha grills me as soon as I hop in the car.

"Relax Keisha. Don't start your shit. She was just asking for directions," I tell her. Keisha sits in the passenger seat steaming. I place my hand in between her thighs.

"You have never looked at me like that," she whispers.

"What?"

"The girl. You've never looked at me the way you just looked at her."

"You're trippin'. I just met the damn girl."

"Whatever Nyce."

"Seriously? Do you want me to take you home?"

"No, I'm sorry. Maybe I am tripping."

I pull into the parking lot of my complex, stick my arm out the window and point to direct Aneesah to the visitor's lot. I spend the rest of my day fucking Keisha but thinking about the mystery girl. I pray to God that she doesn't live here and that today is the first and last time I would ever see her.

The ringing of my phone breaks me out of my sleep.

"Hello," I answer. Keisha is asleep, lying on my stomach as I try to peel her body off of me and leave the room.

"We need to talk," Knuck says on the other end of the phone.

"Where the fuck have you been?" I ask him walking into the kitchen and poring myself a glass of orange juice.

"I'll explain. We need to talk. You home?"

"Yeah but I'll be heading that way soon to drop Keisha off. I'll stop by then," I tell him hanging up. I shower and dress. Keisha and I go to Denny's for breakfast before I drop her off.

"When's the next time I'm going to see you?" She asks, kissing me good-bye.

"Soon. I have some business to take care of."

"Okay baby. I can't wait until you come back and I love you," she says sweetly. I kiss her on the cheek and walk out of the house. I head straight over to Knuck's crib.

"Yo," I greet Knuck when I enter.

"What up?"

"You tell me."

"I did some checkin' around yesterday. Becky called and she told me she was home but never said anything about her being arrested," Knuck says.

"Yeah, I know. She called me too."

"When Jeff first told us that she was locked up, I called the police station. She was being held in a holding cell. I called again later on that week to see how much her bail was. They told me $150,000.00. I waited for her to call me to say she needed bail but she never called. I called again a few days ago and they tell me that they have no record of a Rebecca Sinclair in their database and now all of a sudden she's out. Something ain't right."

I listen to Knuck and am in deep thought as we both take a seat on the couch.

"What are you thinking?" He asks me.

"You already know. What are you thinking?"

"You already know."

"So now what?" I ask.

"I'll handle it."

"And what if we're wrong?"

"I'll make sure we are right first. Just give me a minute," he assures.

"You sure you got this?"

"Yeah. I'm good homie," Knuck says standing up and walking into his kitchen.

"So, we in a drought?" Knuck asks handing me a beer.

"Yeah. Everything is on pause until we figure this shit out."

Knuck and I call an emergency meeting with our people to tell them that we are in a drought and they have to lay low and not sell a damn thing until we give the greenlight. With the drought going on, it gives me time to think. What are my goals? What am I trying to accomplish? I don't want to do this hustling shit forever but getting out is going to be hard. The rules are set. I would have to buy myself out with the promise to never return. How much money do I need to make for me to quit because I know the longer I stay in, the deeper I am married to this game.

When week two rolls around, my corner boys start to get antsy at the money freeze. I'm not trying to pressure Knuck into possibly doing something he is going to regret so I stay patient and urge everybody else to do the same.

I'm in my condo holding a little meeting with Black, Knuck, and Mookie.

"So what's the verdict?" I ask Mook.

"Jeff is still lying low like you asked. I believe that he is safe. He's not working with the cops and Ricky is handling both his and Jeff's territory like a boss. I've watched his moves. He doesn't slip."

"How long are we on this freeze, man? I mean, I'm good but my boys on the corner are acting like hungry niggahs," Black says. I glance at Knuck.

"Just continue to tell them that there is a drought," I let him know. Nobody knows about Becky except Knuck and I. Technically, Black and Mook have a right to know but I don't need them to start trippin' on shit; especially Mookie's crazy ass.

"What's this shit for real? I know we ain't in no drought and I just told you that Jeff is clear. What's really going on? Terry and Bo will take over our shit if we ain't actin'," Mookie informs us.

"Y'all trust me?" I ask.

"Yeah," Black and Mook respond.

"Then trust me. This will all be over soon and fuck Terry and Bo. Their time is numbered," I tell them throwing on my boots. We walk out into the parking lot.

"Should we be worried about somethin'?" Black asks.

"Naw man; we're good. We are asking that you just trust us at the moment," Knuck finally speaks. "And my ass is hungry. What's the fuckin' move?" Knuck asks rubbing his stomach.

"I could go for some steak and eggs my niggah but y'all payin'. I'm in a drought," Mookie jokes.

"Niggah, we are all fuckin' millionaires. Ain't nobody tryin' to hear that shit from you," Knuck says playfully punching Mookie in his chest.

"Yoooo, peep shorty," Black speaks as we all stop to stare lustfully at Aneesah walking through the parking lot with bags in her hands. Her long hair is out and rhythmically dances in the wind. She walks with authority; with confidence as she glides towards us in a long white skirt and a red and white striped shirt that is showing off her stomach. My dick flinches as I try to think about anything else other than making love to her.

"Damn, she bad as shit," Mookie says licking his lips and readjusting his dick. His actions instantly piss me off to the point I catch myself about to hit him. What the fuck is this? I've never been some hatin' ass niggah so why the fuck am I on some type of Captain Save-A-Hoe mission over a broad I don't even know?

"Down boys. I've got this. Y'all married anyway," Knuck says as we watch her approach. Knuck gently grabs her arm as she casually walks by.

"Hey, get off me," she says snatching her arm away from him. Her gesture makes me laugh on the inside.

"You don't have to be so damn nasty Miss Attitude. I was only going to ask you if you needed any help carrying your bags," Knuck says.

"No thank you. I'm good," she responds.

"Are you sure? It wouldn't be any trouble at all," Knuck responds to her while giving his Casanova smile that bitches seem to fall for. I laugh as I watch Knuck try to win her over by using his dimples.

"Knuck man, leave that girl alone," I finally speak. Her eyes are hidden behind a pair of sunglasses as she turns her head and finally notices me.

"That girl?" She quizzes with much attitude. "One, I am a woman and two, this girl has a name. It's Aneesah in case you forgot," she says. I'm not sure who starts to laugh first but me and the fellas burst out laughing at her little attitude. What she said was a little hood but her dialect and delivery screamed suburban white girl. I find it fuckin' adorable and a complete turn on.

"Miss Attitude. I'm gonna call you Tudy," Knuck laughs. I get into character and get my Billy D on.

"Excuse me Miss Aneesah. I am terribly sorry if I offended you. Knuck, leave Aneesah alone. Is that better?" I ask her cracking a smile. She smiles at me, displaying one luscious dimple in her right cheek that makes my dick flinch again as I fantasize about sticking my tongue in it. She walks by us not saying another word and proceeds to walk up the stairs. She has a small music note tatted on her lower back as we stand watching her walk away. I'm impressed and intrigued. She seemed unfazed by the materialistic shit that most females drool over. Each one of my boys; including myself is iced the fuck out displaying our expensive watches and earrings and yet she seemed not to notice.

"Rock, paper, scissors?" Mook asks as we are still stuck on stupid watching her walk up the stairs.

"Shut up niggah. If you don't get your married ass outta here," Black says.

"You married too," Mook reminds him.

"I'm just an admirer. I didn't say I was going to cheat on my wife wit' her. I can look; I just can't fuck," he laughs.

"Fuck that. Rock, paper, scissors?" Knuck asks turning to me.

"I saw her first homie," I tell him hitting him in his massive chest. We hop in my truck.

"Executive decision; give each of the corner boys $1000.00 to hold them over," I tell everybody as we drive to IHOP.

"That's $25,000.00," Mook says.

"I got it," Knuck volunteers.

"Why you be actin' so damn cheap, Mook?" Black asks.

"Cuz I've been broke and that shit is something I never vow to do again and plus Gia be actin' warden over my money."

"Stop cheatin' and maybe she wouldn't clock your moves," I tell him.

"Says the man that was in a relationship all through high school and was never faithful," Mook shot back. I laugh.

"I ain't make her my wife though."

"Whateva. Y'all act like I be doing her wrong all the time. We've been married for two years now and I've only cheated twice," he says like he accomplished something.

"Black, I know your bitch ass ain't laughing. Sabrina always got your balls in her purse," Mook laughs.

"Yup. She does and I ain't afraid to admit it. That's what real love does, son," Black boast unashamed.

I chill with my boys for most of the day. It feels good not to worry about whose doing what on the street. I gotta admit that I am enjoying this little vacation from the game.

The next day as Knuck and I are driving back from one of our stash houses, my phone starts to go off.

"Yo. I got a one-eight-seven on the block," I say to Knuck looking at my text message.

"Yeah. Me too so hurry up," he says. A one-eight-seven indicates that Terry or Bo has been spotted. I drive to the block and see Terry on the corner. I park my hooptie in the middle of the street and hop out the car with gun drawn. Terry sees me coming and bolts as his goons starts shooting at me and Knuck.

"You good?" I ask Knuck. We are hiding in between cars.

"Yeah, I'm good. You?"

"Cool," I tell him. I poke my head out to see three dudes still standing on the corner. I motion to Knuck who reads my eyes and count to three. BANG-BANG our guns go off as we shoot two of Terry's boys in the leg and watch the third one run. Knuck and I stand and walk over to the two idiots on the ground.

"Where's Terry?" I ask pointing my gun.

"Fuck you," the boy answers.

"Wrong answer," I tell him as I shoot the boy in his other leg.

"You want to change your answer?" I ask.

"FUCK," Knuck yells when his hat flies off. "Somebody's shooting from the roof," Knuck shouts as we start to run and dip up an alleyway. We stop running completely when we hear the police sirens. Knuck starts to laugh.

"What the hell is so funny?" I ask.

"They almost had me, man. They shot my damn hat off. If I didn't bend down to hit the kid when I did, I would have been a goner. Shit. I liked that hat too," he laughs nonchalantly completely unfazed by his near death experience.

"That's not funny, Knuck," I tell him. I don't care about me. No, I don't plan on dying any time soon but I almost lost my brother; my best friend and I don't think I would recover from that had the niggahs succeeded.

Now that the cops are out patrolling the area, we walk back up the block.

"Those niggahs done stole the car 'cuz your dumb ass left the keys in the ignition," Knuck laughs as we stare at the vacant spot. I am in no mood.

"Nyce, I'm fine. I hate when you get creepy quiet. We're gonna get those niggahs before they get us. Word is bond."

Later that night, I rush into the gym at my complex to try to burn off this adrenaline. Those niggahs almost killed my best friend today and I ain't having it. I plug in my earbuds and let DMX get me into my workout zone, taking my aggression out on a punching bag. An hour and a half later, I step off the treadmill after my 20 minute run, leave the gym and walk up the path back to my condo. I see Aneesah sitting on a bench bobbing her head to some imaginary music and smoking a blunt. *Oh shit. Shorty speaks my language* I think and begin to walk towards her.

"You sharing?" I ask. She screams.

"Where the hell you coming from?" She asks as I laugh at her high pitch scream.

"Workin' out. So are you sharing or what?"

"I don't know. You seem like a man who takes care of himself. I wouldn't want to corrupt you," she says with a smile. Corrupt me? This girl has no clue as to who I am. I like that.

"Girl, just give me the damn thing. Shit! I've been smoking since I was two," I joke with her. She laughs and passes me the blunt. I inhale the smoke. Damn! She got some good shit. Wherever she's buying from, it definitely ain't from me. I'm almost tempted to ask her who her supplier is.

"You cold?" I ask when she holds her legs up to her chest, wrapping her arms around them.

"A little," she responds.

"I think I have a jacket," I tell her digging inside my gym bag while trying to peek inside of her pajama shorts. I hand over my jacket frustrated that all I got to see was the outline of her pink panties.

"Better?" I ask her when she puts my jacket on.

"Yes. Thank you," she replies sweetly. "So that girl, the one you were with that day at the gas station, is she your girlfriend?" She boldly asks. I almost choke on the weed smoke. Her question catches me off guard.

"Naw! She's just some girl," I answer.

"Some girl, huh? I guess I know what that means."

"And what's that?"

"You're a dog," she tells me bluntly. I laugh, almost dropping the weed. I pass her the blunt back.

"Oh, you just gonna put me out there like you know me, huh?" I laugh. Normally, I would be feeling some type of way that some random chick is already jumping to her own conclusions as to what kind of person I am but she's actually making me laugh because she's right.

"I'm just sayin'. I have an older brother. I know how y'all niggahs do," she says shrugging her shoulders.

"What if I told you that I tell every woman I'm wit' what the deal is? I'm a bachelor not looking for commitment. You can have some of my time when I'm willing to give it," I hint to her.

"Do you really tell them that?"

"Yeah, I do. I don't play wit' people's feelings. I'm not into that."

"But doesn't someone's feelings end up getting played in the end anyway?" She asks passing the blunt back. I watch the smoke seep out of her mouth. Damn she got some sexy ass lips. I think about Keisha and all the other women I've been wit'. I've never fell for them. Don't really have a reason why. Not sure if Jenna's death left a hole in my heart but I've always been the one to leave a chick alone when they become too clingy.

"Typically, yeah. I guess most women think they can handle it," I manage to say. I try to pass her the blunt back but she waves her hand at me to finish it. I start to walk up the path a little to see if she would get up and follow. She does. We are now standing side by side as I slyly check her out in her wife beater and shorts. *Damn. Shorty got body* I think as I watch her ass jiggle through the material of her skimpy shorts.

"You work out?" I blurt out as I discover that my favorite part on her body are her legs and ass.

"No. Why do you ask?"

"No reason. I like what I see. Most women have to work out for a body like that," I tell her licking my lips and dropping more hints that if shorty wants it, she can get it. I will even give her the special and make her toes curl.

"Nyce? Are you flirting with me?" She asks, sweetly singing her words. I lick my lips again and smile but I don't answer her question.

"No, I don't do anything. I used to dance though," she answers. We walk up the stairs and I walk her to her door.

"You know, I live two doors down. In case you need to borrow a cup of sugar or something," I smile. She giggles.

"Shit," she curses.

"What?"

"I forgot my keys," she says. Yeah, shorty wants the D.

"You want to come to my crib to use the phone or something?" I ask.

"Please," she replies sweetly. We take the few steps to my crib. We walk in and I watch her look around. She makes a few faces but doesn't say anything.

"Here," I tell her handing her the phone. I look into her face, I mean really look. This is the first time I am seeing her without sunglasses on. She's fuckin' beautiful.

"I didn't know your eyes are...what color are they?" I ask mesmerized by her silver colored eyes but it's not her eye color that has me hypnotized. I've had plenty of bad bitches with light eyes. It's the fact that her eyes are sad and yet filled with so much life. She's either been through some shit, seen some shit or both.

"I dunno," she answers. "Some say blue; others say gray and some even say silver. I stick with gray," she nonchalantly responds while on the phone with maintenance.

"You want something to drink?" I ask her once she hangs up.

"No thank you," she says handing me the phone and taking a seat on my couch.

"How long did they say?" I ask taking a seat on the opposite couch.

"About twenty minutes. If you have somewhere to be, I understand. I can wait outside for them to come. I don't mind," she tells me, standing up from the couch. My eyes trail her body and I quickly turn my head when she catches me staring. I don't know what the hell has gotten in to me. I'm drawn to her for some reason.

"You cool, sit down. I apologize for staring; it's just nice to see you without sunglasses on. I thought maybe you had a lazy eye or something," I laugh trying to take the heat off of me for acting like a creep. Truth is, I wish she did have a lazy eye so I wouldn't be so damn drawn to her.

"Honestly, being in here, you need to wear sunglasses with all this bright ass white. It's startin' to hurt my eyes," she cracks back referring to my bare walls.

"Oh, you got jokes?" I laugh. She thinks fast on her feet. I like that. "So where are you from?" I ask her wondering why this beautiful black woman sounds so damn white and proper; kind of like my mom.

"Gladwyne. It's a small suburban town in Pennsylvania."

"Where Iverson lives?" I ask referring to the 76-Sixers point guard.

"Yeah," she answers casually. I'm surprised. I've got "clients" out that way. Rich people know how to party. I wonder if she comes from money.

"So are your people loaded or something?" I ask curiously.

"No. Not my people." There's a knock at my door interrupting our conversation.

"Must be maintenance. Thanks for letting me stay," she says standing up and walking out my door. She has me intrigued. Not just sexually but I actually want to know who she is and what's her story. The longer I sit thinking about her, it becomes clear to me that I have to stay away from her. Jenna didn't belong in my world. This girl doesn't belong in my world and I don't want to do anything that would ever hurt her.

"Fuck man. Get it together," I say out loud while pulling out my phone and scrolling through my contacts to see what pussy I can slide into tonight.

SIXTEEN

"Nyce?" Knuck says on the phone.

"What's up?" I ask him.

"I need to see you."

"A'ight. I'll be there soon," I tell him. We are at the end of August and still in a drought. I drive across the bridge to Philly and arrive at Knuck's door. He yanks the door open with urgency as I step inside.

"It's true," he confirms.

"Are you sure?" I ask him making sure that he is 100% certain that Becky has made a deal with the cops. I know Knuck is certain. I just don't want him to be.

"I'm sure. I put a tracking device on her car. She met two undercovers yesterday at the mall. I don't know what she's told them if anything."

"Becky doesn't know where the stash houses are unless you told her," I say looking at him cautiously. I know Knuck wouldn't do that. Knuck lives by the code of the streets.

"Niggah, seriously?" He asks me making a serious face because I just offended him.

"Sorry man."

"I couldn't do it," he says handing me an ounce of powdered heroin. I take the bag out of his hand and stuff it into my pocket.

"You don't have to."

"This is so fucked up." Knuck punches a hole in his wall.

"We don't have to, brotha," I tell him placing my hand on his shoulder.

"Yeah we do," he whispers.

"If I do this, are we going to be okay? Are we going to be straight?" He looks at me.

"We will always be straight," he responds. He hugs me tight before letting go.

"I love you, man," I tell him.

"I love you too," he says giving me dap. I leave Knuck's house and drive back home. Around 7:30pm, I dress in all black and head back over the bridge, driving straight to Becky's house.

"Hey sweetie. About time you paid me a visit," she says all smiles as I enter the garage.

"What you been up to Beck?"

"Nothing. Just chillin'. Do you want a beer or something?"

"Nah. I'm straight."

"Is Knuck not talking to me? I've been calling him."

"He's just been busy. I'm sure it's nothing."

"Oh. Tell him I miss him."

"You good, Becky? You have something you want to get off your chest?" She looks at me for a moment like she wants to tell me something.

"I'm fine Nyce," she finally manages to say. "Do you have anything for me?" I give her a stern look.

"Stop it. I'm stressed out, okay."

"Why are you stressed out Becky? Is there anything I can do to help you?"

"No. Just bullshit. I'll be fine," she says. *Please Becky, come clean* I want to say to her.

"So, do you have anything for me?" She asks again.

"This will be your last time," I tell her holding up the baggie.

"It will…it will…I promise," she says trying to grab the bag.

"Becky, this will be your last time," I repeat to her. She eagerly grabs the bag out of my hands and cooks it in her spoon. She takes off her socks, spreads her toes and shoots up. She rocks slightly and then smiles.

"Best fuckin' high ever," she says, lying her head in my lap. She shuts her eyes.

"I forgive you, Nyce. Tell Knuck that I love him; I'm in love with him and I forgive him as long as you guys forgive me."

"What are you talking about Becky?" I ask jumping up and running over to the cabinet to get the Naloxen. It's gone.

"Becky, where's the Naloxen?"

"I moved it."

"WHERE IS IT?" I yell at her.

"I forgive you," she says with tears running down her face.

"BECKY," I holler at her but it's too late.

"BECKY, WHERE THE FUCK IS IT? REBECCA," I yell as I watch her spit up white shit. Her body violently convulses from a lethal injection of heroin and the KCL poison that Knuck mixed it with. I watch my friend die; a death that I could have prevented; a death that is ultimately my fault. I pray over Rebecca's body although I am pretty sure that God no longer listens to my prayers.

"It's done," I say to Knuck once inside my car and quickly hang up on him. I don't want to talk to him about it. I light a blunt to help ease my mind and make it all the way home before my head, stomach, and heart catches up to me. I shut my car off and run over to the bushes to throw up. I wipe my mouth on my shirt and gargle with a bottle of water I had in my truck.

"Fuck, I'm going to hell," I say as I feel my heart breaking, mourning the death of my friend. I look up at the sky and close my eyes.

"If we confess our sins, He is faithful and righteous to forgive our sins and cleanse us from all unrighteousness. Lord, please forgive me," I recite and slowly open my eyes. I spot Aneesah out the corner of my eye walking out onto her balcony. She's talking on her phone as I watch her in the dark aware that she can't see me from this angle. I watch her in the dark as I stand, yearning for warmth; some form of human contact and love to remind myself that I am human and not this monster that I've become. I watch her in the dark as my mind slowly eases and I no longer hear my own twisted thoughts. I watch her in the dark as she silences my demons that live within me.

Acknowledgements

Thank you to all the book clubs, book bloggers, and the many people who have supported and embraced me thus far. It truly has been a blessing and an amazing journey, and I hope that this book has not disappointed.

Zyire, my son, your mom is still chasing her dreams. I love you more than life itself, and I hope that I am setting a great example in showing you that it is never too late to accomplish a goal.

Jameelia "Jae" Drinks, you truly take my breath away, woman. Who would have thought that from one simple introduction we would become sisters? Thank you so much for being there for me and helping to hold me up when I stumbled. Such great beauty and strength within your soul and that is why I admire and adore you. I know your time is coming, and I will be right there cheering you on. I love you girl.

To dat girl Heather Butler, my literary agent. I cannot thank you enough for all you have done for me. You help push me to limits that I never envisioned for myself. More importantly, you never gave up on me even when I gave up on myself. This process can be frustrating and instead of babying me, you gave it to me raw. Thank you for your continued support and thank you for being my sister-friend. I know that I would not have gotten as far as I have if you were not by my side.

We have so much more to accomplish together and I am looking forward to it.

Christopher Reeder, man, you're like my creative spirit brother. I'm always in secret competition with you when it comes to this creativity thang. We have a movie to make and a soundtrack to produce. Thank you to you and your company, Crucial Republic/Chris Reeder Photography, for all of your hard work. Our trailer was INCREDIBLE and we did dat. I can't forget about your beautiful wife, Andreia Sardo-Reeder who took this amazing image of you that graces the cover of NYCE. Everyone keeps asking me who's the model. LOL.

Miss Silvie Drouillard, you edited the heck out of this book. Thank you for your hard work and commitment. I wish you nothing but the best.

And to everyone else who helped me during this process, THANK YOU!

Made in the USA
Columbia, SC
26 September 2020